Also by Larry Heinemann

Close Quarters (1977)

Paco's Story (1986)

COOLER

BY THE

LAKE

LARRY

HEINEMANN

COOLER

BY THE

LAKE

Farrar, Straus and Giroux

NEW YORK

Library of Congress Cataloging-in-Publication Data
Heinemann, Larry.
Cooler by the lake / Larry Heinemann.—1st ed.
I. Title.
PS3558.E4573C6   1992   813'.54—dc20   91-42052

ACKNOWLEDGMENTS
I would like to express my thanks and appreciation to the
John Simon Guggenheim Memorial Foundation as well as
the National Endowment for the Arts for their generous
fellowship support.
And, too, many hearty thanks to Tom Nawrocki and Fred
Schafer, Asa Baber and especially Pat Strachan for their
indispensable encouragement and timely assistance.

For "240" Gordy McKay

and

W<u>m</u>. Kile Riley

CONTENTS

D I S C L A I M E R

A brief word to the lawyers:
I am told that it is worthwhile to mention that
the story which follows is distinctly a work of
fiction. The remotest, most vague resemblance
between the imagined characters of this story
and real persons, whether man or woman, liv-
ing or dead, is the sheerest accident of coinci-
dence and in no way intended. To say it
plainly, no such persons as these ever walked
God's earth.
By the same token, the instances, episodes,
and scenes of the story are likewise wholly
imagined, and exist nowhere but in air.

Larry Heinemann
Chicago, 1992

He threw nickels around like manhole covers.

—Mike Ditka,
*   speaking of George Halas*

COOLER

BY THE

LAKE

The Friendly Confines

Maximilian Nutmeg was a mildly incompetent, mostly harmless petty crook, always hustling for money. He would wake up in the middle of the morning, listening to the traffic coasting through the stop signs at the corner, and run easy-dough "Max makes a million" schemes through his head. He was born and raised in Chicago—and the saying goes that if you can't find work here, you can't find it anywhere. He'd lived all his life in the same house on North Ravenswood Avenue across the street from the Chicago and North Western Railroad tracks, which brought commuters to and from the North Shore suburbs. (Ravenswood Avenue was named after either a local Indian Chief Raven or the town of Ravenswood, West Virginia, the hometown of one of the partners in the Ravenswood Land Company—which developed that part of the city—*or* after a flock of ravens that fortuitously flew over the partners as they stood at the corner of Leland Avenue and Clark Street sweet-talking each other about all the money they were going to make. Leland Avenue was named for Cyrus

P. Leland, one of the land company partners; Clark Street was named after General George Clark, Revolutionary War hero.)

Lately, Max had been cruising the city's alleys at night with Easy Ed (his shade-tree mechanic running buddy), stealing batteries, truck tools, and spare tires. It amounted only to chump change and walking-around money, but then again it was better than a poke in the eye with a sharp stick, as Max said *many* times, and was better than a straight day job— according to Max, lying drunk in the gutter was better than a real job—working your ass off, dying young, while the guys with the sit-down jobs got rich, lived "north," and went on forever. All of that was true, it was just that Max was getting too old to stay up till all hours.

Well, wouldn't you know, one morning in May Max woke from a dream (interstate; fog; chain-reaction accident), hung over to distraction, suddenly thinking that panhandling was easy dough: Why don't I try that!

The bedroom smelled of Elizabeth Taylor's Passion perfume and the moist potting soil of just-watered African violets—there was a huge wet spot in the middle of the bed. The aromas of boiled coffee touched with cinnamon and fresh-baked whole-wheat bread filled the house. A new litter of calico kittens was playing with his feet through the cotton sheet, attacking his heels, tickling his ankles with their little kitten claws, and tumbling over one another like winter wool socks come alive. He turned his head to the pillow. Why oh why, does Muriel have to make coffee with that junk, Max thought to himself. ("It's just the *teeniest* sprinkle of cinnamon, dear," Muriel, his wife, would say, acting as though it had been a harmless little spill.) A moment later he stood on the bed (because cats were into everything) among the jumble of covers, stooping down (because he was so *tall*) and pulling on his Jockey shorts. The next moment he stood in the bathroom, leaning his head against the high-pitched slanted wall and relieving himself—the mighty sound of warm urine splashing against cold porcelain could be heard throughout the house.

"Any city fool with a horrible face," said Max to himself, out loud, "bundled head to toe in raggedy overcoats and sweaters, long and greasy, horrible hair, swollen feet spilling out of his shoes, runny eyes, and never a decent haircut, can hold his filthy little fingers out to passersby and *beg*!" Max shook himself out. "What I need is a scam! An undeniable gimmick and a good corner!" Max stood in front of the washbasin mirror gazing at himself—pitiful! I must have been drinking dynamite last night. What to make of this face, he thought, and rubbed his chin, enjoying the rumbling sound in his head that his whiskers made.

What on earth possesses a grown man—husband and father, homeowner and taxpayer (few taxes though he paid)—to drink that horrible stuff, Max thought, remembering the lukewarm strawberry Boone's Farm that he and Easy Ed had drunk by the heaving gulp the night before. They'd been sitting on the davenport, watching a Johnny Carson rerun (Jay Leno bullshitting with Bob Hope and ex-quarterback/ex-senator/HEW Secretary Jack Kemp), waiting out of sheer politeness (and intrigued jealousy) for Amaryllis and her new boyfriend to get back from Deadwood Dave's Wild West Saloon.

Max stood on the threadbare bathroom rug ruminating on his latest surefire money-maker. "What I need is a ruse," he said, pointing to himself in the mirror, getting sly. "An excuse."

He ran the hot water, combing out the wavy tangles of his hair with his niece Amaryllis's plastic perm pick. When he felt the warm water rising, he dipped his hands under the faucet and rubbed his face with double handfuls, blubbering his fleshy lips, pinching and squeezing his eyes, turned on the cold water, and leaned down to drink heartily, swirling the water around his mouth and listening as he squirted it back and forth between his teeth, still thinking. Then he stopped and stood as if struck, the same way a yard squirrel will start, whipping its tail, its little heart pounding, suddenly aware it is prey. Instantly he saw it all: standing tolerably well buffed out in his best secondhand suit and spiffiest tie, a gas can, a busy intersection, a money clip, gassing and pitching the passing solid citizens—"Praise the Lord, brother, my car's out of gas and I've got to get back to Buffalo Grove."

Aha!

Of all the nickel-and-dime crackpot schemes, the snide and petty chiseling, the thumb-on-the-scale cheating and small-time shoplifting and heavy-handed out-and-out thievery, this brainstorm was to change the course of Nutmeg family history for generations to come. It couldn't fail; it didn't fail. It was, finally, Max's once-in-a-lifetime, brilliant up-and-at-'em *pièce de résistance—Voilà!*, as the barstool philosophers down at Deadwood Dave's Wild West Saloon would say.

His back straightened, his eyes brightened to a sparkle, he set out immediately for his closet, pulling at his Jockey shorts as he went (Max really packed a load—"A regular wallop!" Muriel liked to brag when she talked on the phone to her sister Raenelle in Valdosta). He passed through the phalanx of cats, passed the hall wall phone (the wall decorated helter-skelter with many telephone numbers—in pencil, Magic Marker, ground-in wet-look lipstick), and went straight back into his room. The closet was behind his dresser so the door opened just far enough for him to squeeze in. He rumbled around inside—decisions, decisions!—rummaging among the winter coats, the boxes of socks, the pup tents and Coleman coolers, and Easy Ed's mechanic's overalls (What the hell are they doing in here? Max thought), until he came up with a plaid button-down shirt, thick-weave corduroys, suede jacket (a little too warm for the weather; But fuck me running, Max thought, it's good enough for this end of the block), and his best fake saddle-shoe Hush Puppies—waterlogged and radiator-dried though they were. A hat and tie were all he lacked. Well, he *could* borrow one of Sweet William's dippy-looking gag ties (William, his nephew, was a retail marijuana salesman and a grotesquely awful amateur musician), but on second thought he picked up a red-and-black bow tie out of his tie drawer and a hand-me-down Totes rain hat.

Max's sister, Belle-Noche, younger by a couple of years, was fast asleep in her bedroom at the end of the hall at just that moment. The Giver of All Good Things had blessed her with the extraordinary gift of an abundantly beautiful body, astonishing in its endowments (men gasped when they saw her—large, high breasts; nipples that pointed up, as the saying goes), surpassing each and every one of her neighbors far and wide, but at the same time had apparently made her as ugly as He could and then hit her with a stick. Built like a brick shithouse, some nervy gossips down at Deadwood Dave's whispered, guffawing among themselves, but positively downright plain and ugly. "Just put a flag over her head and fuck 'er for Old Glory," Deadwood Dave's professional patriots said.

All those years the Nutmegs had lived next door to Verna and Cecil Wheat and their children, Leo and Nadine. Leo still lived at home, sitting around waiting for his mother to *do* for him. In high school Nadine and Belle-Noche had competed to see who could lay the most guys senior year (using rubbers as coup the way Indians used to run up on some poor fool and slap him across the back of the head with a coup stick; touching coup, they called it—*coup*, French for blow). And when the babies started to arrive (out of "nowhere," some of the gossips at Deadwood Dave's said), the two girls competed with who could go nuts the quickest in the morning; who could look the most skinny, run-down, and nervous; who could throw the shittiest diapers the farthest out the baby's bedroom window. Back in those days, Max would come home from work (sorting trash, tires, and other car parts for the Grateful Dead Auto Auctioneers, who also operated a chop shop on the side) and he would know just exactly how his sister's day had gone by how many diapers and little-bitty baby turds littered the front yard. And when he walked into the house there would be beer bottles all over everything, and Belle upstairs in her bedroom exhausted with anger—the baby loose in the living room, crying her eyes out.

Belle-Noche had brought four children into this world (little thanks though she got), not bothering to marry the fathers: Daisy-Lily by Durango Ruby, Petunia-Rose by Jack Locke, Amaryllis by Hollis Buck, and William by Eddie Sailor; each daughter more remarkably endowed and blindingly ugly than the one before, until she got to William—embarrassingly homely and built like a mail bag, ambitionless and talentless, his only genius was freeloading off good old Uncle Max. His development had been slowed, stumped, and withered by breathing solvent from Braithwaite's Paint Company next door (though like every good salesman *he* knew what his customers *really* wanted). The only time Sweet William (nobody called him Bill, or even just plain William) ever looked healthy was in the summer when he had a T-shirt tan. Belle-Noche would stay up half the night, gallivanting all over "hell's half-acre," as Max called it—"dating," she told her mother, Agnes-Ruth—and usually slept until after noon. She was the soundest sleeper in the house and couldn't be roused by a wonking, screaming parade of fire trucks, their mufflers louder than their sirens.

Well! So! Max thought as he stood in front of the bureau mirror, revived, holding up his clothes to admire them. That's more like it, and he threw everything across the foot of his bed and scrounged enough chump change for carfare and lunch from Muriel's one-gallon wine-jug penny jar behind the headboard. Another day, another dollar!

•   •   •

I don't know that anyone ever saw Max work as fast as when he was in the throes of yet another brilliant money-making idea—that's what Muriel always said. And the thought of yet another surefire scheme made Max gleeful and puckish.

He came down the stairs in his shorts, grumping and grunting like an old dog, taking the steps one at a time—each step squeaking—and making his way as best he could (through Amaryllis's cats) to his morning coffee. What possesses a man to invite his whole fucking family to live in his house (such as it was), he asked himself, and turned around the swaying newel post and wheeled into the kitchen. The floor was sticky with furrows of brittle linoleum mastic—the flooring had been laid in 1949, taken up in 1985; the mastic left as is and slick with molts of cat hair, flakes of papery onionskins, and milk-soaked Cheerios you couldn't get up with a blowtorch and a paint scraper.

The warm, fragrant air of the kitchen was suffocating. The house itself, a two-story wood-frame affair, had been built in 1914 by two Luxembourg Catholic immigrant brothers so grateful to be out of harm's way that they went broke before the United States entered World War I, and both died in prison for refusing conscription. Max's house was so dilapidated and frail there wasn't a tight nail left in the whole place. The only thing holding it up was the paint job.

Muriel was busy in the basement with the wash, sorting clothes and singing—

Well, I'm going to Chicago, sorry, but I can't take you!
Yes, I am going to Chicago, sorry, but I can't take you!
There's nothing in Chicago that a monkey woman can do.

When you see me coming, raise your window high!
When you see me coming, raise your window high!
When you see me passing, hang your head and cry.

If you love your baby tell the world you do!
If you love your baby tell the world you do!
There's coming a day your baby will learn to love you too.

Hurry down, sunshine, see what tomorrow brings,
Hurry down, sunshine, see what tomorrow brings,
And that sun went down, tomorrow brought us rain.

You so mean and evil, you do things you ought not to,
You so mean and evil, you do things you ought not to,
You got my brand of money, I guess I'll have to put up with
    you.

—at the top of her lungs, her voice traveling through the cast-iron plumbing and the woodwork to every last corner of the house.

Amaryllis, Max's niece—the youngest, most remarkably endowed, and ugliest of Belle-Noche's daughters—stood at the Cook-Rite stove, her little bare feet already gnarled by a lifetime of cheap hand-me-down shoes. Her eager-beaver boyfriend, Easy Ed Fitchett, sat at the table drinking his first cup of coffee, admiring the dimples of Amaryllis's buttocks through her little purple baby-doll nightie (a weird, nifty riot of 100 percent polyester ruffles and ribbons held together with half a dozen Velcro fasteners that Ed would rip open with his teeth); as far as Ed was concerned, she certainly did have a way with clothes.

"Mornin', Ed," Max said, looking through the cupboards for the clean cups, which were always in a different place. "Good mornin', Amaryllis."

"Mornin', Max," said Ed, straightening himself up from where he sat slumped, looking pitiful, exhausted with a hangover got from the same bottle of lukewarm strawberry Boone's Farm as Max (who had had sense enough to take a couple of aspirin and some vitamin B and C with a glass of water before staggering off to bed). Easy Ed had never heard of such a thing and was too young and stupid anyway, preferring to suck it up, as the saying goes, and gut it out through the puking and diarrhea, the hallucinations and blurred vision, the shakes and staggers and slurred speech.

"Good morning, Unc," said Amaryllis, stirring scrambled eggs in a Teflon frying pan (the Teflon long departed) with a plastic picnic fork.

Easy Ed was one of those eager young men (with a strong back and all his brains in his neck) who never intended to finish high school, so eager was he to get out of the house, so eager was he to make money, so eager was he to make his way and make his mark in this wide world. But he hadn't got very far; just diesel mechanic's school and motorcycle mechanic's school and Mr. Goodwrench school. He could wheel those semi-trailer trucks around the parking lot at the Big Rig Driving School like nobody's business (where everyone called each other "good buddy" and had a CB moniker), but had never been out on the road with one. Twenty years from now his motto would be "Life is hard, and then you die." It had never occurred to Easy Ed to join the army, the navy, the air force, *or* the Marines. " 'Be all that you can *what?*' That shit makes my ass sore," he'd say to the army commercials of guys jumping out of helicopters or driving tanks full-tilt down some *autobahn* during the NBA play-offs or the Super Bowl. "*My* mama didn't raise no fool," he'd say, lifting his feet off the coffee table, talking back to the TV, and pointing to his head. Everyone he'd ever known who'd come back from the army, the navy, the air force, or the Marine Corps had seemed hopelessly muddled, forlorn, and disorganized—victims of an endless psychological harassment of military chickenshit. These guys talked about nothing else but getting laid in Manila, beat up and robbed in Yokohama, stoned higher than a kite in Okinawa, or going to the Hamburg Oktoberfest (a line of men three abreast going in one door of the men's room—two hundred beer-soaked Bavarian Germans standing shoulder to shoulder and pissing into a deep concrete trough—and a great river of steaming yellow piss roaring out the other door). Easy Ed had moved in with the Nutmegs "to save on the rent," and had been sleeping with Amaryllis for going on three months. Amaryllis said with teasing exasperation that he was just a little something to keep her feet warm, but he sure could hustle his ass when the spirit moved him—Which was just about every single damn night, Max thought, What's it going to take to wear that guy out? What made it worse was that Amaryllis was a screamer, and Ed—"Easy" though his name was—was a huffer and a puffer. Ed always grinned when Amaryllis got on one of her jags, bad-mouthing him in that lame, whining way she had. He would grab his crotch with both hands as if grabbing hold of a bushel basket of truck-garden vegetables and say, "Well, everybody knows that a big cat'll scratch you to death, but a *little* pussy never hurt anybody." Which of course would make Amaryllis stand bolt upright at the sink, fetch a sigh, and stick out her tongue, pouting snidely, just a breath away from smashing the piled-up glassware with the Ekco soup ladle; "A lot *you* know, Mr. Ed!"

Ed sat at the kitchen table dressed in one of those woodsy, flannel logger's shirts bought in the secondhand Salvation Army Red Shield store at Clark Street and Bryn Mawr Avenue (named for a town on the Reading Railroad Main Line outside Philadelphia). The shirt was virtually brand-new—Easy Ed knew how to shop, you understand—originally owned by a Mercedes-Benz salesman at Loeber Motors, the kind of sense-lessly rich city kid who never got west of Clark Street, much less Kedzie Avenue (named after John Hume Kedzie, partner in the Ravenswood Land Company, who died stinking rich in 1903), and had never *actually* camped a single night in his life ("It gets so *dark* out there!"). Easy Ed was the hopeless sort of fool who would wear a logger's shirt with wide red suspenders *and* a two-inch leather belt. Now, the dress code for plain working stiffs in this world is pretty sloppy and go-to-hell, but no self-respecting logger (*don't* call them "lum-berjacks," bub) would be caught stone dead in suspenders *and* a belt. If you're a logger, a tree cutter, say (they get to knock off early), and you wheel your Silverado half-ton (known among pickup truck entrepreneurs as "a heavy half with a short box") up to the Bear Creek Tavern (decorated with slimy seed hats and famous chain saws, greasy and smelling of scorched sawdust and burned oil, hanging significantly from the high cross beams on leather straps and baling wire) wearing suspenders *and* a belt, why, those Bear Creek alcoholics would lift you up by the hair and the ears and arms and legs, take you to the woods out back—"What the hell kind of goddamn tourist are you, *pal*"—and lacerate the proverbial dickens out of you. Loggers also wear distinctly gratuitous hard hats—they like to claim—flattish and wide-brimmed like pith helmets, except heavier. "Total fucking useless, ask me," any self-respecting tree cutter will tell you. "Why, you start cutting on a tree and the thing gets to quaking and shaking, cracking and ripping and snapping, all sorts of dead bullshit comes down on you. More than once I seen a big piece of the top come loose. And if that chunk (big as a Buick sometimes) hits you, why, there ain't no pissant little hard hat gonna save your ass. *Stomp!*—you go in the ground tight as a nail."

Max grabbed Amaryllis's Disney World mug—hand-painted with all the "cartoony" characters, bought for a nickel at a garage sale back of Paulina Street near the Chicago Transit Authority's Howard Street elevated train yard—and scooped up some of Muriel's famous coffee with a soup ladle. (Paulina Street was named after the venerable and capricious wife of real-estate developer Reuben Taylor; Howard Street was named for Howard Ure, banker and real-estate mogul, whose family donated the right-of-way to the city.)

Muriel always got up at the crack of dawn and made the

coffee in a four-quart soup pot, campfire fashion. Boil the water, dump in some coffee—always the cheap, on-sale kind, and ground so coarse you'd have thought it came through a rock crusher—let it steep, then stir it around to settle the grounds as well as can be expected, and let everyone help themselves. Years ago she somehow got it into her head that Max *liked* grounds in his coffee. Max himself could never imagine where Muriel got that idea, but never got up the gumption to ask. "Better leave well enough alone" was his motto.

Amaryllis's pet ferrets, Big Daddy and Betty, slept in their big chicken-wire cage—big as an easy chair—among shredded newspapers and cedar shavings, which made them sneeze, and smelled up the house with a musky tang worse than thirty years of cat pee. In a house full of cats, Max thought, what the hell is Amaryllis doing with ferrets; and what the hell *is* a ferret, anyway? They look like a cross between a water rat and a rock monkey, except they have those sneaky little ferret faces and sneaky little burglar eyes. And the way Amaryllis cuddled them (Big Daddy and Betty slithering and squirming around in her lap worse than snakes) was a display of affection Max could barely tolerate. "Why doesn't Amaryllis grow up?" was all he would say on the subject. He looked from the ferrets, sneezing like water sputtering out of a faucet, to Easy Ed, blowing on/slurping up his coffee, and was sure Amaryllis had strange taste. (Max often watched the two of them going upstairs to bed and thought to himself, They don't come any dumber than Easy Ed.)

Max stood in his underwear, sipping coffee through his teeth and rubbing his skinny chest, his long, bare feet sticking to those furrows of pebbly linoleum mastic, daydreaming and contemplating his anticipated fortune out the back kitchen window. (Muriel had once read an article about getting rich quick in the *National Enquirer*, by Dr. Carl Hudgins, whereby a body could meditate about stacks of cash by "seeing it in your mind" and "dreaming about it vividly." She had read the whole thing to Max one night, and Max—a man willing to try *any* gimmick, no matter how stupid or humiliating—tried it regularly.) The mushy grounds in the coffee always baffled Max, sticking between his teeth. Why didn't Muriel use the Mr. Coffee he got for her at the flea market on Racine Avenue? (Named after a river in Wisconsin, French for root.) "What the fuck," Max said to himself. "It's only a buck!"—*that* was Max's motto! In an instant he was back upstairs, working his way through the cats, which wandered around as if looking for something they'd lost, back to the bathroom. He shaved, took a shower (Max always shaved before he showered), splashed some woodsy after-shave on the back of his neck, and then carefully dressed, trying his damnedest to tie the big red-and-black bow tie.

Max had once given serious consideration to growing a beard, had tried it for a weekend, then Monday morning had taken a good long look at himself in the mirror and said, "Naw!" It hadn't occurred to him then, but there was something satisfying about having to look himself in the eye every morning (intrinsically both curious and mysterious, an act of reassurance and self-discovery at one and the same time; looking himself in the eye every morning had never bothered Max). He'd shaved his face clean and felt much better, though Muriel was disappointed because, she said, Max's beard tickled her in the most delightful way.

He stood in front of the bureau mirror (he could see himself only from the ears down), with his big bony feet flat on the floor, tying and untying it. But the knot was always lumpy and he couldn't for the life of him make the tail ends even—either they drooped or the whole arrangement was crooked, or the bows were too skimpy and the tail ends too long, making him look like some horse's-ass Colorado cowboy. "Balls!" he said, making a face in the mirror, and grinned like a certified madman trying to please the staff nurse by taking his meds with an emperor's magnificent flourish.

("See? I can take it," you say, knocking back that little Dixie cup of uppers and downers, etc., like a shot of schnapps. Gulp! "Ah—that's mighty tasty!" But when you walk away don't let them see you jerk and twitch, flailing your arms and curling your fingers, whispering gibberish the instant the rush hits—Brrr! Woof! Wow! *Wham. Bam. Thank you, ma'am!*—just smile and wave! And not ten minutes later the whole ward is cool, calm, and collected, licking its lips, chain-smoking Virginia Slims, and watching Oprah Winfrey gush and brag about her latest diet with a bland and absorbed concentration that would make the State Board of Health stand tall and point with pride—"Ladies and gentlemen, observe! These nuts are no trouble at all!")

Max stood in the doorway of the bedroom. *"Muriel!"* he yelled out the bedroom door and down the stairs at the top of his lungs. The wood of the house hummed, scattering the cats in all directions—some slammed against the wall, knocked senseless; some stampeded to the bedrooms; some to the bathroom (leaping headlong into the tub or scaling the drooping plastic curtains); some ran pell-mell down the stairs; and some of these galloped clear to the basement, where Max kept his collection of filthy old storm windows got from long-demolished houses during his alley-scrounging days. (Every time Max went to the basement to check the water heater or show the gas meter man the gas meter, he stood among beer bottle boxes of priceless trash and admired the stack of storm windows, saying out loud, "Money in the bank.")

"Muriel!" Max boomed again, "I'm having the devil's own time with this *tie!*"

Doughty, intrepid, and buxom little Muriel (grateful that Max did not throw chairs down the stairs like her deaf father had to get her deaf mother's attention) bustled all the way up from the basement to the bottom of the stairs in the entryway, wiping her hands on her cotton apron, looked up into the darkened hallway where the cats staggered cross-eyed and woozy as if coming out from under an earthquake, and said, "Dear?"

"I said, *Muriel*, that I'm having the devil's own time with this *goddamn* bow tie. Can you help me?" said Max, begging and childlike, stepping out into the hallway, looking down in the direction of his wife in utter selfish helplessness, and scattering more cats with his feet. Max was always perplexed about where all the cats came from, as if they had been acquired through prayer. And he hadn't the faintest idea who had invented the bow tie but suspected it was some ignorant jackass with five thumbs on each hand—probably a Polack or a limey or a frog; "Just the sort of mean, dumbshit trick for a frog. What's more strange is that the rest of us go along with it," said Max to the cats crouching behind Muriel's hand-lotion jar and big fluffy powder puff, though this matter of the bow tie was also a matter of costume, as Max well knew. "I can do most things, you'd think I could tie one goddamned little bow tie."

Muriel Nutmeg (née Kincaid) was one of those hopelessly cheerful, endlessly smiling, keepsake-hoarding wives the Germans call *Hausfrauen*, who polish and scrub (except for the second-floor hall wall phone numbers), rake and prune (the yard looked like a garden—neat and spiffy, if pathetic), scrape and paint seven days a week, racking their brains among the Four Basic Food Groups to keep everyone in the house interested in meals and reasonably well fed. She was wife and mother to the whole house; the work (the cooking, cleaning, washing, fetching and toting, the errands, deliveries and pickups, the sickroom nursing) stretched endlessly before her like the ruin in the broad aftermath of an east Texas tornado. Her efficient good cheer made Belle-Noche's teeth itch and the green snake of envy coil around her heart more than once. Muriel had a vast collection of cookbooks—the culinary history of her marriage—Betty Crocker, Chinese, Filipino, French country cooking, New Orleans, pioneer West, Tex-Mex, and Thai; tofu, vegetarian, traditional firehouse, white trash, holiday parties, barbecue, "intimate" dinners and buffets; fast meals, slow meals, easy meals, complicated meals, meals that marinated for days, stove-top stir-fried, or boiled to death. Food articles and recipe clippings by the basketful were shoved in among the pages, some as bookmarks and others for the hell of it. Muriel was forever culling recipes from *Women's Day, Woman's Delight, Woman's Circle, Woman's Complete World, Woman's House & Home, Woman's Women, Modern Woman, Savvy Woman, Working Woman*, and all the rest. There were recipes held to the Kelvinator with brightly colored plastic fruit magnets, Scotch-Taped to the spotless (if dilapidated) woodwork, stuck to the cabinet doors with Super Glue. Muriel always had something on the stove, even if it was only a tub of water to keep humidity in the house, winters. And long ago Max had accustomed himself to surprises at dinner—"What the hell is this, Muriel?" he'd say as he sat down and pulled in his chair, looking at his plate of vegetarian goulash and macaroni and cheese over sticky rice, for instance. He was dutiful beyond description —good old Max—ate whatever Muriel put in front of him, and always cleaned his plate. Belle-Noche thought it was a miracle he wasn't fat. Max and Muriel had first met at a Senn High School seniors' sock hop, and Muriel was instantly, longingly infatuated. They got married two weeks before graduation. Muriel loved Max to distraction, especially during their frequent lovemaking episodes. She would fall asleep, exhausted, cuddling him in utter dreamy and helpless satisfaction. Max—for his part—had always thought Muriel was great in the sack, and loved her, too. Max really enjoyed games and Muriel was a good sport; both of them particularly fond of Spy and Beaver & Bear (the first rule was: the first to hit the mattress buck-naked gets to be on top, except when they played Bride & Groom or Comfort the Widow). Muriel had the notion that their union would befuddle the nosiest, pickiest Freudian (Jungians were able to take care of themselves; New Age Pentecostals were just hopeless). They had been together thirty-one years, and for all their horsing around had produced but one child years ago, Robert (tall and skinny like his father), whom Muriel called Bob and Max called Boy. Robert left the house every morning at 7:00 sharp (he still lived at home, the apple of his mother's eye). He worked at Walgreen's (the corner of Western Avenue and Granville) as a stock boy ("But not for long, Ma," as he'd been saying for years)—the only person in the house right that minute with a straight job. (Western Avenue, the longest street in the city, was so named because at one time it was the city limits; and Granville was named for Granville Temple Sprout, one of Chicago's first teachers, though experts differ and no one seems to know why the city used his first name.)

Robert had been conceived the night of September 22, 1959, when Bill Veeck's White Sox beat the Cleveland Indians 4 to 2 to clinch the American League pennant. (Robert bragged about it in that lamebrained way folks will brag that they were conceived at Woodstock or the day that What's-his-name set foot on the moon or the night Richard Nixon re-signed rather than be impeached.) The Sox were in Cleveland; the future Hall of Famer Early Wynn was the starting pitcher. Gerry Staley came on in relief late in the game. In the bottom of the ninth with the bases loaded and one out— everyone in Chicago expecting the Sox to fuck up and blow it—Cleveland's Vic Power hit into a double play. Shortstop Luis "Little Looie" Aparicio picked up the grounder smoothly, kicked second for the force, threw it to Ted Kluszewski (the first player to cut the sleeves off his shirts so his biceps would fit through the armholes) at first for the double play, and the Sox clinched their first pennant since 1919, when the World Series ended with the Black Sox Scandal—Shoeless Joe Jackson banned from organized baseball for life. Roly-poly Mayor Richard J. Daley—a lifelong Sox booster who grew up a short walk from Comiskey Park; a man whose stone-dead, white-bread imagination seemed to shrivel and deaden everything he touched—met the team when it returned to Midway Airport, along with the thirty-piece Chicago Fire Department Band and tens of thousands of screaming, hysterical Southside fans. (Mayor Daley would boost anything that made him look good but didn't cost him a nickel.) Fire Commissioner Robert Quinn, an old Bridgeport drinking and poker buddy of Mayor Daley's (fellow member of Bridgeport's Hamburg Social and Athletic Club), was so tickled about the whole thing that later that night he cranked up the civil defense air-raid sirens to celebrate. (Bridgeport is a working-class neighborhood of Irishmen, Lithuanians, and Poles just north of the old Union Stock Yards—now gone.) The whole city ran amok, half of them celebrating the first American League pennant in forty years and the other half (who didn't give a shit about baseball) thinking, What the fuck?—World War III?—*Great Balls of Fire!*—Duck and cover! White Sox fans all over the city thought, That just fucking figures, the minute we win the goddamn pennant it's the goddamn Russians and their goddamn bombs, oh my aching fucking back! Max and Muriel went to bed for one more roll in the hay, and *bingo!*, Max hit the bull's-eye and Muriel got pregnant—to which Max had said, "That's just great. The Sox win the fucking pennant and we get fucking pregnant." Muriel had wanted a houseful of kids, but try as they might, all they got was Robert.

Muriel climbed the stairs (when Max had *that* tone of voice it usually meant trouble), shooing the cats along with waves of her apron—"Move along, boys and girls"—and pushed Max back into their bedroom. "Now, Max sweetheart, you just stand *still*," and she took hold of the funny-shaped tie ends as if they were the reins of a stagecoach team and she was commencing a cross-country sojourn from St. Joe to Cheyenne, working them back and forth under his collar— he could feel the heat on his neck and hear it whiz against the fabric of his shirt. Was there nothing this woman could not do?

"Chin *up!*" she said, and then with the deftest flipping of wrists and mysterious over-and-under gestures, she had the tie snug and straight as a die in a jiffy. Max tried to watch her, staring down his nose and almost crossing his eyes, but she moved so fast and his view was so distorted that he couldn't make anything of it. And all the while she worked she was grinding her hips against his crotch, hinting (she could be a terrible tease, overpoweringly buxom and coquettish and virtually irresistible), until Max said, "Muriel, *I* have work!" reciting his agenda for the day. She listened to Max's latest money-maker with the solid and worshipful attentiveness known only to the truly faithful, then snapped the ends of the tie and slapped him on the shoulders, where his tattoos were, to signify that she was done.

"There, Max. Don't you look handsome! Anything else?" she asked, and looked up at him with her bedroom eyes, cuddling him luxuriously with her pillowy breasts, teasing him more. "Muriel, there is *work*!" said Max (thinking he needed incentive rather than comfort and encouragement just this minute), and sat on the bed to pull his socks over his long, thin feet—the toes bony and pink (they always reminded Muriel of the chicken necks you got with the giblets packed in roasting chickens). Muriel, dismissed with a wave of a sock, went back to the basement, smiling uncontrollably on her way downstairs in anticipation of some good clean fun that night. Max finished dressing in a wink—shooting his cuffs in the mirror (Muriel thought he looked mighty handsome all dressed up), scrounging through his sock drawer for his lucky Art Deco dollar-sign money clip, and snatching his Hush Puppies from the top of the radiator—then went out to the garage to fetch his gas can, shouting down into the basement (announcing to the whole house and half the paint factory next door) he'd be home by six.

The door of the garage was always tricky, and Max worked the big silver key in the lock, leaning on the door for some time. Finally, it gave way and in he went.

There hadn't been a car parked in the garage for many a year. From rusty fishing gear to piles of tires, many an odd object from Max's alley-scrounging days had found its place under the roof of Max's brick garage, stacked to the rafters (everything half ruined but "utterly priceless")—the roof itself collapsing like a grave; long flaps of brittle tar paper and rolled roofing hung down from between rotted planks. The detritus of all this littered the floor, fine and powdery enough to use for mulch. Max rummaged around for some little while, among the steamer trunks and cardboard boxes of paperback books, the rusted-together decimal tools and player-piano rolls, until he finally found the two-gallon Johnson outboard motor gasoline can—Johnson, a brand of motor made by Outboard Marine of Waukegan that had been pouring PCBs into Waukegan Harbor for scores of years (until 1978, when the courts told them to cut it out; in some sections of the harbor the PCBs had reached 500,000 parts per million), poisoning the fish and anyone who ate them far and wide. The spout was rusted solid into a gooseneck curve as tight as a tricycle tire, the can dented more than once, but here it was—Max holding it up to the sunlight coming through the roof, checking for leaks—in as good shape as it was years ago when he first saw it: a giveaway at a yard sale in good old Winnetka on the North Shore.

He locked the door behind him and walked off to the Thorndale Avenue Chicago Transit Authority Elevated station, swinging the gas can like a lunch pail. (Thorndale, named for the Pennsylvania hometown of developer John L. Cochran.) He stopped at a submarine sandwich place to get himself some lunch, telling Jesus (pronounced *Hey*-zeus) a roast beef with everything—including hot peppers, sweet peppers, fried onions, jack cheese, and Louisiana hot sauce—he stuffed the whole thing (wrapped in butcher paper), looking like a rolled-up *Racing Form*, in his coat pocket.

•   •   •

Walking down Magnolia Avenue near the Bethany Evangelical Lutheran Church (Missouri Synod) in the Edgewater neighborhood well south of Loyola University (the only university in the world named for an El stop, as some of the dropout deadbeats at Deadwood Dave's Wild West Saloon might say), Max looked like a parody of Mark Twain or Kurt Vonnegut, tall and lean. (Magnolia Avenue is named for a Chicago River tugboat, whose skipper, Joseph Gibson, is credited with saving many lives during the worst hours of the great Chicago Fire in 1871, when ships burned to the waterline and dockside warehouses burned to the ground.)

Max diddy-bopped with long strides and swinging arms —shoulders dipping, head lolling—his wavy, wiry hair sticking straight up like the thick fur of a spaniel. He had a pleasant, happy-go-lucky smirk on his face, his bony wrists stuck way out of his sleeves, and the fake buck-leather nap of his Hush Puppy saddle shoes was as smooth as well-combed, greased-back hair. He felt so happy and optimistic he burst into song:

> *They're gonna nickel-and-dime me to death.*
> *They're gonna nickel-and-dime me to death.*
> *I can tell by your friendly face,*
> *You're gonna nickel-and-dime me to death.*
> *I give a quarter to Gizmo the street bum.*
> *I give plenty to ComEd and Ma Bell.*
> *I give bankers three hundred of my very best,*
> *And they're gonna nickel-and-dime me to death.*

His lanky legs moved him along like a late-inning Wrigley Field day-game crowd making for the exits when the home team pitching goes flat (even the spitters and split-finger fast-balls sailing out onto Waveland and Sheffield Avenues on the fly; even Mitch Williams, who once said he pitched as if his hair was on fire, having a bad day; everyone in the ball park watching the slugfest with uhs and ahs) and all they want to do is "get to the car and beat the traffic." (Waveland Avenue was so named because in the old days the lake used to spill over onto the street in rough weather; Sheffield Avenue was named after Joseph E. Sheffield, developer in Lincoln Park and one of the founders of the Chicago, Rock Island & Pacific Railroad.) Max paid his dollar fare at the Thorndale El station with a benign smile—"What the fuck, it's only a buck"—and trooped upstairs.

The panorama of rain-washed, run-down housing stretched in every direction. Westward, just across the alley that ran along the El tracks, was the Illinois National Guard Armory, where the weekend warriors in their camouflaged fatigues (what the fashion experts at Deadwood Dave's would call K mart cammies) gathered to juice around in the gymnasium, playing soldier but no doubt able at a moment's notice to defend our borders from all comers to the death. Farther west, across Broadway Avenue (named after New York City's famous theater district, the Great White Way), the barren roofs of two-flats (gray rolled roofing and make-do cold-tar patches around the dead-red brick chimneys) stretched for miles—lace-curtain Irish, neat-as-a-pin Orientals, and first-generation Eastern Europeans too old and sick and stupid to move—their thirty-year mortgages paid off thirty years ago. They were sitting on gold mines, run-down eye sores though they were, with hedgerow evergreens gone wild-ass years before the kids were out of the house, and out back cascades of day lilies had killed the grass from the back of the house out to the alley cement. Getting the owners up and out would be like clear-cutting a Santa Fe River cypress bog with nail clippers.

East and south across the street was the George B. Swift Grammar School, where overworked teachers, all good union men and women, tried to inculcate thousands of years of history, mathematics, science, and other trivial odds and ends to students (forty to a room) so hopelessly bored and harassed it boggles the mind. How many people do you suppose died for the concept of zero? How many centuries was it before Christians discovered the Virgin Mary? Whose signature(s) appear on the Magna Carta? Just how much did Christopher Columbus cheat on his maps, distance, azimuth, compass correction, likely landfall, so he could sell his idea to the Spanish Crown? True or false: Sodium pentameter is ordinary table salt. Multiple choice: Who is the President of Nicaragua? Juan Valdez. Daniel Ortega. Roberto Clemente. Enrico Caruso. Doña Patrona Violeta Chamorro.

And farther east was the wall of lakeshore high-rises along Sheridan Road, where ordinary folks—rich of pocket but dead of imagination—lived one on top of another in little-bitty apartments high above the park that stretched south along the lake; people the rest of the city both envied and despised. (Sheridan Road was named after Civil War hero General Philip Sheridan, who once said, "The only good Indians I ever saw were dead Indians.") In summer, when the weathermen say, "Cooler by the lake," *this* is exactly what they mean, except none of these people can get their windows open. They're the first ones in the city to see the sun in the morning, little good though it does them.

A midmorning four-car "A" train came, rocking and rolling back and forth on its springs and scraping against the edge of the platform—the thick planks slathered with fresh, aromatic creosote. The doors flew open on their complicated hinges with a slam and a bang. The conductor stuck his head out the window, looking fore and aft. Max trotted along the platform and then popped aboard as if he were sidestepping a roller coaster. He had given up sitting in the first car or the last car ever since a motorman had rammed the rear end of a train a couple of years before, the head end car clipping the anticlimbers of the last car on the train ahead and plunging the first two head end cars to the street below. This happened near the end of the afternoon rush hour above the corner of Wabash Avenue (named for the river) and Lake Street (named for the lake)—those first two cars falling like rocks to the street, killing several passengers and innocent passersby, and scaring the living shit out of most people and the holy bejesus out of everyone else. For months afterward people would cross the street at Wabash and Lake, look up, shudder, and hurry out of harm's way. The accident was every child's worst nightmare fear of riding the El—you're five years old and can stand on the seats, just barely squeeze your face against the glass, look down and see nothing but air, then thick and solid pavement thirty feet below.

Max and his gas can sat down in one of the middle seats behind two little old ladies, dressed in their ever best (clothes and shoes they'd been nursing along for fifteen years—letting the dresses out, letting them in, letting them out again), going downtown to cruise Marshall Field's department store. It was Tuesday, and there was always a cooking demonstration in the kitchen department, the audience afterward invited to eat whatever was prepared—some weeks, good; some weeks, eh?

Bernice and Fanny would browse aimlessly through the store, wandering loose until noon, fingering everything and buying nothing. They would gossip about everything under the sun, killing time until the show—attend and watch, listen and eat with the blue-haired, Gold Coast bag ladies dressed to kill, who'd gathered to mooch a free lunch—then adjourn upstairs to the Walnut Room, the perfect place for two little old ladies to idle over hot weak tea, resting their ankles, while badly trained waitresses and busboys hovered over them, eager— positively drooling—for a tip.

Bernice and Fanny had been neighbors for thirty-five years on Glenlake Avenue (named for Glen Lake, New York), west of Broadway, "Well away from those rich snoots on Sheridan Road" was how Bernice put it. They'd raised families of boys (machinists and bakers and Wyoming ranchers), sons who'd failed at a thousand jobs, sons who'd married women so stunning the mothers had to wonder what the attraction was, sons who'd married women so manifestly plain, "misshapen and gawky"—*fat* was the word Bernice used—you also had to wonder what the attraction was (young women, let it be said, who produced children by the armload), sons dragged off to the Korean War and not heard from since. "Well, at least we know he ain't dead," Fanny's husband, Bernard, had said in 1955. "Otherwise we'd have got a telegram by now. But where that boy's got to is anybody's flipping guess." Both Bernard and Frank (Bernice's husband) had "passed on"—Frank carried away by lung cancer in 1982 and Bernard dead of a heart attack while shoveling snow the winter of 1979, the year there was one blizzard after another and it was always cold and the snow "never went away." There was plenty of ground water *that* year. The trouble was, Fanny said later, after she'd calmed down, evaluating the whole situation pragmatically, the trouble was he died early that winter, but it kept on snowing so that it piled to the windows (the winter of '79 was famous; it even had its own T-shirt), with no one to shovel—"I wasn't going to shovel the stuff, and all the kids on the block were too lazy to come around and ask," Fanny had said.

Bernice agreed right then and there it was a pity.

Bernard was a big man who loved his pirogis and his roast pork (a little lean with lots of juice), his TV baseball and his horrible cigars, and when he died—which came as a great surprise to him and everyone else, as he clutched his heart and keeled over into the snowbank—Fanny cried her eyes out and said Bernard had a heart as big as all outdoors. The Cook County coroner took one look at it and said, "He had a heart big enough to hold as much blood as a Volkswagen crankcase holds 30-weight oil." (Not everyone in the Coroner's Office got that joke.)

Fanny and Bernice sat facing the front of the El car, just in front of Max and his gas can, with their purses in their laps, their collars up around their ears, long feathers in their hats, and the toes of their tightly laced, hard-worn, little-old-lady shoes just touching the thick-rubber, "easy-care" flooring, talking a blue streak with their little whining voices.

"There he was kicked off the gymnastics team for horsing around in the shower, and nothing to do after school," Bernice said, snapping the clasp of her purse open and closed. "So I said, 'Well, *Walter*, why don't you get a job. Earn a little pocket money. Help out around here.' And *he* said, all smug and snippy the way he always was, 'Ma, there ain't a decent job for a kid within an hour's bus ride from here. Leave me be.' This was back when there wasn't a McDonald's on every street corner that would hire kids who don't know how to work and pay them nothing, like there is now! Nowadays you can hardly throw a rock and not hit a McDonald's. Walter's out in Denver now, selling cars, the last I heard. What kind of work is that for a grown man? Married to some hussy from Baltimore."

Fanny twirled the strap of her purse around her thumbs, tired of Bernice's endless complaints about Walter, whom everyone on the 1300 block of West Glenlake Avenue knew was a hoodlum and hooligan, smoked that marijuana, and played those nasty kissing games in Gustelfout's garage, "which was never locked, heaven's sake," with the oldest Raushman girl—the one that came home mighty pregnant from that college in Kalamazoo two years later. "Well yes, now, Bernice, that may well be true, hussy and all, but as I was saying, did you read in the paper the other day that Richard M. Daley said he wasn't sad or sorry or regretful he missed the candidates' debate?" Richard M. Daley, oldest son of the late Richard J. Daley (once asked in a court of law what his occupation was, the elder Daley replied, "*I am* the Mayor of the City of Chicago").

Fanny said, "He stood there with a straight face and said that if he'd been there, he would have felt or looked or actually been, oh, I can't remember his exact words, like a slice of baloney and cheese between two pieces of Wonder Bread. Can you believe that? He actually said that?"

"Well, Fanny," said Bernice, "that's just his trouble, this matter of the straight face. I mean, did you ever just turn off the TV sound and take a good long look at him. Why, his face *ain't* straight. It's sort of squeezed off to one side, like a funny lemon. When he screws up his face like that, his talk is a little slurred but plain enough—I've heard that he had a speech coach—but when he lets his face go straight and talks, why you can't hear or understand a blessed thing he says,

'Duh cit' 'n' its pro'lums.' Isn't that the truth? And I heard another thing. He had to take his lawyer's test three times before he passed it. Now, I mean, taking your driver's license test three times to pass is one thing, and Jerome took his Army Induction Physical three times before he passed—and a lot of good *that* did him—but the lawyer's test? Now, Fanny, let me ask you a question. If it was life and death, millions, *billions* of dollars, sue the everlasting daylights out of some fast-talking, pea-head banker who cheated you out of your whole life's savings and family fortune, would you hire some 'third-time's-the-charm' lawyer who couldn't keep a straight face and talk plain at the same time, just because he had his father's name (God rest *his* soul), except for the *J* and the *M* part? And now he's going to be mayor and run the city, may the saints preserve us!, despite the fact he is cute and looks about as harmless as that old bloodhound—what's his name?—in that Disney cartoon *Lady and the Tramp*."

On and on they gassed about anything that came into their heads: about the mayor's election and the neighbors; where their children had gone to; and competing with each other with nasty stories of their husbands (Can you top this?). Bernard was the sloppiest dresser that ever lived, couldn't keep his shirttail in, was always stepping on his shoelaces and tripping over his trouser cuffs, tracked mud in the house from all over creation, had the most bizarre hobbies—one year it was pigeon racing and woodshop down at the Broadway Armory, another year it was stamps and train watching, the year he died it was restaurant tours and origami—bought *all* his clothes at the Sears, Roebuck, and when the family piled into the De Soto for their summer vacation trip to Kentucky Lake he drove like some mad Russian (swatting the kids with a rolled-up newspaper when they got antsy, tumbling around like puppies: "I just want to get there. You kids shut up and sit down! Count cows, for God's sake!"). Frank talked in his sleep and could wolf down a dinner so fast it was as if he tipped his plate up and just sucked it in. "After all that work, he made it look like it wasn't worth eating. Why I worked so hard in the kitchen is beyond me!" said Bernice. "*Birth*day cakes, anniversary steaks, Thanksgiving turkeys, Christmas leg of lamb, Easter ham, Wrigley Field Opening Day hot dogs—snarf-snarf-snarf." Max sat in back of them wiggling his nose like a pig rooting for grubs. " 'Thanks, Ber, great eats!' 'You're welcome, dear. Seconds?' Fanny, Frank was the father of my children—may he rest in peace—and at least he brought his check home every Friday and was home every night of the week besides, but why I would waste my breath and ask that man if he wanted seconds is beyond me."

Both women had hats with long, slim feathers, and every time one turned her face toward the other, touching her sleeve for emphasis, the feather—dry and slightly oily at the same time, like the backs of Amaryllis's cats—would brush across Max's face. Halfway through the story about Bernard's heart attack—Bernard disappearing like lost luggage into the head-high snowbank above the rose hedge; his soul departed this earth half an afternoon before Fanny thought to look out of doors—Max changed seats with the gas can, put a foot up on the baseboard heater, laid his elbow on his knee, his chin in his hand, and stared out the window.

By that time the train had traveled south quite a bit, past Graceland Cemetery, where truckloads of rich and famous people were buried. From Potter Palmer and George Pullman, Cyrus McCormick and Philip Armour, to Jack Johnson and Augustus Dickens (youngest brother of that writer guy Charles), Allan Pinkerton (Lincoln's private detective) and

Timothy Webster (hanged from a pear tree in Richmond, Virginia, for a Union spy); people with streets named after them—Harrison, Altgeld, Fullerton, Wacker, McClurg, Root—even the first male child born in Chicago (died here, too). Heavens to Betsy, Max thought to himself, that's a lot of dead people. The tall, thick concrete cemetery fence along the rising railroad spur next to the El tracks was decorated with grotesquely elegant graffiti—*Kill the Poets, Gay Pride, Stones Hood!/Honky Fags Die, Cynthia Loves It*, and whatnot—along with a huge sign nailed to one of the overhanging trees about eye level with the train:

NO DUMPING

VIOLATORS SUBJECT

TO PROSECUTION

There was a jog in the tracks for Sheridan Road and then the train headed south past Wrigley Field, "the friendly confines," as Ernie Banks used to call it. Home of the Chicago Cubs (lovable losers, the doormat of the National League since time out of mind), owned as a tax write-off by Philip Wrigley, the guy who made a whopping fortune selling chewing gum—imagine that? The Cubs' only tradition until 1988 (when lights were installed) was day baseball played on real grass, and they hadn't finished anywhere vaguely near the big money since 1945, when every able-bodied man in Christendom was off fighting German Nazis and Japanese fascists. On the way home El train commuters could see the W (win) or L (lose) pennants flying from the top of the only hand-operated scoreboard in the National League.

There is a curious, unacknowledged tradition in the Wrigley Field bleachers. When the visiting team hits a home run, the bleachers rise in a body to catch it—arms outstretched, mouths agape—which they almost never do on the fly, then shags it down (by this time the guy is dogging it around second, grinning like an ape about his batting average and the RBI), but before the guy reaches third someone throws the ball, a priceless souvenir anywhere else, back onto the field and it dribbles across the infield before the guy is halfway home, taunting the pitcher with his shuffling little jaunt. This ritual is never shown on TV, and good old slurpy Harry Carey never mentions it ("Bad for baseball"), and it never makes the papers; the fan who threw it is taken downstairs by the "security men" (which the public-address announcer makes a point of describing as "off-duty policemen") and given a scalding lecture about acting like a gentleman (or a lady), sportsmanship and all that other bullshit, then generally let go. The bleacher bums seem to be saying: We would rather die a bunch of dirtbag winos, motherless and unloved, than accept this gift from you; go ahead, help yourself to the RBI; take the goddamn pennant, see if we care. *We* have day baseball, played on *real* fucking grass.

(In 1985, Max had somehow got hold of a "Charlie Hustle" Pete Rose homer, when he was making his run for Ty Cobb's record for lifetime hits. Rose, a notorious switch hitter, was standing in against Lee Smith, a tall and ugly, notorious fast-ball pitcher. With a count of three and one, Smith tried to blow one by him on the outside corner and Rose hit it into the left-field bleachers. Max wept as he tossed it back—five thousand haranguing bleacher patrons chanting: "Hits? Yes. RBIs? No"; others screaming at Max: "Throw it, you fool, or we'll kick your ass from here to Chinatown" and "Charlie who? Charlie who?" There were many offers to buy Max many rounds of beers, and when Max wound up and threw it back onto the grass there were hearty cheers from everyone in the park—the TV camera busying itself with a shot of Cubs manager Jim Frey looking mighty sad, inconsolably perplexed, and inexplicably philosophical. Meanwhile, back in the left-field bleachers, Max could not be consoled, as rip-roaring, shit-faced, falling-down, sloppy drunk as he got—a Pete Rose homer, for Christ's sake! The next day Belle-Noche told Max that when he went to the bleachers he should carry an old, raggedy baseball for just such a moment, then instead of throwing back the "real" one, he could heave the nasty, hideous old used one; Max had to laugh at the neat, sufficient logic of it. Four years later when Rose got banned from baseball—basically for being a jerk—all Max said was, "It figures.")

At Belmont Avenue (named for the Battle of Belmont in the Civil War, when General Grant marched three thousand Union troops into Missouri and was defeated by rebels commanded by General Leonidas Polk) everyone changed trains, the north/south subway for the Ravenswood El (the one that went around the Loop for which Downtown was named). Then the train headed south again, stopping first at Fullerton Avenue to pick up the first of the rich people from Lincoln Park—professors, TV producers, trendy storefront retailers, professional artists (like unlicensed English majors who suddenly declare themselves poets)—you know, the *comers*. (Fullerton was named for Alexander N. Fullerton, son of a banker, who came to Chicago in 1833 a lawyer and real-estate speculator with plenty of money in his pocket, and made a whopping fortune selling lumber.) Then the train dove into the subway, and by the time it got to Clark and Division Streets (so named, the story goes, because it divided Goose Island in half), Chicago Avenue (named after the city itself; experts say it is an Indian word meaning wild onion), and Grand Avenue (an old Indian trail once known as Whiskey Point Road), there was standing room only—everyone gazing out the standee windows—*serious* Gold Coast rich people; the movers and shakers, the bankers, the Rush Street tourist saloon owners, the exchange brokers, the small-time city patronage lawyers, and that kind. (Rush Street named for Dr. Benjamin Rush, a signatory of the Declaration of Independence.)

Just my meat, Max thought to himself, now with his banged-up two-gallon Johnson outboard motor gas can in his lap, sharing his seat with the night bartender from Mother's (the *grand*mother of all the singles' bars on Division Street). For twenty-eight blocks Max's mind had been blank, lulled into stupidity by the swaying of the train and Bernice and Fanny's endless deluge of trivial gossip.

When the train pulled screaming into State Street (named for the state, *the* downtown shopping district virtually invented by Potter Palmer in the late 1860s) and Washington Boulevard (named for the President), half the passengers stood and faced the door, shuffling forward in the aisle. It's a kind of desperate, grasping compulsion, you know, standing at the door long before the train gets into the station—as if the train were going to get there any quicker and they were going to get out the door any sooner. The conductor, Statue Mosby, married to a schoolteacher and thirteen years on the job, with decent seniority, stood at the far end of the car with his brass key in the lock that worked the doors, smiling and nonchalant, regarding the commuters and shoppers with a stupendous, roaring boredom known only to those who pass eight times a day through the State Street stations (Washington, Monroe, Jackson, and Van Buren; some CTA officials

will tell you it's the longest subway station in the world). After
a while the vast parade of Midwest humanity becomes a
blur—human beings as work.

How would you like it if tens of thousands of people came
trooping through your office while you were trying to work,
sitting down in your chairs to sleep or sitting on the radiator
and staring out the window, reading trash paperback best-
sellers, sucking on grapefruit wedges, talking sheer incom-
prehensible gibberish, staring off into space like zombies,
overdressed, exhausted, standing bump up next to you—
somebody's crotch at the back of your head—and nosing
through your work over your shoulder; and when they got
up, leaving newspapers, candy wrappers, book bags, shopping
bags, Walkman radios, discarded clothes, beer cans, Affy Tap-
ple sticks; a very *smell.* There was even a coterie of homeless
"persons" (as the police blotter called them) who traveled the
trains night and day, summer and winter, rain or shine. You
have to wonder how bank tellers regard money, since they
handle it all day, or what cooks think of food, or what cops
think of the law, or what DJs think of music, or what pit
miners think of coal after shoveling it eight or ten or fourteen
hours. Statue's only concern, as Insull Irby brought the train
to an easeful halt and Statue let his window drop open and
snapped the switches that flipped open the doors, was that
everyone get off as soon as possible without breaking their
goddamn necks.

Half the people got off, Fanny and Bernice included (with
their purses and their umbrellas and plastic mesh shopping
bags), telling each other to be careful as they lurched and
jostled along and warning everyone that *here* were two little
old ladies who wanted *off!*—the other passengers tolerating
the two of them with an exasperating "That's-life-in-the-big-

city" catch-all shrug. Another half got off at State and Monroe (named for the President), racing for the escalators. Then at State and Jackson Boulevard (named for the President) yet another half got off—Max too! And in an instant Max and his two-gallon Johnson outboard motor gas can and his Art Deco dollar-sign money clip made their way through the subway platform musicians (down-at-the-heel cello players, acoustic guitar-playing folk singers, dazzling tap dancers wearing spangled dinner jackets, and coronet and saxophone players come there to practice) and were up the dingy stairs and onto the street, the State Street Mall—the smell of caramel popcorn and articulated bus fumes and greenback cash everywhere —out among this world's solid citizens once more. Max looked up at the grimy old buildings and the new construction, knowing that in a few hours he would be filthy rich, dripping with cash. He took a breath and whispered, "Ah!" and felt like rubbing his hands together in sheer glee.

This definitely wasn't like Max's bus driving days, when State Street was bumper to bumper with buses and the diesel fumes hung in the air like the pall of smoke hanging over the debris of a demolished building.

Max lollygagged down to Jackson Boulevard, ditching the crowd he'd come up the stairs with. He checked his tie and hat in a store window (snapping the brim for good luck), crossed the street, then crossed again coming north along the wide brick State Street promenade. Then he started in.

He saw a small thin young man dressed in a trench coat and carrying a *Sun-Times* under his arm coming up the stairs at the head of another crowd and walked right up to him, but then halted, almost embarrassed—suddenly he didn't know what to say.

Inspired by extreme and anxious panic, Max held the

gas can up where the guy could see it and blurted out, "Say listen, I'm in a bind," ad-libbing. The guy in the trench coat stopped to listen, wondering what sort of distress this strange man could be in, a man looking slightly foolish in a big tie and holding a gas can for dear life, as if it were a ladder rung. "I've done a very stupid thing," Max went on. "I just got into town, parked my car, and went to a meeting. I went to claim my car," and Max pointed south and east, signifying a city parking garage on Wabash Avenue around the corner and down the block out of sight, "and discovered I'd left the house without my wallet." Max wanted the guy (Gary Fuqua, an actuarial trainee with Lembke Corporation) to see the wallet left on the dresser, chockful of money and papers and tax-deductible receipts, spare keys and photographs of the wife and kids, discolored business cards collected from all the collar counties, and a loose deck of bright plastic charge cards. Gary Fuqua looked Max up and down as if searching for the bulge of his wallet. Fuqua wore a Burberry trench coat with more straps and buckles than he could ever use, a fifties flattop (what local barbers call a "boy's summer haircut"), and walked with a slight jerk from a dislocated hip he'd got playing flag football in high school.

"But that's not the worst of it," Max said, moving the story along. "Now I find out my car's out of gas." And Max held up the gas can and rattled it some—flakes of rust and insect husks, loose at the bottom, rattled with a shushing sound—empty. "The point is, I've got to get to (uh) Buffalo Grove for a sales meeting by two o'clock." Max made a large gesture of looking at his Timex. "I don't have much time to spend on this, and a quarter won't do. Could you help me out with a couple of bucks." And again he indicated the gas can with his eyes, meaning that he had to get to Buffalo Grove *fast.* Tens of thousands of dollars were at stake; hundreds of jobs from one end of the country to the other. Gary Fuqua walked on, listening to Max's tale of woe, eyeing him severely but seeming to understand the clothes when Max mentioned "sales"—Yeah, just like you'd expect one of those salesmen guys to dress; figures; remembering Terry Rippy, the Fuller Brush man who came to the house four times a year to flirt with his mother and sell toilet articles and such as that; *he'd* always dressed "funny." Much to Gary's own amazement (virtually unable to resist) he whipped out his wallet and plucked a single from the stack, folded it in half—the money flat and stiff—gave it to Max, and kept walking. "God will bless you, sir," Max said as Gary walked across the street and disappeared around the corner at Adams Street (named for the President; Gary feeling uncommonly good), going toward the U.S. Gypsum Building.

Max could hardly believe his eyes, and stood on the sidewalk staring at the folded paper. He wanted to paste it up somewhere, the way saloon keepers would tape their first dollar above the cash register, as if to say, "Hurrah! Huzzah! Hoo-ha! Max, old buddy, old pal, we're in business!" and dance a little jig.

Easy! Max thought to himself. This is easy. Why didn't I think of this before?

In his time he'd been a golf caddy (his first job ever, where he learned one of life's first and most cruel lessons—women are lousy tippers), an Andy Frain usher (rock concerts were such a drag, but not as bad as the auto show), a car hiker for the Grateful Dead Auto Auctioneers ("The Best on Western"), and screamed himself hoarse as a beer concessionaire at Comiskey Park ("Beer here! Hey, *beer!*"). He drove a North Side bus for the Chicago Transit Authority out of the

North Park car barn (the money was positively righteous, but the uniforms never fit, the heat in summer was withering, and the bus-riding public were such assholes). He'd scrounged alleys as a pickup truck entrepreneur cruising for refrigerators, stoves, storm windows, and such as that (a lot of back work but very lucrative!)—trying his level, mildly incompetent best to keep body and soul together, food on the table, and the dogs away from the door. In his day Max had also driven a Checker cab, but was a terrible driver—a true menace—and never got the hang of cheating—or cutting corners, so to speak (as many times as Belle-Noche tried to explain it to him; Belle was not a good teacher and Max was a lousy student). But never in his life had money been this easy.

All the rest of the morning and into the afternoon he worked his way up State Street to Lake Street, then over to Dearborn (named after General Henry Dearborn, veteran of Bunker Hill, and President Thomas Jefferson's Secretary of War) and down to Van Buren (named for the President), over to Clark and up as far as the Greyhound Bus station across Randolph Street (for some obscure reason named after Thomas Jefferson's cousin John Randolph, Virginia's U.S. Senator in the 1820s), from Richard J. Daley Plaza, kitty-corner from City Hall—a building that looked like a mausoleum or a World War II Maginot bunker—stopping strangers and passersby and hustling them with his sad tale of cheerful incompetence and once-in-a-lifetime woe. Max worked the entire loop grid from State Street to Wells (named for Captain William Wells, hero of the Fort Dearborn massacre in 1812) and beyond—about three hours it took him.

As the day wore on, his story became more elaborate. He was a poor hapless schnook who never made a mistake in his life, nothing to check his steady rise and calm, safe suburban life (Just the perfect, healthy, righteous atmosphere to raise children, wouldn't you say?); he wanted people to see Max the family man, Little League coach, buyer of church raffle tickets, amateur camper, woodsman, and jogger, and backyard gardener (Max's big, juicy Early Girl and Beefsteak tomatoes the envy of the block—out of this world!). He wanted them to see all that and more—except this morning I did a really silly thing: I was in such an all-fired hurry to leave the house and get to this early meeting ("*You* know how enthusiastic salesmen get. You *know* how much nonsense these breakfast meetings are"), crank up the old Beemer, and get into town with all my sample cases and no hassle, I flat out forget my wallet on the dresser. Silly, silly me.

Sometimes he was the Buffalo Grove computer salesman, sometimes the Freeport municipal lawyer (come to town on township business—something about water rights and state-mandated utility easements), sometimes he was the Burlington, Iowa, wheat factor (never been to the *big* city and plenty anxious) come for a Board of Trade business luncheon and a late-afternoon ball game (courtesy of Muffin, Trunks & Chaffee, Attorneys at Law), and sometimes he was the career navy man (which also explained the weird clothes), just retired and come to Chicago to look up his creep of an ex-brother-in-law and punch him out for doing his sister wrong fifteen years ago—the brother-in-law one of those shits who went out for a pack of smokes and never came back. No story seemed too farfetched and fantastical or just plain *crazy*, and it always brought in plenty of dough. Walking down Franklin Street (named for Benjamin Franklin, American Revolutionary patriot, etc.), crossing Madison Avenue (named for the President), Max finally wondered if these people wouldn't believe the plain, flat-out honest truth: I'm a harmless petty crook and this—the two-gallon Johnson outboard motor gas can, stupid hat and goofy tie, the Hush Puppies, the aggressive innocent begging—*this* is what I do for a living. The idea of telling people the truth was suddenly irresistible, like the Sears Tower window washer who suddenly gets the undeniable notion into his head at the ninety-second floor that he could just hop over the safety bar and step back from the scaffold, float in air, and admire his work. But Max was able to restrain himself admirably.

Sometimes Max talked to one person, sometimes several, and sometimes he drew a crowd, especially at street corners, waiting for the walk light—Max beseeching them with his earnest and guileless ineptitude. He was capable of doing and saying virtually anything with a straight face (the way street-smart dope dealers, serious gangbangers, and poker-faced lawyers bullshit cops and judges)—that—who knew?—it just *might* be true. Some listeners thought him a pathetic trashy fool, some believed every last word of his pitiful little story, some (whose own pitch was more high-toned and lucrative) instantly recognized a comrade-in-arms; some were so impressed with the whole expression of his body and tone of voice and unshakable (if slightly hilarious) sincerity—the whole wacky theater of it—that they couldn't help themselves. Duped or embarrassed, amused or entertained, nearly everyone whipped out his wallet and coughed up some cash.

You see more and more beggars these days, anyway, loitering in the park, panhandling with hands shiny with dirt, mumbling about you helping them scrounge enough change for a meal—"A *quarter* will do."

There are the "blind" guys who hang around outside the El stations rattling a paper coffee cup of brand-new Eberhart pencils, not saying anything and certainly not expecting anyone to actually *take* a pencil.

And not too many years ago an old blind black guy named Arvella Gray used to stand at the corner of Grand Avenue and State Street in front of the Jazz Record Mart with a paper coffee cup safety-pinned to his shirt, playing a steel acoustic guitar. He used to hang out around Maxwell Street, too (that street named for Dr. Philip Maxwell, a state legislator known as the "Falstaff of the Chicago medical profession"). In his time Gray had been a Mississippi River roustabout, among other things, and once got two fingers shot off during an attempted stick-up. He'd stand at the top of the subway steps, cranking out blues tunes with the three fingers he had left on his strumming hand for the homebound coat-and-tie commuters (songs by Blind Willie McTell and Peetie Wheatstraw, Big Maceo Merriweather and Robert Nighthawk, and a bunch of other old-timers who lived fast and died young).

The song he dearly loved to sing was an old McTell tune:

Ticket agent, ticket agent, which a-way is my woman gone?
"Describe your woman and I'll tell you which road she's on."

She's a long, tall mama, five and a half from the ground,
She's a tailor-made woman and she ain't no hand-me-down.

Mama, if you ride the Union Pacific, I'd ride the Santa Fe,
When you get to Memphis, pretty woman, look around for me.

Take my advice, let all married women alone,
'fore their husbands grab you and beat you ragged as a cedar
*   tree.*

I want to tell you, pretty woman, exactly who I am,
When I walk out that front door I hear that back door slam.

And when he would finish singing each song he'd twang-a-twang that guitar of his and shimmy some to make the change in his cup jangle.

Then there's the one beggar in town who really works at it, standing on his knees, staked out at the foot of the down escalator at the Chicago and North Western Railroad station, his voice cracking, a little handmade sign around his neck UNEMPLOYED HOMELESS VETERAN, saying to the blur of passersby stepping, homebound, off the escalator, "Say, I need a little money for dinner. Say, I'm a homeless, unemployed veteran and I need some money for a meal. Say, I need a little money for a meal," and pausing every now and again to get his breath, lean back on his heels to give his knees a rest (like a catcher between pitches), and wipe his face with the whole of his sleeve or the tail of his shirt—a very hard dollar that guy works for.

But Max and his gas can were terrific, raking in the bucks, and hardly broke a sweat.

Whatever the multitudes of solid citizens thought of Max and his strange clothes, his pitiful little gas can, and his sorry little tale, by the middle of the afternoon he had more money than pockets and was rolling the bills and stuffing them into the Johnson outboard motor gas can. Max traveled up one street and down the other, looking in the coin-return trays of each and every pay phone he passed. And try as he might, still he didn't find anywhere he could sneak to and take a look at all that geetis—he was itching like crazy to take it out and touch it, face and fold it, count it and caress it. But he didn't trust ducking into an alley. So late in the afternoon he boarded a Ravenswood train at the renovated Quincy/Wells station (looking like the bright, snappy restored antique it was;

Quincy named for President John *Quincy* Adams), and home he and his gas can went, smiling and jaunty.

• • •

Max arrived home in a jiffy—"a New York minute," some of the clock-watching loafers down at Deadwood Dave's Wild West Saloon would have said—and when he walked in the door, he could smell a very good dinner cooking in the oven and boiling on the stove.

"Welcome home, Max, we're glad to see you!" said Muriel from the kitchen. "Did you have a good day, dear?"

"Yes, Muriel, it was just *fine*," Max said, and took his two-gallon Johnson outboard motor gas can straight to their bedroom (Just *fucking* fine! he thought to himself) and stashed it under the chest of drawers, hung up his coat, took off his tie (trying in the unraveling to see how it was that Muriel had tied it in the first place), washed his hands in the sink, changed into his housework overalls and slippers, and came downstairs. He gave Muriel a big hug and a big sloppy kiss on the lips, copping a feel as she stood at the stove while he was at it, said, "Did I *ever*!," got himself a bottle of Augsburger dark from the back of the Kelvinator, and went out to the glassed-in sun porch to smoke himself a cigar. (Muriel made Max drink dark beer because it was "healthy," and did her best to put up with the cigars—godawful cheap, smelly torpedoes though they were.)

When Muriel rang the little bronze dinner bell for dinner, the whole house—cats and all—came to the table, dawdling around their chairs until everyone was present. Muriel sat at the end of the table closest to the kitchen in case she had to fetch anything; Max sat at the other end, with his back to the ferrets. Max's loopy old mother, Agnes-Ruth—who always spent the morning in her attic garret talking to herself—sat to his left.

Agnes-Ruth (née McPhee) had come to Chicago in 1938 with Darl Dwayne Nutmeg, her husband, from Jessamine County, Kentucky, looking for work—and found plenty. Every afternoon at 4:30 she came out on the porch with a tumbler of gin and a pack of Kools and sat in the high-backed car seat and watched the Chicago and North Western commuter trains zoom and roar by, chain-smoking and sipping her ice-cold gin, talking to herself and the occasional passerby about how much she had loved Darl and how much she regretted it when he was killed in an industrial accident (a flat car of planed lumber tipped over on him; when the police peeled him off the freight-yard roadbed he looked like a hairpin), but that the insurance money certainly had been a blessing and a comfort—even if the insurance company had taken the devil's own time sending her the check—measly though it was, it *was* all they could afford; she told strollers that every time she went to the racetrack with Verna Wheat, her neighbor, who'd since moved to Alaska, she thought of how handsome Darl was, but that it was God's will he was snatched from this life in his prime, though the worst part of the whole tragedy was having to sleep alone in the attic with all those blankety-diddle cats Amaryllis let into the house, and the fact that Darl—who had been the handsomest man in Jessamine County, you see!—was not here to enjoy all that good money.

After half a pack of smokes and an eight-ounce tumbler of gin, Agnes-Ruth would be on a roll and feeling no pain.

Next to her was Belle-Noche, dressed for the evening, and Petunia-Rose, passably ugly and the oldest of Belle's ugly daughters (a part-time barmaid at Deadwood Dave's Wild West Saloon). On the other side of the table sat Daisy-Lily, middling ugly (studying nursing at Midwest Industrial Arts College), Amaryllis (stunningly ugly and so dumb she was virtually unemployable, but if you asked Easy Ed, a great piece of ass), and Sweet William, who was so dim that Max had to stare in wonder at how he had made it into adolescence. (He had made it, Sweet William would reply, by selling retail marijuana.) Then came Easy Ed, who had the habit of eating everything with a tablespoon which he held with his entire fist. Robert—the "Boy"—was not at the table, because right then he was out making extra money delivering phone books; it seemed to Muriel that he was never home for dinner. Amaryllis's cats wandered in and out, rubbing up against everyone's legs, sniffing for scraps—some purring louder than diesel engines at idle. The ferrets wrestled in their cage, tumbling over one another in a parody of a cartoon alley cat fight and yipping at the tops of their little ferret lungs.

When the platter was passed to Max—everything always passed to the left—he said, "Muriel, what is it this time?" He was looking at a heaping pile of small, coffin-shaped rectangles the color and texture of toasted-coconut ice-cream bars.

"Max dear," Muriel said at the other end of the table, smiling, "these are turbot fish sticks, aren't they nice, and this is creamed corn with sweet red peppers, and this"—she passed the piping-hot serving bowl to Daisy-Lily (the bowl got for 15 cents at a garage sale on Winthrop Avenue near Foster Avenue in Uptown)—"*this* is stir-fried broccoli with almonds and butter sauce. Don't you like it? By the way, dear, how did it go today?"

(Winthrop Avenue was named for John Winthrop, first

governor of the Massachusetts Bay Colony; Foster Avenue was named for Dr. John H. Foster, real-estate tycoon, who came to Chicago in 1835 to settle up his brother's affairs when he was shot and killed by a drunken soldier.)

Max picked up his knife and fork, and hardly knew where to begin. "Well," he said, cutting his pile of fish sticks and spreading some of Muriel's homemade horseradish on the edge of his plate, "it was like taking candy from babies. It was like finding money in the street. It was like having people come up to you and push money into your hands." And he told everyone his astonishing story of how he had spent his day—without actually telling them the approximate cash amount, his "guesstimate" he would have called it—gesturing with his knife smeared with horseradish and breading crumbs high into the air and out over the serving bowls, popping his eyes at every punch line. And when he was through, Sweet William said, "*Wow*, Unc, that's a great riff!" (On top of everything else, Sweet William was a terrible amateur musician— a member of a New Age–Heavy Metal amateur garage group sometimes called Riot with Padding or The Great Train Robbery or Douse Da Glim.)

After dinner, after boozing it up a little with Easy Ed (watching the TV news and talking back to the utterly handsome anchor people and street reporters), Max threw the cats out of the bedroom (like a newspaper delivery truck helper shoveling bundles of Sunday supplements off the back of a truck), turned on the BreezeKing window fan, and commenced to count his money.

If there was one room in the midst of the chaos of the Nutmeg house on which Muriel lavished all her exquisite and minute attention, it was her and Max's bedroom. There were plenty of pillows on the bed, which was covered with a thick comforter decorated with dogs of every age, size, and description. The headboard was an enormous bright red, crushed-velvet affair that did not squeak. On the ceiling above the bed was a large mirror—Muriel liked to watch the muscles in Max's rear end work and his toes curl while they were screwing; she liked to see her ankles crossed over the small of his back; she liked to see her hands spread wide on his back and the reddened nail marks she made across his shoulder blades.

The one thing Max loved to do was count money—though he'd seldom seen so much of it. He put his blazer back on, the pockets stiff and bulging with cash (a little wine-drunk and bubble-headed). Then he began prancing and mincing around the room—between the bed and the dresser, the foot of the bed and the door, the wall and the bed—dipping his fingers into the pockets, pulling out little clumps of crumpled-up bills and sprinkling them over the bedspread, where wolfhounds napped, Afghan hounds leaped over stone fences chasing bears, and Labrador puppies crouched ready to pounce on ragged house slippers. He danced his little jig over to the dresser, where he kept his antique tin of Players cigarettes and his stash of Northern California sinsemilla, popped the tin open, and took out a neat, expertly rolled joint—Muriel called them cigarettes, Amaryllis called them doobies, and Sweet William called them "the accessory" (in a parody of heavy-metal punk-hip)—and "cranked" one up, as Amaryllis would say, with a strike-anywhere kitchen match. At first glance a body wouldn't expect that Max was the sort of degenerate heathen to use "recreational pharmacology" (as some of the out-of-work, overage gangbangers down at Deadwood Dave's liked to call it), but there you are, as the saying goes; there is more than one peculiar contradiction in this world; there are times in this life when there are astonishing surprises at every turn. Max had learned to smoke marijuana when he tended bar at the Glenview Naval Air Station Officers' Club back in the days when dope was *good* for you. Smoking it made Max mighty horny, of course, but it just gave Muriel the giggles (which to her resembled the hiccups) and was an integral part of their bedroom games.

> *Get a little* high,
> *And then we play* Spy

was how Muriel put it as she stalked around in the dark wearing her white fox fur hat. In an instant Max felt light-headed and airy as a fawn, and the BreezeKing window fan blew a fragrant, watered-lawn smell into the room. Max wistfully imagined it was the smell of money and continued to take great sucking, he-man lungfuls of the joint and toss money out of his pockets, onto the bed, tiptoeing around in a kind of parody of a clown waltz—the only way he knew how to dance—his long, thin basketball player's hands floating limp and elegant in the air. In no time at all he was higher than a kite and plenty cross-eyed. Sometimes he flipped handfuls of money over his shoulder, sometimes he sprinkled them as if he were a kid scattering sand at the beach, sometimes he threw them as if trying to shatter rocks—aiming for the heads of the dogs (dachshunds and poodles and miniature collies)—and sometimes he imagined himself to be Michael Jordan leaping with remarkable poise and superhuman elegance across half the backcourt to reach up with his ape-like arms (tongue hanging out, huge feet fluttering the way Michael's do) to slam a righteous, breakaway lay-up. Max hadn't had so much easy fun with money since he'd found an old metal ammo box full of passable-looking counterfeit twenties and fifties that time he delivered a 1965 Buick Electra to Kaiser Brothers Dodge Sales in Valparaiso for the Grateful Dead Auto Auctioneers. What a hell of a train ride home that had been. Now, *that* was some party, Max thought to himself—Max pouring the money all over a naked and squirming, voluptuous Muriel from a bushel basket; Muriel uproarious with hysterical giggles half the night (everywhere he touched her she was ticklish); Max beside himself with glee as he held her by the wrists, above her head, and pushed the money around with his nose, "interrogating" her. (The ammo can of genuine counterfeit was still around the house somewhere—probably in the basement.)

When Max got fired from the Grateful Dead, the umpteenth shitty job he'd had, he came away with another one of his rules of life: All you need to be a used-car dealer is a bunch of American flags, a couple of strings of 100-watt lights, and a guy working for you who knows how to wash cars.

After Max had emptied all the money from his pockets he kicked the two-gallon Johnson outboard motor gas can from under the dresser. He looked at the spout and suddenly realized that he was going to have trouble getting to the cash. This was not some ceramic piggy bank where all you had to do was stick a table knife into the coin slot and shake it around, working the knife until the money came dribbling out—No, no, Max thought to himself, a body could shake that goddamn gas can all day and all night and all the next day and never would you liberate a single dollar bill. Max stood in front of the mirror in his house-repair bib overalls and blazer, mighty perplexed; all that money so close and yet so far. Still and all, there was only one way to do it, though it would be killing the goose that laid the golden egg—he hated to, but there it was. He set the gas can on the bed and went down to the kitchen and fetched the Mixmaster electric can opener—a contraption as big as a four-slot toaster. Back upstairs he plugged it in and set it on the cedar chest under the fan. Then Max clamped the gas can into the machine and turned it on. Never had Max heard such a noise come out of the electric can opener since he'd bought it at the Kane County Flea Market in 1974 for three bucks, but he'd had to haggle and argue with the guy (a Hines Lumber Company yardman from out near Palwaukee Airport in Wheeling) until he was blue in the face. A horrible grinding and crunching and squealing that set all the dogs off back of the alley and made babies start from their sleep up and down the block (there were suddenly new babies on the street—Muriel couldn't account for them, there were just more).

A long time it took that machine to work its way around the bottom lip of that gas can—goddamn those Johnson people, thought Max, impatiently biding his time, watching the blade make its way around the bottom of the can, which curled up like humidity-soaked shirt cardboard. Money began spilling out like popcorn from an antique movie theater popcorn maker, but soon enough the machine was finished and turned itself off. Max poured the crumpled-up bills onto the bed and threw what was left of the two-gallon Johnson outboard motor gas can over by the door so Muriel could throw it out with the rest of the day's trash. Then he went around and picked up loose money from the floor, scooping it up as if it were confetti.

All that dough made a mighty handsome pile on the bedspread, bits of rust and dust, the corpses of dead bugs, and all.

He sucked down the last of the joint, knocked the glowing tip off into the ashtray, and ate the rest, gulping it down with a dry mouth. (That's what Max thought most wonderful about smoking "the truest herb," as Sweet William called it: you didn't have to keep it cold; foam didn't go up your nose and spills didn't dribble on your shirt; it didn't make you pee every five minutes; you could smoke it till you fell asleep in the chair and set the house on fire, but it never gave you a hangover; you didn't make a racket when you threw it into the street—you didn't have to worry about recycling the god-damn thing, anyway—just smoke that sucker down to the lips, knock the ash off, and eat the son of a bitch! Max thought that was mighty elegant.)

Then came the really fun part—the counting. He sat on the bed, plenty light-headed and dreamy, and proceeded to unravel, uncurl, and unfold all those crumpled, well-knotted, double-dog-eared pieces of paper. Some of the money was brand-spanking-new, some was as limp and sticky as a nasty old handkerchief, but most of the bills were simply middling well used. No matter. Each and every one he smoothed out on his leg and laid down—reading the notice across the top of each one (FEDERAL RESERVE NOTE) on the border just above THE UNITED STATES OF AMERICA, keeping an eye out for the old silver certificates, which were actually worth money. While he was looking, Max couldn't help but see the little notice under the word UNITED that read, *This note is legal tender for all debts, public and private.* Isn't that the truth, Max thought to himself, just isn't that the truth. It took him considerable time to get through all of it, Max not bothering to count any just yet. When he had the money all straightened out, he faced all the bills the right way (each loose stack about as thick as a bar of soap)—Max had what could pass for a spiritual reverence and uttermost respect for money. He loved to handle cash; loved to touch it and rub a handful of it with his thumb; loved to fold a handful of it in half and feel the easy bulge of it in his front pocket (next to his crotch). For all the endless day-in, day-out supreme aggravations of driving a CTA bus, Max's one compensation (and few there were) was that he handled money.

Then, in a kind of mindless, idiot ecstasy, he picked up a pile of cash and counted it, using both hands—passing each bill from one hand to the other with his wetted thumb, like you see the guys do at Arlington International Racecourse betting windows. And as he moved the money with his thumb he counted out loud by tens:

> *One, two, buckle my shoe.*
> *Three, four, shut the door.*
> *Five, six, pick up sticks.*
> *Seven, eight, lay them straight.*
> *Nine, ten, begin again!*

On and on he counted, mincing around the room in front of the BreezeKing window fan—a beautiful litany, a mantra, an exquisite and wonderful poem. He counted the money with superb concentration and admiration, and laid each handful on the bed. Sixty, seventy, eighty . . . hundred fifty, hundred sixty, hundred seventy . . . two hundred (taking a long sigh, and then a break to get himself a tall glass of water from the bathroom). On and on he went, giddy, smiling to himself over his shoulder in the mirror, so pleased with his day's work he could hardly keep from laughing out loud. He was well into the three hundreds when he came to the last stack. Never in all his born days had George Washington, that grand old patriarch and patriot, soldier, statesman, Virginia land and slave owner, looked so handsome and sartorial, Max thought to himself. But, and here he chuckled and grinned big and sly in the mirror, what the fuck, it's only a buck!

When Max had it all counted and stacked and everything was sitting pretty, it came to $357; and it all looked mighty fine.

That was when Muriel came in, closing the door behind her with a conspirator's calm. Everything down in the kitchen shipshape, clothes washed and folded and put away, and the whole house glowing like a well-lit Christmas ornament. Muriel, who didn't altogether approve of begging with a gas can—"shenanigans," she called it—looked at Max and looked at the rumpled stacks of greenbacks and had to admit she was impressed. She gave Max a big hug (and a big kiss on the lips), the like of which he couldn't rightly recall, and left him gasping and breathless. Then she stood in the middle of the bed, like an acrobatic aerialist just come down from another triumph on the high wire to take her bows—large and extravagant; *voila!* (also *hup!*)—had her clothes off in an instant, and stood there in all her naked and abundant glory. Max could never decline an invitation like that.

There was going to be plenty of nasty high jinks and good clean fun tonight!

Let's Play Two

Max woke from a dream with the biggest shit-eating grin you ever did see—Muriel already "up and at 'em," as Belle-Noche would say (with a petulant snarl, grinning and jealous). The night before, Muriel had helped him bundle all that dough (bound with rubber bands) and hide it under the loose maple plank under the bed; then she just about fucked him silly—Muriel, as it turned out, could keep up with Max just fine—celebrating their astonishing good fortune on her hands and knees with her rear end up in the air.

Another day, another dollar! Max thought to himself in the full light of day, and fumbled around, searching under the bed with his fingers for his Jockey shorts. He stood on the bed—out of the way of the cats—to pull his shorts on and then went to the bathroom. Once again the mighty sound of warm urine was heard throughout the house—and everyone knew that good old soft-touch Uncle Max was up and about. Max grinned at himself in the mirror, the smile spreading over his face the way a pleasant odor fills a room. If you stood on the railroad tracks across the street and looked in the window of the upstairs bathroom (the only bathroom in the place), you could point and say, "Now, *there's* a man keen to get to work"—so sure was he of making a killing (as they say in the Soybean Pit over at the Board of Trade while drooling over crop failures and trade embargoes, famines and hurricanes, and civil wars). Max just could not wait to get downtown once more. He dressed in a jiffy, this time in well-buffed wing-tip shoes, a Hart Shaffner & Marx three-piece suit, and a madras breast-pocket handkerchief—the whole ensemble got for a song at an apartment sale on Belle Plaine Avenue (French for "beautiful field") just west of Clark Street—and straw Panama hat, which, Sweet William, when he saw him in the kitchen, called Max's "Florida Dope Dealer's Hat."

For several years now Sweet William had made a fair living selling Baggies of marijuana back of the garage, out of the trunk of his mostly mint-condition '54 Plymouth, taking anything handy in trade—cash or goods. Sweet William's work was a kind of running gag the whole family pulled on Grandma (who never left the house except to sit on the porch and commiserate with the world, holding her glass of gin in one hand and her pack of smokes in the other), saying that William was "working on the car, which was going to be worth big bucks someday, Ma." (Max and Muriel and Belle-Noche called her Ma; the grandchildren called her Gunny.) Agnes-Ruth was none the wiser—though it did seem to her that Sweet William dressed too well for someone always puttering with a car, but she explained it away by commenting to passersby, "Well, you know how *men* are!" Sweet William got his start in the retail marijuana business almost the minute he got his valid driver's license—and immediately dropped out of Senn High School ("Who needs this shit?" he said

when the principal called him into his office one more time;
the school named for Nicholas Senn, Swiss-born physician
who was the Illinois Surgeon General during the time of the
Spanish-American War)—traipsing off to Stark County, Indiana, where the most godawful but mildly intoxicating hemp
grew wild along the gravel road ditches and out back of the
barns and equipment sheds of abandoned farms, and could
be got for the trouble of pulling it out of the ground—roots
and all. Stark County hemp was to the marijuana culture what
Bull Durham was to the ready-roll cigarette trade or Richard's
Wild Irish Rose (which some people think is rosé) was to wine
merchants. It was fifty years ago during the big war that
farmers had been given seed and a guaranteed good price for
their hemp—which the United States Navy somehow turned
into rope. Sweet William and his very best friend, Clarence
Gatewood, would cruise the Stark County backroads ("Oh,
the girls of Koontz Lake, eh, Clarence?") in Max's old '48,
straight-8 Pontiac, harvesting the hemp plants with pruning
knives—everything shoved in the trunk until it was tighter
than a drum. What horrible stoop work that was! Sweet William and Clarence drove U.S. Route 41 all the way back to
the house. Then they'd lay it out to dry in the attic, telling
Gunny Agnes-Ruth it was a valuable and precious herb—
which, to hear William and Clarence (and Amaryllis) talk, it
certainly was. And Agnes-Ruth, doting on William as she did,
certainly thought he was an enterprising young man, which
of course he was. After a couple of years, Sweet William got
tired of selling Stark County hemp ("Which was 100 percent
total shit," William said many times, " 'cause you had to suck
down a whole bunch to get any kind of a decent high, and
pity the poor rubes who bought it"), took what was left of his
profits, bought a 1968 Chevy two-door, and bumped into a

guy at the Taste of Chicago by the name of E. J. Cavanaugh, who owned a shack and a couple of acres just off Highway U.S. 1 near Tavernier, Florida, just south of Key Largo. Over a bratwurst and a Berghoff beer Cavanaugh took many elaborate pains to explain to Sweet William, who was paying for the lunch, that all you had to do was take a boat out into the Gulf and the square grouper (as baled marijuana was called down in that neck of the woods) just about jumped into your boat. Cavanaugh threw back his head, laughed right out loud, said it was easier than grenade fishing, *and* more lucrative. Not fifty feet from where the Buckingham Fountain (named for Clarence Buckingham, killed in World War I) was squirting water high into the air, Sweet William and Everett Jackson Cavanaugh struck a deal, spit on their hands right then and there, and shook. After that, every couple of months Sweet William would hop in his Chevy and drive down Interstate 65 to 25 to 75 to U.S. 41 to Route 1 (the main drag between Miami and Key West), down to Cavanaugh's place in Tavernier, and buy with cold hard cash a bale or two of Colombian marijuana—which, Cavanaugh said as they stood on the porch of his ramshackle shotgun house, washed ashore every once in a while and lay as thick as suds along the rocks or the undergrowth. Then Sweet William would dress up in a gaudy Hawaiian shirt and one of those straw Panama numbers he called *his* "Florida Dope Dealer's Hat," and drive back North, as innocent-looking as the day is long—always taking his own sweet time; visiting the Kennedy Space Center, Disney World, Mammoth Cave near Bowling Green (Kentucky), the Barton Museum of Whiskey History in Bardstown, and the Swine, Poultry and Cattle Museum in Indianapolis. Then he and Clarence would divvy up the whole caboodle in little Baggies, and sell it out of the trunk of his Plymouth to those nutty suburban kids who'd drive all the way in from Highland Park and Arlington Heights and Northbrook and Lake Bluff (and such places) to do "a little business," as Clarence called it. And the way those dumb suburban kids smirked and cackled and carried on, you'd have thought they were really getting away with something; William always thought them uproariously "wholesome," and they would look at Clarence and Sweet William and think city kids unbelievably "hoody." Then one year not long ago, Clarence got a wild hair up his ass and joined the Coast Guard. "The Coast Guard?" Sweet William had said. "What the hell you gone and joined the *Coast Guard* for, Christ's sake?" and Clarence had looked at *him* funny and said, "'Cause it suits me just fine, that's why."

· · ·

When Max got all dressed up he sure did look spiffy, though the suit was just a little wide at the shoulders. He took a handful of cash out of his stash, caught the Clark Street #22 bus up to Zayre near Touhy Avenue (named for Patrick L. Touhy, real-estate millionaire who was with Mayor Carter Harrison, Sr., when he was assassinated October 31, 1893), and bought himself a brand-new one-gallon gas can, the cheapest thing he could find—one of those big red numbers about the size of a $100 dictionary that said G A S C A N on the side and C A U T I O N : F L A M M A B L E on the other—and caught the El train at the Howard Street station, where the north-south trains, the Evanston and Skokie Swift trains all met.

Max arrived downtown planning to work the east-west streets, his totally arbitrary reason being that the people who used the north-south streets wouldn't be caught stone dead going east or west. It was a warm and sunny day—the Loop bursting with commerce, Max bursting with glee to commence his work.

So off the train he got at Jackson Boulevard and walked down to Van Buren Street. No sooner had he turned the corner, heading west under the south Elevated tracks toward the main Post Office, than he started to work—"Say, listen, I'm in a bind . . ." First he was the computer salesman from Buffalo Grove (since he had memorized his pitch so completely). Then he was the corn factor from Burlington (and limped some first on one leg, then the other for kicks). *Then* he moved on to a story about his brother's wedding in Zion and how he had stopped off to pick up his tuxedo—"Haven't been in a tux since I was in high school, but *hey*, my brother is my brother. A preacher he is, and marrying a wonderful girl who my dear old sainted mother positively loves to death, and there isn't anything I wouldn't do for him. I'm in the wedding party. I'm in from St. Paul. I left after work yesterday and drove straight through, and stopped off to pick up my tuxedo. Well, pooh, I must have left my wallet in the men's room at the 76 station outside Janesville. The first time in my life I've ever done anything so forgetful and childish. Can't get the tux, can't get my car out of hock, and now I discover I'm out of gas." He offered to show skeptics his Buick Century parked at the city garage just around the corner. What a fix; what a bind; what a dummy I am! "Called my brother's church, then the parsonage, to get somebody down here to help me out, but nobody's answering the phone. Can you beat that? Be a *pal*, help me out with a couple of bucks."

And just the same as the day before, patent attorneys, washerwomen, street-corner newspaper guys, rookie cops, bartenders, Post Office employees, bakery and beer truck delivery men, tourists and the odd, casual passerby, not to mention what the mouthy gossips down at Deadwood Dave's Wild West Saloon called monkeys ("good-looking broads who hang on to their silly-ass City Hall office jobs with their tails")— virtually every solid citizen that Max rubbed up against dug deep out of sheer remarkable generosity (many a cheerful donor discovering his largesse at that very moment) and shelled it out for this best of brothers who drove all bloody night to attend his youngest brother's wedding—"The best-looking of the six of us, *and* the last to get married, that *lucky* dog," Max said. The women Max importuned nearly wept for joy when he told them how handsome was his brother, Charles Francis McNair, and how ravishingly beautiful was his any-minute-now, soon-to-be sister-in-law, Rebecca Scott Krautlander. A real babe, Max told the older guys with a wink. Max seemed to intimate that McNair was a better name for Rebecca Scott than was Krautlander, though no one could say later—when they were telling friends of their strangely memorable encounter with Max ("What a remarkable man he was," they'd say)—how that idea had come into their heads.

As the day wore on and Max traveled with the one-way traffic out Van Buren, in toward the lake on Jackson, out Adams, in Monroe, out Madison, etc., the story got more elaborate and fantastic, and the Loop's solid citizens seemed unable to resist, hauling out their wallets left and right. You might have thought Max was selling shares in some infallible double-your-money-right-this-minute, get-rich-quick scheme—as if the instant they gave him a dollar he was going to reach into his suit, *some*how, *some*where, pull out a big bundle of dough, and give them back two; it was amazing!

Charles and Rebecca had met at the annual church retreat at a Trappist Monastery in Kentucky, Max told people; had corresponded with long letters about various interpretations of lengthy Bible passages; had inexplicably fallen in love; had suddenly found themselves traveling to meet each other more or less halfway (Bellefontaine, Ohio; nice and quiet, definitely out-of-the-way; a town whose claim to fame in the Rand McNally was that the first concrete pavement in the continental United States was laid there in 1891)—she from Clarksburg, where she had a secretary's job at the power company; he from Pistakee Lake, where he was the congregation pastor at the First Church of the Brethren, having indulged in lengthy missionary jaunts to Malaysia on the side. Somehow—neither Charles nor Rebecca could recall it exactly—one night they'd found themselves completely disrobed (shoes and clothes discarded all around the room) and sleeping together, to the sheer unadulterated relief and complete satisfaction of both, between discussions of biblical minutiae. These weekly Bible seminars and tutorial sessions went on for months. And when the families finally discovered what was what between those two, Mother McNair had been justifiably mortified; Charles's Piskatee Lake parishioners were indignant, outraged, and huffy; but Toland Krautlander, father of the bride, was positively, righteously furious and threatened to sue until his wife, Louise Anne, told him to pipe down—Rebecca was finally going to be out of the house: "And thank God for *that*." What could they do now to save Rebecca's sterling reputation (and Charles's gold mine of a job) but get those two married as soon as possible.

Neither Rebecca nor Charles objected in the slightest.

Max snidely whispered to the men, as they hauled out their wallets and handed over their contributions to the great work, that now Charles was going to get laid all the time,

Praise the Lord!, and Rebecca was going to be a missionary preacher's wife—something she'd had her heart set on since she was a little girl.

The blur of gulled solid citizens never fazed Max—not Hovey Curry with his money all knotted up like a wad of gum (listening, distracted, to WBEZ's pledge-week broadcast); not Milo Stibbins, an actor with a day job moving furniture for Carlo Brothers Movers, who gave Max all quarters; not Loretta Spokeshave, with her Seven Deadly Sins Gallery shopping bag of antique kitchen gadgets, fumbling in her purse for her wallet (the woman practically speechless with pity: "What a terrible shame to miss the wedding, Mr. McNair"). Max raked in the cash, never batted an eye, and was just hitting his stride. This was great!

Then about 12:30, as Max was winding it up with Horace Lejeune, a Speed-Demon bicycle messenger on his way to traffic court on North La Salle Street with some paperwork and a check from "some vice-president guy" at Continental Bank, Max saw in the filthy alley doorway of an office building an object in the corner of his eye that was to change his life, and the lives of *all* the Nutmegs, the minute he picked it up. (La Salle Street was named after French explorer Robert Cavalier, Sieur de La Salle, who came through Chicago in 1682, traveling south on his way to discover the Mississippi River, etc.; he was murdered by his own men in 1687, basically because he behaved like a perfect asshole.)

Max thanked Horace for the dollar—the kid leaning over the handlebars of his stripped-down cross-country Schwinn with the bill of his Sox hat turned to the back of his head (the way kids do nowadays) and holding his wallet significantly— " 'preciate it, young fella." Max waited until the kid hopped back on his bike and pedaled off, then turned and walked over to the edge of the sidewalk by the corner of the building and had a closer look.

At first he couldn't exactly make out what the object was, such was his eyesight, but suddenly he figured it out.

The thing was a round, fat, gray-leather lady's wallet, scuffed aplenty and frayed around the edges; a thing as big around as a Captain Nemo's five-dollar submarine sandwich. Max stood flat-footed and gawked unashamed at it—hypnotized, transfixed, immobile—as if it were a beggar's corpse.

To the casual passerby—of which there were plenty at just that moment—Max seemed perplexed and preoccupied, as if suddenly struck with the terrific inevitability of terrible fate; sunk in the awful conundrum of pitiful, exasperating choice; a man staring down into the abyss of horrible, gasping inevitability. To some observers he was the good and faithful white-collar workingman summarily dismissed after twenty-three years in a top-to-bottom corporate housecleaning, with nothing to show for it but a wishy-washy, noncommittal "To whom it may concern" letter of recommendation (written with the fuzzy distinctions and meaningless, ritual compliments of a befuddled high-school book report) and a shoe box— which strangely resembled a gas can—of desktop trinkets and trivial memorabilia. Others saw Max, the tricky investor, who wagers and connives once too often and is ruined between the opening of the market and lunch hour by cleverer and more ruthless ex-clients, who conspire to bankrupt him for the sheer pleasure of seeing him walk from the trading floor stone broke—a ruined man, and good goddamned riddance. Still others imagined the sickened and ashen nausea of a guy who'd seen one too many clams and had slugged down one too many Bud Lights at lunch—Isn't it a shame that some people have no discipline and no feeling for others, they seemed to be saying; that man needs to find Jesus.

To Max it seemed that he must be dreaming; that he and the wallet were suddenly and completely and utterly invisible and alone—even though Max was seen and vividly remembered by scores of people—Sharon Sheppard included.

Then Max got cagey. It can't be I'm the only person who has seen the thing. The wallet was very fat, and the leather and metal, though dusty, gleamed like a beacon. He cocked his head and stared at it, like an inquisitive but skeptical hound. This is perhaps a test of some kind, he thought, and he looked up and down the street for the local CBS network television remote video camera truck (a plain white van with an antenna on top that looked like the twin barrels of some newfangled, death-ray antiaircraft gun). Max and Easy Ed had once watched Mark Schaefer on Channel 2 News ("The *Deuce*," as anchorman Bill Kurtis would say) do that very thing—leave a little girl's cheap plastic wallet on the street near Water Tower Place (one of the few edifices to survive the Chicago Fire of 1871, and spy, taping how this guy or that guy had dealt with it. *That* had been something to watch—ho, ho, ho, Schaefer mugging and winking at the camera—all those Christmas-shopping Michigan Boulevard rubes flipping through some little girl's wallet with her autographs and her classmates' pictures and her notes passed back and forth (the *i*'s dotted with hearts—a very nice touch, Mark), her name, address, and telephone number, *and* a nice clean ten-spot—presumably shopping-spree money, a gift from good old lovable soft-touch Dad.

Max stared at the wallet a long time (the way extraterrestrials might stare at the bizarre spectacle of a three-ring circus), imagining all sorts of horrible, wonderful things, before he moved a muscle.

.   .   .

And just as he was standing there, a woman in a red dress came by, walking from the Chicago and North Western station to meet her husband for lunch. Her name was Sharon Sheppard, and her husband, Miles, worked in the Kluczynski Federal Building on South Dearborn. (Fort Dearborn was located at the intersection of Michigan Boulevard and Wacker Drive, where, in 1812, the Indians massacred every man, woman, and child, except for John Kinzie, one of Chicago's original solid citizens, who snuck out at the last minute and died in his bed stinking rich many years later; Wacker Drive was named for Charles H. Wacker, wealthy brewer, tireless civic do-gooder, and director of the World's Columbian Exposition in 1893, who helped save the lakeshore from the Illinois Central Railroad turning it into wharves, factories, and railhead docks—thanks Chas.). Miles had a federal appointment—a great patronage job—as director or chief manager of all the federal courthouse bookstores in the entire Mid-Continental Region (MidConReg, as they called it in Washington, D.C.; from Ohio to Nebraska, Alabama and Texas to Michigan and the Dakotas; twenty states). His federal salary, along with discreet kickbacks in the form of legal retainers and personal loans from guys who had somehow got it into their heads that Miles had "clout," enabled Miles and Sharon to live in Winnetka, with a country home in the north Wisconsin woods near Rhinelander. They also received contributions (in the form of a large annual Christmas check) out of sheer unadulterated pity from his father, Frederick Sheppard, the paper-cup manufacturer (whose company also made dime-a-dozen notepads designed specifically for air force bomber crews and NASA manned space missions). Twenty-five years ago Frederick had hired some crazy engineer (who taught drafting and calculus at the University of Colorado School of Mines) to develop gummed paper that would stick to everything *but* wouldn't burn. The elder Mr. Sheppard sold the 50-count pads by the truckload at $4.00 a 3 × 5″ sheet—the family fortune assured, because as everyone knows, once you have a Defense Department contract it's harder to get rid of than cats or squirrels.

Sharon and Miles met on the street and walked hand in hand to Binion's Restaurant on south Plymouth Court (named for the town of Plymouth, Massachusetts—the second permanent European settlement in North America), just down the way. When they were seated in the Hob Room and Sharon had settled herself petitely and was playing with her turtle soup (the specialty of the house) and saltines, she told Miles about the remarkable sight of a man in a three-piece suit holding a brand-new gas can looking into the alley, forlorn and sickly (as if on the verge of heat stroke), on Randolph Street—wasn't *that* queer—and thank God in Indian Trail (a very snappy neighborhood of Winnetka where everyone lived in a big house with fabulous "art" on every wall) you don't see such things very often. But Miles, who had recently purchased a portfolio of touchy stocks as thick as a phone book without telling Sharon and was understandably edgy and skittish about it, excused himself, got up immediately, and went to the men's room where the pay phone was (the male patrons could whiz and talk on the phone at the same time). Miles hastily called his broker and sold everything—so suspicious was Sharon's story and his instant surmises about Max; Miles's broker was mortified but compliant. "The whole thing sounded fishy to me," Miles later told his old DePauw Law School roommate one night when he called to talk, "so I decided to dump everything before the old shit hit the old fan and everyone at the club is saying, 'Well, old shithead Miles sure stepped on his dick *this* time!' " Miles came back to the table feeling much better (as if he had just moved six or eight feet of impacted bowel). Later that week, when Sharon found out what Miles had done—after the stocks had practically spiked off the graph, the stocks worth a fortune; Miles totally stupefied and chagrined—she just turned her head and looked wanly out the bedroom skylight, gathering the hem of her ruffled peignoir in her lap, finally understanding only too well the old folk adage about the difference (and preference) between being born lucky and being born rich. She stared out the window and thought about what her mother had told her that day in May 1969 when she announced that she and Miles were going to be married. He had driven up to Indiana University, from which Sharon was shortly to graduate, telling her excitedly and bluntly he wanted to get married—Miles back then supposed one had to get married to get laid. Sharon, tickled and horny, had gone straight home that weekend with the happy news. Her mother had come into the bedroom dressed to the nines for dinner at the club and talked with Sharon until twilight—the house dark, quiet, and eerie. Finally, when all other reasonable, rational argument had failed, her mother had bluntly said, "Dear, don't. Miles is just not smart."

•   •   •

It was 12:45 when Max finally made his move. He had slowly gone through all his options, so to speak, and decided to pick up the wallet and help himself. Max, my man, this ain't nuthin' but a lady's wallet, Max thought, so what the fuck, it's only a buck.

No one back at the house on North Ravenswood would have been surprised.

Virtually everyone walking by looked at Max with a sort of embarrassed and pathetic curiosity; a man so despicable and raunchy, thoroughly and irremediably disgusting and ugly, that everyone within a block and a half would have said that here was one of that goddamn George Bernard Shaw's *un*deserving, lazy, and ignorant poor—well dressed though Max was.

Let's shoot the sorry son of a bitch and save the taxpayers a whole bunch of money. That's what Area #1 patrolman Fausto Gottschalk, high-school graduate and ten-year veteran of the force, said to himself as he cruised by in his air-conditioned squad car, dry-sniping Max with his trigger finger and laughing big, haw, haw, haw. (I *eat* big and I *shit* big, 'cause I'm a *big* man, Fausto always said of himself.) He was one of those cops who had a definite opinion about the Chicago Police Department's logo on the side of his squad car: " 'We Serve and Protect' *me*," he always said, pointing to his head with his trigger finger. "Everybody's guilty of something, and it's up to me to find out what!" he would say. His other in-fallible motto was: "Keep kicking in doors, there's *got* to be something nasty behind one of them." Max sure did look like easy pickings—helpless; probably stoned on some kind of newfangled dope—standing there with his back to the curb.

Oblivious to everything going on behind him, all in one motion Max stepped forward, bent down, and picked up the wallet—it was surprisingly hefty, like a fireplace log—and started walking briskly north through the alley with his bright red gas can in one hand and that heavy, solid, gray-leather lady's wallet in the other.

And it was as if by picking up the wallet Max had pulled a cork of some kind. That afternoon and into the night the whole city sneezed up voided warranties, screaming mad-fit chain-reaction car accidents (in Castilian Spanish and Genovese Italian), bungled chump-change stickups, political suicides, known felons let loose when boxes of incontrovertible evidence suddenly disappeared, second-shift wildcat strikes, bank failures, landfill blowouts, wholesale firings, and plant closings; vast ripples of deep-anger contention and stinging blood-oath vengeance—exquisite permutations of appalling circumstance. There were spontaneous trash fires and construction mishaps, design failures and pavement collapses, market dips and righteous lawsuits thrown out of the courts, kitchen-knife murders and run-aground grain barges, children abandoned and blood-kin betrayals of all sorts—everything right down to ruined celebration dinners, fucked-up haircuts, dropped third strikes, skinned knuckles, and drunks falling off the stools at Deadwood Dave's. Chickens of every size, kind, and description come home to roost. More than one cop shook his head and thought it was the night of the full moon, and years later told their grandchildren, "What a hell of a night *that* was!"

Max loped right along, swinging those gangling arms of his, and went straight to Garvey Court (named after E. Garvey, another one of those nineteenth-century get-rich-quick real-estate guys)—a little bit of a street that led straight to lower Wacker Drive.

Max dodged traffic across the underground thoroughfare called lower Wacker Drive and stood in the dim, weird shadows behind one of the Chicago River bridge pylons at La Salle Street.

Max flipped open the wallet and unzipped the space at the back where any reasonable person kept the money and picked out the cash with his thumb and first finger just as easily and carefully as if he were picking lint from a sweater.

Lo and behold, there were *eight* one-hundred-dollar bills—a great deal of money.

"Goodness gracious," Max said to himself, whispering and virtually breathless, so remarkably astonished was he. "Good golly, Miss Molly, and fuck me running!" The look of all that money in such a slim pile boggled his mind. He looked skyward to the filthy underbelly of upper Wacker Drive, where long, stringy dollops of road tar hung down between the water-damaged concrete seams. This was more money than Max had seen in one pile since he sold ruined air conditioners and junk typewriters out of the trunk of his Dodge four-door Aries K—and *good God*, that was years ago; until today the best day's work he'd ever done! He forgot his gas can, forgot the crumpled dollar bills in all his pockets, forgot everything in the world except this scruffy gray wallet and these eight crisp one-hundred-dollar bills. He circled around the high concrete barricades and found a park bench along the river promenade, dusted it off with his handkerchief, and sat down, suddenly uncomfortable and queasy, cramped and hot in his Hart Shaffner & Marx three-piece suit complete with four-in-hand China-red regimental tie (sweat running down the middle of his back). His wing-tip shoes felt like red-hot iron boots. He crossed his legs and put the wallet in his lap and looked at the eight one-hundred-dollar bills in the palm of his hand. Like an unbeatable hand of draw poker, he thought to himself (Go ahead, Max, bet the farm and everything else that isn't nailed down on this one, you can't fucking lose)—the bills were utterly new, sliding against each other with the faint raspy sound of #000 emery cloth.

Max had worked at one job or another since he was eleven years old, but when was the last time he had *found* money? When he was a kid he used to go to the church parking lot after the summer carnival and kick around for change dropped under the Tilt-a-Whirl and the Ferris wheel and such, and in Lincoln Park along the lake sometimes you just walked right up to it, and when he was a CTA bus driver there was always money unaccountably left over at the end of the day. (Back in the days when the drivers still handled money, any total under the tally had to be made up out of their own pockets—Sorry, *pal*—but any money over they were supposed to turn in just the same—ho, ho, ho, fat chance! Just like many another driver, Max *never* bought his own dinner.)

But $800, wallet and all, now *that* was something. "Heavens to Betsy and fuck me running," Max repeated out loud. If yesterday had been his best day's work *ever*, then this was unspeakably *fine*. "Hurrah, huzzah, hoo-ha!" Max squealed, and winked all around.

Then he got suddenly sly and conspiratorial, glancing upriver at the screwy-looking twin circular Marina Towers and the warehouse-looking *Sun-Times* Building (like a huge, silvery refrigerator cardboard box thrown out in the alley), then downriver to the Merchandise Mart (built in the late twenties; once the largest commercial building in the world, surpassed only by the Pentagon, and bought for taxes-due by Joseph P. Kennedy—nice going, Joey). Max looked above at the ornate concrete railing along the sidewalk of upper Wacker Drive. He looked at the money in his hand—eight big ones; eight hundred smackeroos, as Easy Ed would say

—and began to count it again and again from one hand to the other, wetting his thumb time after time, and the stash always totaled eight. He chimed again and again:

One for the money,
Two for the show,
Three to get ready,
And four to go.

On the face of each bill was an engraved portrait of an older Benjamin Franklin, sagging flesh at the neck, curly fur collar; half bald, with shoulder-length, hippie hair. This was the guy who stood out in the rain to fly kites, was a printer, signed the Declaration of Independence and helped write the Constitution, and got a job with the new government as our first Postmaster General (a very good patronage job in those days). Franklin looked up from each $100 bill, slightly cross-eyed, it seemed to Max as he looked closer, as if about to say in that phony a-penny-saved-is-a-penny-earned, mealy-mouthed *Poor Richard* way of his, "Listen, Max, always take an older woman for a mistress. Everything else being equal —and assuming you know what you're doing—they're so *grateful*! Oh, and by the way, keep the money but throw away the wallet." This from the man who represented our revolutionary government in the royal court of France, where he was regarded with curious awe and chivalrous jealousy as some kind of noble savage, like many a strange-looking celebrity nowadays. The elegant and noble ladies of the Versailles Court just couldn't keep their knees together when he sashayed into a room, try as they might. The story goes that he couldn't keep his zipper zipped to save his life, but apparently won the United States many a favor from the French, who couldn't *stand* the British, no matter how many of their women Franklin slept with. (Some of the slobbering, alcoholic old history buffs down at Deadwood Dave's Wild West Saloon would wheel around on their barstools and say the Americans could have got the same thing if they'd sent a deaf-and-dumb wheelchair corpse, but would drink a toast to Ben—"that sly, peppery old rascal"—just the same.)

On the back of the hundred was Independence Hall, portrayed as if standing by itself surrounded by trees in a park out in the countryside somewhere instead of smack dab in the middle of downtown Philadelphia. High in the air above the bell tower were the words IN GOD WE TRUST, as if it were an advertising banner trailing behind a slow-cruising biplane circling high above Soldier Field, say—hard-charging, grim and gimpy, lippy Bears' coach Mike Ditka looking sky-ward, saying to himself and any second-string benchwarmers standing near, "Yep! That's what it takes, in life, by God! And if not, we'll stomp the living shit out of these greaseball Green Bay cheesehead palookas us-selves. *Won't we?*" The story goes that when the Continental Congress was trying to hash out the Constitution in the summer of 1787, the city fathers decided to lay straw and horseshit (what historical experts would later call barn straw) on the street cobbles in the square out front of the hall to keep the incessant, raucous hubbub of carriage and wagon traffic from disturbing the great work, so that the great men from each of the great original states of the Union gathered in the chamber abovestairs wouldn't have to argue and negotiate and piss and moan at the top of their lungs and could hear themselves think without putting their hands over their ears. It must have been mighty strange work, with all the windows flung open and that peculiar odor hanging as thick as fog, while those guys tried to nail down

what three co-equal branches of government were actually
going to do and prevent the others from doing, and which ten
things ("stuff" in the modern parlance) went into the Bill of
Rights.

When Max got tired of fooling with the money, he folded
it up, creased it precisely, and put it in his shirt pocket. He
picked up the wallet and proceeded to rifle carefully through
it. There was a small deck of credit cards—American Express,
VISA, Marshall Field & Co., Lord & Taylor's, Kroch's and
Brentano's, Carson Pirie Scott & Co., and the like; combs
and bobby pins and safety-deposit-box key; scraps of paper
and matchbooks with numbers and addresses and brief reminders written on them; spare keys for a GMC car, a Master
lock, and what was probably the basement door key (just in
case); Triple-A Motor Club tow-away card, newspaper clippings and family photos; Band-Aids and rubber bands; and
in the side coin purse were single earrings, small "product
sample" lipsticks, a collapsed box of Chiclets, a long-tined
black-plastic teasing comb, and a small tube of Crest travel
toothpaste. The driver's license said her name was Loretta
Spokeshave of Snuffy Lane in Northfield. She was born in
1952, 5 feet 6 inches tall, brown hair and green eyes, and
weighed 125 pounds. Her accompanying photo looked
atrocious—Max would never have recognized her on the
street ("if she crawled up and bit him on the leg," as Belle-
Noche would have said). He looked on the back and saw that
she had donated her whole body and all the usable organs for
use as transplants and such as that—so generous, Loretta
was. An "anatomical gift, effective on my death" was how it
was written, signed by her (she had a pinching little signature) and witnessed by her neighbor Sophia Haupt. (Loretta
had dragged Sophia with her the last time she had her license

renewed and got Sophia, a very accommodating woman to be sure, to witness with her signature this generous act of spirit; in the event of Loretta's death her body would simply disappear.)

All that was well and good—library cards, old photographs, long-past dentist appointment reminders, Cash Station receipts, her husband's business cards (Henry Spokeshave was not a doctor, he just had a whiz of a signature), not to mention the small fortune in cash. But then Max found a letter folded up and stuck behind a ragged flap in back of the money. It was from a guy named Jean-Claude—a love letter. "Well, bless my soul," Max said right out loud.

My dearest Loretta,
It seems that I can't wait for our Tuesday and Thursday meetings. I love you so. I lie awake at night and think of nothing but your beautiful body. Your breasts, your thighs, your feet. I've made a permanent reservation so we don't have to embarrass ourselves at the front desk anymore. See you in Room 1407 at the usual time. Don't forget to bring the feathers, the blindfold, the choke-chain dog collar, and the baby oil. I have lined up the air mattress and bought a bottle of surgical soap.

Love,
Jean-Claude

The number 1407 was circled in red pencil.

The handwriting was so round and precise, done with a fountain pen—no doubt a Mont Blanc, Max thought later, worth a small fortune brand-new—that the guy had to be an engineer or a banker or one of those old-money, Lake Forest guys who just sign remittance checks as they come in and forward them to their estate managers—which, as it turned out, was an excellent guess.

Max read the letter and clucked his tongue—tsk, tsk, tsk—smirking as he admonished Loretta for fooling around with naughty old Jean-Claude. But what on earth were the feathers and collars and baby oil and air mattress for? And why a bottle of surgical soap? Max had to chuckle at that one. He looked at the money again. These were serious times, he thought, and this is serious money. Max, never a man to ponder long about anything, gazed at the money a good long time. What now?

He straightened his back and sat up. It was a case that seemed clear: put everything but the greenback cash back in the wallet and toss it over the side into the river (the very same river where on St. Patrick's Day a couple of Chicago City Streets and San. payrollers in a motor launch would pour bag after bag of green dye off the fantail and stir it with the propeller). Who gives a shit if Loretta has to apply for her driver's license, credit cards, and such all over again? Who gives a shit if she can't remember the room number where Jean-Claude will meet her with his air mattress and his bottle of soap, so has to "embarrass" herself asking for it one more time at the registration desk, carrying a Nike gym bag of accoutrements and appurtenances?

Then Max again caught sight of her driver's-license picture—the too bright face, the ridiculous eyeliner, the sparkling/glistening lipstick, the knot of a Gucci scarf at her neck, the reddened, watery eyes, the limp hang of her hair (the photograph had been taken in late February, a time of the year when all of winter's multitude of endless exasperations both large and small made everyone in the city surly, spiteful, and short-tempered)—Loretta's whole pathetic expression, which seemed to ooze mute blasphemy at the well-oiled, chickenshit incompetence of the Secretary of State's brain-damaged lifers who shoveled the paperwork around and took the pictures. "Vote Republican," Loretta seemed to be saying, standing with her hands at her sides drawn into fists. "And *this* is the thanks I get. Just wait until I get home and Henry hears about this! But at least I have my little Tuesday and Thursday afternoons with Jean-Claude!"

Then Max looked at the money again.

Hadn't someone once said there was a sucker born every minute; hadn't someone else said a fool and his money are soon parted? Wasn't there an old saying, "Get the money"? Hadn't some famous dead poet once said, "Money is a kind of poetry"? Several other pithy, homespun homilies came to mind—all remembered from Max's youth, when Agnes-Ruth would lecture him at dinner while spooning out the rice and beans and deep-dish tuna pie. But the more Max thought about it, the more strange sympathy he had for the woman —she was a human being, after all. Sitting there on that bench along the promenade of the Chicago River, his body shivering and his brains whirling at all the contrary possibilities, Max suddenly had an attack of scruples, something he hadn't felt since before he was old enough to vote (not that he ever did anyway). It's hard to say how these things happen and what sort of neuroelectronic glitches are responsible, but there it was—much the same as bumping into an old lover after twenty years, two marriages, and half a dozen kids. And even though Max was a mostly harmless petty crook—his job had always been to lie, cheat, and steal (indifferent though the results always were; in Max's case it was a line of work that barely paid)—he finally, absolutely, could not conceive of missing the look on her face when he returned the wallet intact—money, credit cards, hairpins, letter from Jean-Claude, and all. Besides, he thought, Muriel would be over-whelmed with pride at his act of honesty and generosity (he'd really cash in with her for that!); maybe *she* could figure out what the dog collar and baby oil were for.

The instant his mind was made up, Max did not waste a moment. He packed everything back in the wallet, rose with a vigorous jerk, bustled up the stone stairs to upper Wacker Drive, and walked east to Dearborn Street to catch a north-bound #22 Clark Street bus—leaving his gas can beside the bench, singing a jaunty Little Walter blues tune about the portraits of all those dead Presidents on paper money and what each bill can and cannot buy. Halfway to the bus stop, halfway through the song a second time—something about Lincoln parking your car, taking Jefferson to the track and bringing home a big bag of money, and everybody in love with half a dozen or so famous dead guys—Max broke into a snappy little jig that startled and embarrassed the other people on the street.

It was past the middle of the afternoon. The first of the p.m. rush-hour CTA buses were just turning at Harrison Street (named for the President) south of the Loop and en-tering the gauntlet of late-afternoon traffic, heading back north. Max waited at the corner of Wacker Drive and Dear-born Street with his dollar in his hand.

As he boarded the bus with three other passengers, thirty-three blocks north at Wrigley Field the Chicago Cubs and the New York Mets were just starting the top of the ninth inning, Cubs down 3 to 1, and the feeling in the ballpark was intense. Harry Carey was bragging about the excellent Cubs pitching but moaning and groaning about the game's sloppy hitting—leaving so many men on base—"Oh, my ach' back," said

Harry, who'd had a stroke the year before and now often spoke without finishing words. Steve Stone, an ex-pitcher (and Cy Young Award winner) who smoked big ugly cigars and had a genius for terrible puns, cautioned everyone about the effectiveness of the bunt—"The true test of a man *is* a well-laid bunt," he was saying—and coaching Vance Law, the Cubs third baseman, to play up on the grass (not that Law, who wore glasses, heard him).

Max paid his fare and sat down just forward of the rear side door next to a woman with a cardboard box of live lobsters in her lap (the animals scratching at the inside of the box with pegged claws) and watched Earl Mack, badge #5844, with twenty-one years' seniority, glance down into his outside rearview mirror, release the brakes, and take off through the intersection when the traffic light turned yellow. Max sat in a dumb funk, excited and depressed, with Loretta's scuffed-up wallet in his lap—*all* that *god*damned money; kiss it good-bye, Max! "Ah me!" he said out loud. As the #22 lumbered up Dearborn Street toward the Newberry Library, the ball game at Wrigley Field was just finishing up; the Cubs losing 5–4 to the Mets on sloppy base running and a Darryl Strawberry fly ball lost in the vines (a stand-up triple); the traffic soon bumper to bumper in every direction.

It's goddamn game day, Max thought, Jesus!

•   •   •

Before Max embarked on a life of harmless, petty crime, he had many a job, but the worst career decision he ever made was to become a Chicago Transit Authority bus driver, his last and worst attempt at real work. After three days of filling out forms and being inspected by some hack doctor, the receptionist's gofer finally called his name and he was

taken into a small side room. A man in a cheap suit, with a
nose broken in so many places it looked like a dollar sign, sat
behind a gray metal desk (with a well-dented modesty panel),
Max's application folder spread out before him.

How many miles had Max driven in the last year? Oh,
about thirty thousand for the Grateful Dead Auto Auctioneers.

Any accidents during that time? Well, thought Max, looking at his shoes, if you didn't count that time a '65 Chevy lost
its steering on the way to Fort Wayne and sideswiped a couple
of hundred feet of fence along the Interstate ditch, or a '62
Pontiac with no brakes that nearly killed him on a downhill
outside Galena, or the couple of dumbshit farmhouse yard
dogs that suddenly got it into their heads to chase him the
summer before when he was taking a Volkswagen to East
Moline (or the other trivial road kills—dogs, cats, deer, pos-
sums, woodchucks, and whatnot). No, Max didn't think he'd
had any accidents at all.

So Max got the job. And right from the first day Max was
your worst bus driver nightmare come true. The CTA super-
visors (all old guys who well remembered the streetcar days)
kept haranguing him and the other new drivers and the summer college kids with the *fact* that they were public
servants—the emphasis on *servant*—which basically meant
they had to sit and take whatever workaday bullshit the bus-
riding public meted out. But none of the stiff-necked lectures
bothered Max in the slightest. He tore up transfers, threw
people off his bus, "breezed" the stops when he felt like it,
and generally drove the bus like a bulldozer, so that by the
end of the summer (this was 1968)—and the famous Democratic National Convention—Max definitely had an "attitude" (as the beer-mug psycho-babble experts at Deadwood
Dave's would say) and was having accidents all the time. His

first streak was three accidents in three days that July. Thursday, he drove over a guy's left front fender, with his rear duals, coming off the Fullerton Avenue exit of the Outer Drive with a p.m. rush-hour "swinging load"—so named because when the bus was full to the doors it tended to swing back and forth on its springs. The next day, Max swiped the entire right side of a brand-new 1968 Cadillac De Ville four-door with the whole forty feet of his bus at McCormick Boulevard (named after Robert "the Colonel" McCormick, publisher of the venerable *Chicago Tribune*) and Devon Avenue (named for a train station on the Pennsylvania Railroad line outside Philadelphia). He mangled the guy's car like you'd rip open a bag of corn chips. The very next day, Saturday, he broadsided a Plymouth Valiant trying the light at Western and North Avenues, bounced the guy off his front bumper, and pushed in the entire right side of his car—a woman on the bus knocked out all her front teeth on that stainless-steel handrail across the top of the seat in front of her. (North Avenue was so named because it was at one time the city's northern border.) Later that week, in a driving rainstorm, he ripped a T-bird's door right off its hinges on Broadway in front of the Curtis Candy Company—yanked the door right out of some guy's hand with the lip of his bumper.

Broadway Avenue had to be unique in the world. The #36 passed through eight neighborhoods—Rogers Park, Uptown, New Town, Lincoln Park, Old Town, the Near North nightclub district, Downtown, and South Loop. Coming through the Loop during rush hour almost killed Max: the buses bumper to bumper, the propane and diesel fumes withering and nauseating, the homebound commuters frantic to get aboard anything that moved and grab a seat. On a Saturday night Max could have a little of everything on his bus: working stiffs, sloppy drunks, straight couples out for a cheap date, screamers, gay guys cruising, cross-eyed Bible-thumbing rednecks, old black guys with watery yellow eyes wearing shabby greatcoats, kids with long hair out to howl, young women who would cruise with him all night, sleeping on the long back seat, and in the morning want to go home with him. *That* was always a puzzlement and a temptation, even though Max got plenty at home, but Max figured they had to be a little kinky and probably crazy.

On Clark Street Max got mostly ordinary working people during the day, but on game day—"Fuck me running," Max would say—Cub fans. Win or lose, on those days Clark Street was an incomparable aggravation a body couldn't compare with anything else. Miles of bumper-to-bumper fans—most half-smashed—trying to make it out of the big bad city in one piece. Traffic backed up from Wilson Avenue (named for Sanitary District lawyer John P. Wilson, whose fortune helped establish Children's Memorial Hospital) all the way south to Diversey Avenue (named for Michael Diversey, brewer and philanthropist) and beyond, where he picked up the rush-hour traffic the rest of the way. What a grinder.

Western Avenue was split into two routes: North Western from Howard to the Ravenswood El at Leland Avenue was like working the wheel in a gerbil cage—many, *many* round trips; it left you breathless. Long Western from Berwyn Avenue (named for a train station outside Philadelphia) to 79th Street was like working the Union Grove quarter mile in *slow* motion—an endless, unvarying blur of storefronts and automobile dealerships that made your mind smooth and rendered your imagination stone dead. Back in the streetcar days, the old-timers said, two round trips was an eight-hour day—and the "Red Rockets," as the streetcars were called, were some of the fastest in the country.

Damen Avenue was a residential street, plain working stiffs who knew where they were going and just how long it took, and after everyone got home at the end of the day nobody went anywhere; they sat on their stoops, drank their beers, and waited for their houses to cool down. (Damen Avenue was named for Father Arnold Damen, a Jesuit priest. The story goes that he was in New York City the day the Chicago Fire of 1871 began. When he heard the terrible news that the whole city was in flames, he fell to his knees and prayed, "Dear Father in Heaven, chiefly known to me by thy rod," to spare his church; that if God and His only Son, Merciful Jesus, did that marvelous thing, the good father, His humble servant and priest, would cause a perpetual light to burn in the place as witness to the Lord's everlasting compassion. Forthwith, God spared Holy Family Church, and the good father was good to *his* word. To this day a number of candles—in later years exchanged for light bulbs to keep down the expense— shine before the image of Our Lady of Perpetual Help.)

What *really* got Max was Sheridan Road, and the little blue-haired old ladies wrapped to the ears year-round in fur. They'd stand at the curb with one hand on the rail inside the door and one little foot on the step, while Max was trying to "make" time (Max was *always* trying to make time), and ask the same questions a million times in their sweet, croaking, little whiskey voices. "Does this bus go *down*town?" "Do you stop at the Art *Institute*?" "Do you go by the *Drake* Hotel?" After a while Max would just lean over the fare box and say, "No, we don't go anywhere *near* there," jiggle the door to shake their grip, close the door, and take off.

That summer, word had apparently gone out far and wide that the CTA would hire just about anybody who arrived under his own power. Twenty or thirty foreign students showed up looking for work—Persians and Arabians, Indians and Pakistanis—all from the University of Missouri School of Mines, petroleum engineering majors. Most barely spoke English, much less drove, and more than a couple had not only never driven anything before in their lives but couldn't speak a lick of passable English. One of the Iranians, who went by the name of Ted and kept telling stories of the Shah's SAVAK (the secret police), got so exasperated he wore a large button on the side of his hat:

I AM

A DEAF-

MUTE

One night after Max pulled in after an especially aggravating shift, standing at the money-counting tables toting up the day's receipts, he asked one of the old-timers why the people on Sheridan Road were so fucking dumb. The old guy was pouring his quarters out of old Alka-Seltzer bottles—$10 per jar, exactly—and replied, "Well, son, I'll tell you, those people have been a pain in the ass with the same goddamned questions for the thirty-five years I've been working here. Seems to me they've got all that money and no brains. The poor dumb clunks on Damen Avenue may be factory-job, shit-brained high-school dropouts, but at least they don't pester you with dumbshit questions, everybody knows where they're going and when to get off." That was certainly true, Max thought. On Damen you never had to call out the streets—not that he did anyway.

Near the end of Max's tenure as a bus driver (as he was coming quickly to the end of what patience he had left), he was driving south on Sheridan in early August and pulled up to the bus stop at Irving Park Road (an old Indian portage to the Des Plaines River named for author Washington Irving). Some folks on the bus were just out for a cool ride along the lakeshore of a hot summer night, some were going down to Grant Park (named for the President) for one of the last summer concerts, some were going God-knew-where. Max picked up a kid dressed in cotton wash pants, crummy house slippers, and a filthy T-shirt, carrying a large brown paper bag of shoes. The kid sat in the first seat opposite Max—always a bad sign. It had been a peculiar summer, but the kid had such a goofy grin and a funny haircut Max should have known something was up. He had no money for fare, though by then Max couldn't have cared less, but as Max made his way downtown the guy solicited all the women who came aboard—"Can I go home with you?"—clutching that wrinkled bag of shoes and dipping his head funny when the women walked by. Max drove and plotted; finally he had had enough. At the corner of Sheridan Road and Surf Street (so named because it dead-ended right at the lake at one time), he hopped into the drugstore and called the dispatcher.

"Yeah? Run number?" the dispatcher said, first thing—paperwork *was* paperwork. Max gave him his number.

The dispatcher said, "What's on your mind tonight, bub?" Max told him a funny-looking guy had got on his bus (Sheridan Road was at the other end of Irving Park Road from the Dunning State Mental Hospital) and looked plenty "goofy." Could it be that this squirrel had walked off the grounds at the hospital, caught the Irving Park bus, rode it to the end of the line, and boarded Max's?

"Where you at?" the dispatcher said. Sheridan and Surf, Max told him.

"How soon you be at Michigan and Chicago?" the dispatcher wanted to know—about twenty blocks; the stop in front of Charmet's Restaurant (now long gone). (Michigan Avenue, Algonquin for great water, was named for the lake.) Max could hit the Outer Drive, run the lights from Oak Street to Chicago Avenue, and pull up in front of Charmet's in a jiffy. About two minutes, Max said. (Oak Street was, of course, named for the oak tree.)

"We'll have some people there to meet you," the dispatcher said.

Max got back on the bus and in a large voice announced, "This bus is express to Chicago Avenue. Anybody getting off between here and there, get off and get the next bus. He's *right* behind us"—which was what the drivers said, regardless. Nobody moved a muscle. Max dropped into his seat, put the bus in gear, and drove straight to Chicago Avenue. And the instant he pulled the bus up to the curb it was surrounded by squad cars and paddy wagons. Two huge, beefy cops, dressed in leather jackets and motorcycle helmets, came in the back door and said, *"Where's the nut!"* in such large and roundly harsh voices that they made Max instantly regret ever having bothered about it. Max turned in his seat and pointed to the kid, sitting next to the front door, looking as small and harmless as the day is long—looking as though he knew he was in for a *Guinness Book of World Records* ass-kicking. The cops lumbered up the aisle, each grabbed an arm, lifted the kid out the door and into the alley at the back of Charmet's, and threw him into a paddy wagon. A CTA street supervisor came aboard and was jawing (the guy would have to write up an incident report), and while they were talking Max could see out of the corner of his eye that the cops were punching and kicking the everlasting bejesus out of the kid—This'll teach you nuts to stay where you belong! Stomp-stomp-stomp!

On top of everything else that summer there was even an earthquake, of all things, the only one in the living memory of any of the Nutmegs (Chicago or Jessamine County, Kentucky). The New Madrid Fault (pronounced *Ma*-drid in Missouri) runs along the Mississippi River into Arkansas; some of the self-educated geologists who hang around at Deadwood Dave's predicted that when the fault blew, the Mississippi River—the third largest waterway in the world and "the commercial lifeblood of the nation," as Benjamin Harrison once pontificated—when that sucker blew for good, the river would "get 'swallered' up," and the Great Lakes and *Chicago* would become "the commercial lifeblood of the nation," though one sorry old coot slammed down his shot glass and cautioned everyone in Deadwood Dave's not to waste their breath or ruin their sleep sitting up nights waiting for that particular apocalypse. One Sunday morning, Max and Muriel were sitting up in bed having their morning coffee—laced with a bit of whiskey—when the house began to "shake, rattle, and roll," as Belle-Noche would later describe it. Muriel said, "Max honey, don't shake the bed so while I'm trying to sip. This coffee's *hot*." The windows rattled in their frames; the dishes rattled in the kitchen, sliding together on the drainboard; the cats wobbled on the floor.

But the absolute last straw of the summer came during the famous Democratic National Convention. That week Max drove the #36 and #22 buses down through Lincoln Park and back of the Hilton Hotel. At North Lincoln Park there was a row of crummy stores (there's a concrete high-rise at the corner now). During the day two live models performed in the window of a shop selling those grotesque Carnaby Street clothes. They would move and strike a pose, freezing for a moment, then move again and pose again. It was the damnedest thing Max ever saw—those guys never batted an eye. There was always a bit of a crowd standing there, watching with the same stupefied, curious satisfaction as Blackhawk hockey fans at the Stadium waiting for someone to throw the live chicken onto the ice from the high balcony seats and the fights to break out. There was always a bit of a crowd there, watching the models, waiting for the bus. Across the street in the park were the Yippies and other kids, lounging and swapping "war stories," and platoons of cops with their squad cars and paddy wagons and their three-wheeled motorcycles parked along the sidewalks and bike paths, leaning on their guns in that way that cops have. Max could easily imagine the banter and talk—in the full light of day—the cops ending the conversation with "See you at eleven, kid." The street action wouldn't begin until after dark when the park was "officially closed."

In the evening Max got in the habit of wasting a light coming south at Lincoln Park West (a bit of a side street named for the park, along the western edge) and leaning forward in the driver's seat, scrunching down, looking out through the park under the trees for floodlights and silhouettes—skirmish lines of cops or Guardsmen and clouds of tear gas. One night the cops threw tear-gas canisters; another night they borrowed a tear-gas machine (built like a mosquito abatement fogger) from the Illinois National Guard. The machine was mounted on the back of a robin's-egg-blue Streets and San. dump truck and cruised through the park after the cops had ordered the kids to clear out (enforcing what amounted to a brand-new law—Lincoln Park neighborhood folks had been sleeping in the park in hot weather, camping out, screwing, and carrying on after 11:00 since well before Max was born), blowing a huge billowing cloud of gas as solid as a smoke screen downwind. (Later, Chicago police lifers said that the tear gas worked so well during the convention that they should have used more of it sooner.)

The other memorable incident occurred either Wednesday or Thursday—Max, later, was never certain which. It was a cool August night, cool enough for a jacket—strange weather for Chicago—and late in the evening. He came down Clark Street past the corner at Webster Avenue (the sight of the S-M-C Cartage Company garage, where on St. Valentine's Day in 1929 five guys from Al Capone's gang—dressed as cops—shot seven of Bugs Moran's gang; one of the victims was asked who did it and he replied, "*Nobody* shot me"; the wall was later bought by a German "collector" and moved to his house, reassembled brick by brick; Webster Avenue was named for Massachusetts Senator Daniel Webster, who visited Chicago exactly once in 1837). Max cruised alongside the now deserted park, down through Old Town and Near North, and on to the Loop. He was not wearing his CTA hat—a violation of company rules for which he could receive a blowhard, chickenshit lecture by a street supervisor. And because of the chill he was wearing a thick wool shirt (got at a garage sale on North Winthrop for 75 cents) as a jacket over his short-sleeved CTA shirt. When he came to the corner of Clark and Congress Parkway (named for the entire U.S. Congress), south of the Loop, he saw something that astonished him. CTA chartered buses were parked bumper to bumper along all four curbs of the parkway from the Elevated tracks at Wabash Avenue to the old La Salle Street railway station —what is now the Midwest Stock Exchange. The buses were darkened, and there were many of them, perhaps fifty or more, filled with platoons of cops in full riot gear, no doubt several thousand. And as he looked down and over the scene, a queer feeling growled in his belly—somebody was definitely going to get a royal ass-kicking tonight, and it definitely wasn't going to be Max.

As far as Max was concerned, the Yippies and the radicalized McCarthy kids and anybody else who had a mind to could run screaming through the streets, hurling bags of dog shit and rocks and Wiffle balls and loaves of bread—and anything else they could rip out of the ground—goading the cops who, you'd have thought, had reached the limit of their astonishing fury a couple of days before. The kids and cops could chase each other to kingdom come, Max thought right then and there; he would drive his pull-in trip (the run paid 10.6 hours—and that was time and a half after eight hours), cash in, and call it a day. Max sat in his bus at the right-hand curb, waiting anxiously, almost desperate for the light to change so he could get the hell out of there.

On the sidewalk near his front side door, a platoon of cops stood with black leather jackets and sky-blue motorcycle helmets, nightsticks, and killer eyes, with big black leather straps around their waists hung with pistols, stainless-steel handcuffs, cans of Mace, etc. One of the cops suddenly caught a glimpse of Max through the glass of the doors. Max looked young and kind of wimpy (being tall and skinny like he was) dressed in civilian clothes. The cop's whole body shivered and his nightstick shivered, and then all the cops standing with him in rank and file *shivered*, then *moved* toward Max. The cop's imagination and intent were clear: Max had somehow sprung loose from whatever massacre was in progress elsewhere—perhaps the very same one in front of the Hilton, perhaps farther down Michigan Boulevard, perhaps over at State and 18th Streets, where comedian/activist Dick Gregory stood in front of a phalanx of Illinois National Guardsmen, in full sloppy NG regalia, bayonets at the ready (scared out of *their* little civilian minds); Gregory inviting "everyone down to his place" on the South Side—several thousand hairy-assed, yippie demonstrators standing behind him, ready to party. According to this skinny little cop, Max had killed the driver—some decent working stiff, churchgoing family man and solid citizen, homeowner and taxpayer—by spilling a Mason jar of genuine Owsley acid on him, stuffing him down into his shoes, and shoving him down the fare box; hijacked his bus (loaded to the windows with contraband TNT with box nails for shrapnel), and was going to ram the lobby of the Hilton (where the delegates were staying) and blow the whole thing up, once and for all! To keep from getting stomped right then and there, Max leaned over the slender fare box, grabbed his hat from the dashboard, and showed it to the cop—*big.* Then he pulled down the collar of his wool shirt over the CTA shoulder patch on his shirt to show him and all his cop buddies, Hey, hold it, whoa! Easy does it! I'm one of you guys!

The skinny cop dropped his truncheon and eased up.

But Max thought things looked mighty grim. All that week the cops kept smiling and saying to the folks at the receiving end of their nightsticks and heavy, discrete bursts of Mace, "We've got our orders, pal!"

When the traffic lights at Congress Parkway changed to green, Max swung a wide, lumbering left turn then and there—from the right-hand curb, an act of such astonishing violation of the traffic laws that Max thought himself lucky indeed to drive away from the intersection with his whole hide. He sat at Congress Parkway and Dearborn Street (a one-way boulevard going north) and thought to himself, Fuck me running, but understood full well that if he got a ticket for such an outrageous flaunting of the law the company had lawyers at the traffic courts, and if you showed up in a clean uniform, the judge let you off. All it cost you was going to work early. (Actually, the only cop in the city who would give you a ticket for anything was the guy at Michigan Boulevard and Chicago Avenue, who ran his corner like a hallway monitor at St. Charles Reform School for Boys.)

Max turned left up Dearborn and that was it. At the end of the next pay period (just after the convention a week later) Max turned in his time and quit. He never worked for wages again, except for a number of brief stints at the Grateful Dead Auto Auctioneers and *only* when absolutely necessary.

Max sat on the northbound #22 making its slow and steady way through the day-game crowd, staring off into space and glancing every now and again at the box of lobsters in the lap of the woman next to him, and blessed the day he kissed off the CTA job once and for all; I must have had rocks in my head to take that job, Max thought to himself as he watched Earl Mack's rising temper when the bus approached Clark and Addison Streets (day-game ground zero). (Addison Street was named for Dr. Thomas Addison, a Londoner who first described a disease of the endocrine glands, Addisonian anemia.)

•   •   •

Meanwhile, back at the Nutmeg house, Belle-Noche was up for the day, getting dressed and ready to go out for the evening with her new boyfriend, Oscar Wendella—who she met one night while she was barhopping from Weeds to the

Get Me High to Sam's Saloon to the Cantina del Muerté and beyond.

Like everyone else in the house, except Muriel, Belle-Noche had had many a strange job. She once worked as a stripper at The Cove out in Bensonville—past Chicago O'Hare International Airport (named for World War II Navy aviator, Edward "Butch" O'Hare, winner of the Congressional Medal of Honor, whose old man ran the Hawthorne dog track for Al Capone; Mayor Richard J. Daley called it "O'Hara Field" until the day he died). Belle either worked with blue feather fans and a Sousa march or a sailor's dress-blue bell-bottoms and all, accompanied by "Anchors Aweigh," and ended her act buck-naked except for a navy-blue kerchief. Between sets she was expected to "waitress," serving the patrons (mostly out-of-towners brought to the place from expense-account hotels around the airport by cabbies paid $10 a head). There were perhaps a dozen mezzanine booths at the back (where the only light was provided by the night-lights along the steps and the EXIT sign above the fire door). The girls were expected to sit and drink with these weirdly horny businessmen, padding the tabs to a fare-thee-well. The owner of the place, Blaine "Fireplug" Honeycutt, liked to sit at the end of the bar near the cash register, where he could keep an eye on the till; a clever bartender could steal better than a week's pay in a single night's shift from right under your nose. Blaine liked to brag to the regulars and his barfly cronies that some of the broads were so dumb that the only thing their mouths were good for "was to stick a dick in." And plenty did—for fifty bucks a shot. "They're so dumb," he would say, "they think their bullshit dancing is *art*."

But Blaine wasn't that smart himself. He could never

keep track from week to week of which cops got how much in payoffs (a body doesn't write such things down), and so the place would get raided from time to time—especially in election years. In the squad car on the way to jail the cops would sometimes apologize, saying they were sorry but he'd missed a payment and they had to make it look good for the chief, who was one of those ex-Cook County sheriff's department lifers who decided to retire to the easy pickings among Bensonville's solid citizens. During the raid the girls always grabbed any old thing they could find against the chill of the night air, were run through night court, bailed out (a condition of their work), and back at work the next night. When the cops arrived at The Cove (with sirens wailing, tires screeching, and gravel flying)—perhaps a dozen and more in eight or ten squad cars (armed with search warrants, fire axes, and sledgehammers), paddy wagons, and a Fire Department ambulance just in case someone got hurt if the cops had to use gun play—when the cops arrived it was chaos, pandemonium, the whole place was up for grabs; every man for himself, so to speak. The patrons, caught flat-footed, were released immediately on their own recognizance. The bartenders and light-show technicians took off for the basement and the walk-in freezer. The girls hid under the booth seats, in the air-conditioning ducts, climbed out the washroom window, and ran across the lot to the Amoco station down the road, or simply lit out the fire-door exit behind the "dressing room" and ran into the woodsy pasture back of the place. The next evening, when Blaine opened for business and everyone arrived, they all had stories: what a fucking mess the cops had made looking for food service, zoning, and fire code violations; how cold the fucking meat locker was, and whose bright idea was all those huge boxes of ice cream; couldn't Blaine do something to make the window in the ladies' can easier to open; the night cashier at the Amoco was a fucking lecher and would call a cab for the consideration of some oral flourishes, so to speak, administered on the spot; how funny and dreamlike the whole scene had looked from behind the trees in the woods out back—the chase lights on the neon sign over the front of the place, the squad cars' Mars lights, clicking, flashing amber and red-orange and blue (shining on the black leather jackets and the badges, the guns and serious patent-leather shoes as the cops milled around the cars, patting everyone down, leering and flirting, cuffing everyone for show, and escorting them into the paddy wagons); how bored and stupid was the night-court judge; what an ignorant slob was Horace Beeman, Blaine's lawyer-buddy (arriving at court with his briefcase full of serious cash dressed in his long, blown-dry hair, plaid suit, and saddle shoes)—"What kind of a shithouse lawyer is he?" the girls would ask. Everyone gathered at the bar for a pick-me-up before the doors opened, all talking at once. On these occasions Blaine was always embarrassed, paid the bail and fines, and stood everyone to the top-shelf liquor, considering the whole sorry episode the price of business—the way aircraft and weapons manufacturers factor in bribes and kickbacks and other wholesale six-figure baksheesh as the price of selling planes and tanks and other such "produce" here and overseas. But then, considering that a credit-card bar tab could run these out-of-town solid citizens $100–$300, and the girls could run three hundred of these woebegone suckers through the place on a weekend night, business was good.

One time Belle-Noche was caught buck-naked between changes when the cops burst in all the doors at once—a serious election-year bust ("Blaine must have really screwed up with his calculator *this* time," Horace said later). The only thing Belle could think of was to slip into a cedar-lined garment bag that hung from an iron pipe opposite the vanity mirrors in the dressing room. She zipped it up as best she could and crouched (like an Egyptian tomb wall engraving) with her feet wedged together at the bottom in an armload of dirty laundry. One of the other girls' sheer shawls of sequined spangles dug into her back. She didn't dare move a muscle and hardly dared breathe—her hands held together at the neck—while the cops (beefy and gruff for show) rousted everyone in the place. The next night, when everyone gathered at the bar for their traditional top-shelf pick-me-up, Belle told the story of how she escaped, how she shivered from the chill, how the circulation stopped in her feet and legs, and how she hobbled around in the dark when everyone was gone and the lights were turned off, and how, since she was locked in (the doors and windows sealed with the sheriff's department evidence stickers), she spent the night sleeping on one of the back booths wrapped in towels and coats.

In all the time she worked there, no one ever topped that.

When she got too old for The Cove, she worked in a North Chicago restaurant near Fort Sheridan called Wiley's, with large, round tables and heavy captain's chairs, where the lunch-rush gimmick was a waitress dressed in "Continental" lingerie—"Whatever the hell *that* is," Belle used to say. Perhaps half a dozen women at a time worked there. The only real clothes they wore were dark, sleek pantyhose, and they were expected to make four changes and more during the lunch hour—the whole thing advertised in the weekly *Reader* newspaper as a "Fashion Extravaganza!" Some of the women understood only too well what a sneering humiliation the whole business was—serving half-pound burgers soaking in red juice, greasy french fries, kosher pickles soaked in heavy brine, and dry salads, while showing off their bodies—and went about their work with a straight face and a stiff neck, ignoring a hundred blunt and leering stares. After working at The Cove, Belle-Noche thought this gig was a piece of cake. But some of the women (who didn't get the joke) moved lithely and smoothly around the room, served the food and poured the coffee refills, flirting like crazy and cranking their tips—and seemed to enjoy the attention (the tips *were* righteous, you understand). When there was a birthday all the waitresses gathered at the table with a small cake and candle for the "birthday boy" and sang the song. Some of the women dated customers on the side, and never lasted very long. Back in the kitchen the Mexicans leered, cackling in Spanish, but left the women alone (it never occurred to Belle-Noche they might be illegals). On the other hand, Wiley was always pestering the new girls to go shopping with him—"to pick out some new ensembles," he would tell them—and Wiley was scoring like crazy.

Belle's last job of any sort was Jell-O wrestling at the Whoopie Palace, a cinder-block roadhouse bar on U.S. Route 41 west of Kenosha, Wisconsin (Orson Welles's hometown, by the way), just over the state line. This was in the middle 1970s, before the toll road was built and the legal drinking age in Wisconsin was still eighteen (for beer). College kids, Fort Sheridan soldiers and Great Lakes sailors, and guys tired of cruising the Rush Street nightclub singles bars would drive up 41 to the place. (Rush Street was named for Dr. Benjamin Rush, signatory of the Declaration of Independence, Revolutionary War patriot, the man who talked Thomas Paine into writing *Common Sense.*) There were always plenty of Illinois plates in the Whoopie Palace parking lot on weekends.

Just north of the line, by a hundred feet or so, was a large lighted Blatz sign on a tall ironwork tower—you could see the thing all the way to Lake Bluff. The Whoopie Palace was set up like a South Carolina dog-fight arena, with a plain wooden bar along one wall (serving beer only), tiered benches, low, industrial-strength tables well bolted to the floor, and a large blow-up kiddie pool in the middle of the linoleum floor. Klieg lights (with colored gels) hung from the ceiling. The owner had papered the walls and half the ceiling with centerfolds from *Penthouse* and *Hustler* (staple holes and all—a vast collection of beavers and breasts that must have cost thousands), and the walls and ceilings were well shellacked with polyurethane. The rubbery kiddie pool was laid over old gym mats and half-filled with Heritage House Jell-O (Dominick's Supermarket house brand); some nights green, some nights red—whatever could be bought by the case. Harmon Huskey and his wife, Judy, the owners, made the Jell-O, thickened it with cornstarch, and added palm oil to make it more viscous and shiny under the lights. The place opened at 8:00 p.m. (there were late-afternoon matinees on weekends and holidays), long-necked bottles of beer sold for $4.00 a crack, and smoke soon filled the room. Harmon officiated, wearing a black-and-white-striped referee's shirt and a huge silver whistle. He stood on the ringside runway (bordered with a knee-high plywood splash board so the patrons wouldn't get Jell-O on their spitshines) just inside the lights and announced the first bout in a raucous parody of a prizefight master-of-ceremonies, reciting "The Marquis of Shrewsbury" rules, as he called them:

1. No choking.
2. No holding the opponent's head under.

Other than that, no holds were barred. Behind the bar Judy

switched on the tape recorder, and slow and husky, nasty-sexy blues with whiskey-voiced, squat-naked, let's-get-down-and-get-some screaming guitar solos and gut-busting saxophone riffs played on half a dozen Bose speakers scattered around the room. Belle-Noche would step out into the ice-blue spotlight at the end of the runway wearing an industrial-strength flowered bikini, with her long bleached-blond hair done up in a Scandinavian braid (wrapped in a bun at the back of her head)—well girded for "battle." She would stand stock-stiff, with her hands on her hips, with a serious game-face scowl—Belle's remarkable endowments and athletic legs plain to everyone in the place. She looked like an Amazon; everyone gasped and was mighty impressed. For the five months she worked there she "fought" Renee Twilly, a young African-American woman from Milwaukee. Renee, like Belle-Noche, astonished men with her worldly endowments but was petitely Rubensesque. "Short and fat. A cross between a fireplug and a brick shithouse," as the afternoon loafers at Deadwood Dave's who'd been north to check the whole thing out would say. The instant the two women stepped into the kiddie pool, Jell-O squeezed between their toes and covered their ankles, and as soon as "they went to work," they sloshed and slipped, slithered and splashed, throwing each other over their hips and whatnot—a mad, wild parody of Wrestlemania showmanship—and in no time had slimy, gooey Jell-O in their hair, their ears and noses, inside their too-small halter tops (their astonishing cleavage bursting) and tightly cinched bikini bottoms (cut high on the thigh). There were hoots and shouts, and Harmon kept blowing his whistle now and again for the hell of it—the one unwritten rule was "No one gets hurt"—Belle and Renee eyeing each other, laughing and grim: "What a shit job this is; your turn to take me down";

then one or the other would go flying and land on her back in the Jell-O with a loud *ker-schlup!* If Belle or Renee looked up during the performance—and could see through the slime of Jell-O—all she would have seen were beer bottles and eyeballs. After fifteen minutes of harmless foolishness and pushing and shoving, Harmon would jump up, throw his arms out with a circus ringmaster's flashy grandeur, and declare the winner—to a rousing chorus of cheers and boos; the grotesque and bawdy irony of a tall white woman cat-fighting a short plump black woman (Renee was the color of molasses caramel) not lost on *this* crowd. The two women would wipe the Jell-O out of their eyes, slick back their hair, squeeze it off their arms and legs, shake it off their feet, and retire to the dressing room to shower and change, waiting an hour for the next bout. Meanwhile, there was nothing for the patrons to do but drink, feed double quarters to the jukebox, and settle their nickel-dime side bets. In the back Renee spread out on the couch and studied her accounting textbooks (the books were always the same; she was always repeating the same bookkeeping course); Belle-Noche drank coffee, played solitaire, and called home to check on the kids with Agnes-Ruth—phone calls that always ended in screaming arguments. And if ever any women came to the Whoopie Palace, they behaved the way Australian working-class women did on dates—sat in the cars in the parking lot while the men went inside to drink with their buddies.

No wonder Belle-Noche had such a peculiar regard for men.

Ubi Est Mea

(Where's Mine?)

When Max got off the bus and came swinging up the street with Loretta Spokeshave's big fat wallet under his arm, Agnes-Ruth was sitting in her high-backed Dodge camper seat on the run-down porch and sipping from a tumbler of iced gin and chain-smoking her Kools (flicking the ash over the weather-beaten railing into the evergreens and tossing the butts into the tulip bed along the brick wall of the paint factory next door). She'd been clucking her tongue loud and long to the rush-hour foot traffic about Darl Dwayne's poker buddy James Earl Jones—"But not *the* James Earl Jones"—and how that nasty James Earl was famous on the block for cheating at cards; how it was that James Earl and Darl Dwayne got into a fight one Friday night and chased each other all over creation, rolling around on the embankment (Agnes-Ruth pointing to the grove of mulberries across the way to the Chicago and North Western Railroad embankment—"railroad dirt," as she called it); how they thrashed the stuffing out of one another with fists like "knotted-up, nasty old dish towels"; how sticker-brush burrs and cinder clinkers stuck to the seats of their pants; how both had to be taken to the hospital; and how they kept sniping and scratching at each other in the car, until James Earl's wife, Honey Jean (who was driving—they had a Kaiser four-door back then—and who was "not small," as Agnes-Ruth always said), slapped James Earl so hard with the back of her hand she knocked the complete set of false uppers out of his mouth.

Agnes-Ruth jabbed the air with her cigarette, as if shoving pins into a corkboard, and rolled her bleary little eyes, trying to describe Honey Jean driving like a drunkard to Ravenswood Hospital, jerking the wheel this way and that to dodge traffic and racing through red lights. Max could hear Agnes-Ruth's narrative exhortations half a block away; all Max could remember of James Earl was the day Honey Jean found him dead on the couch in front of the TV, and when the men from the funeral home came to take the body, they could barely get the gurney out the door—James Earl was so fat—and how James Earl looked so funny, him being dead and all.

Amaryllis had the ferrets airing in a Havahart woodchuck trap Max had picked up years ago at a farmers' market in Logan Square (named after Civil War general John A. Logan) for a buck-fifty—Big Daddy and Betty wrestling around like socks in a tumble dryer and snapping at each other's snouts, just beginning to come awake. Agnes-Ruth had her legs crossed at the ankles and when she puffed on her cigarette would swing her arm out over the evergreen bushes in case any ash fell off.

That afternoon Easy Ed and Amaryllis were out cruising alleys in Hegewisch in Ed's old Chevy tow truck, stealing batteries—they'd be back in *plenty* of time for dinner. (The extreme southeast neighborhood was named for Achilles Hegewisch, president of the United States Rolling Stock Company, a part of the city separated from the rest by vast tracts of heavy industry, rail lines, toxic landfills, and whatnot. In 1883, when the plant was built, Hegewisch wanted to build a company town on the order of George Pullman's, and did, though it never acquired the same quaint and homey prominence, perhaps because of the odd pronunciation Chicagoans gave it—"Hedgewitch.")

Robert was out delivering Donnelly Directories—there were plastic-wrapped pallets of phone books all over the side porch. Sweet William had gone to make a delivery in DuPage County—special customers, you understand. Belle-Noche was finally up for the day and dressing for the evening in the upstairs bathroom, "making herself beautiful" for her date that night; Max could see her silhouette on the plastic curtains and heard her singing between tightly pursed lips:

> *Round and round goes the great fucking wheel,*
> *In and out goes the big prick of steel,*
> *The huge brass balls are filled with cream,*
> *And the whole great gizmo is run by steam,*
> *Burma-Shave!*

It was a song she'd learned from her Uncle Carl, Darl Dwayne's brother, who'd brought it home from Europe in 1945 and would sing it around the house when he had a snootful and was feeling "hornier than a five-peckered billy goat," as Darl Dwayne used to say.

Belle-Noche was currently dating Oscar Wendella, a precinct captain somewhere or other on the South Side, and a payroller with the Chicago Park District, who supervised the flower beds in Grant Park (between Michigan Boulevard and the Illinois Central tracks) across from the big Hilton Hotel with a stiff rake and a long-handled ditch spade. He drove a 1978 Cadillac (pitted with rust like freckles), loved the ponies at Arlington, Maywood, and Washington Park, and always seemed to have plenty of money—kept in a loose roll in his big pants pocket. Oscar was one of those guys who had a hard time keeping his money in a bundle, so every time he showed it off—"Whipping out his wad," he called it—money spilled all over everything. He was a little bit of a guy with plenty of meat on his neck, a fuzzy head of hair, and a thick, brushy mustache. And the way Oscar drove, always showing up at the house well before quitting time, made Max wonder if he wasn't in on "something"—either Downtown, as the jealous busybodies at Deadwood Dave's would say, or out at the track along the backstretch.

Max walked up to the porch with Loretta Spokeshave's gray leather wallet in his hand and sat down on the top step, weary and careworn (assuming an expression of perplexity and doom), loosening his shoelaces (his feet were *killing* him), slacking the knot in his China-red tie, and unbuttoning his vest—suddenly feeling much relieved—and called into the house for someone to bring him a beer and a cigar.

Muriel stood in the kitchen, stirring soup, and thought Max should not wear shoes that pinch, and that a hot footbath of Epsom salts would do just the trick.

"Welcome home, dear. We're glad to see you," Muriel said from the kitchen, bustling around working on dinner. Max could hear her open the Kelvinator and feeling for the coldest bottle of beer—Muriel was one of those people who think that drinking out of cans is "common"; she thought it distasteful when she saw men in the neighborhood idling on their porches with cans of beer wrapped in small paper bags.

"Ma, I got to talk to you about something," said Max to Agnes-Ruth (trying to get his mother's attention), and was about to launch into his strange tale of woe, leaving out a thing or two—We mustn't upset Mother was Max's motto—when Muriel hustled out with an unwrapped Dutch Masters panatella, a box of Swedish Lancer stick matches Raenelle had sent her as a souvenir of her twenty-fifth wedding anniversary Hawaiian vacation, and a frosty bottle of Augsburger dark (a good, cheap American beer). She handed him the cigar, the matches, and the beer, then tousled Max's hair, gave him a warm, bosomy kiss on the top of his head, and struggled to sit down on the stoop next to him with her apron composed across her lap.

Max sat very still and tried to explain to his mother and Muriel about the money and the wallet, and what should he rightly do (as if Agnes-Ruth had any brilliant ideas; he just wanted to hear himself talk and try to figure out the whole weird episode), displaying the wallet, fanning out the hundred-dollar bills, and showing Agnes-Ruth and Muriel the fistful of charge cards. He told the two women how the wallet had been lying on the alley bricks next to the steel fire door of a building on Randolph Street; how he apparently had been the only person who had seen it and he felt as if he were invisible—one of the strangest sensations of his life (part sexual ecstasy; part angina; as close to an intellectual epiphany as Max was ever going to get); how he had taken the wallet and sat on a bench next to the river near La Salle Street and pondered the money both hard and long; how it was the kind of cash (only cleaner and neater) he hadn't seen since he parked cars in that house lot a couple blocks north of Wrigley Field, when all those wholesome suburban rubes would come to town for a ball game and give him fivers and sawbucks that looked as if they'd been scrounged from a trash basket. (Don't people know how to handle money? Max had often thought to himself. What the hell do they teach people in these suburban schools, anyway?)

Agnes-Ruth sat back in her chair and looked at him sort of diabolically funny. Muriel waited patiently for the point to the story. And Belle-Noche, upstairs, pricked up her ears at the mention of eight one-hundred-dollar bills and leaned over the bathtub (her good ear to the window) while cinching her stockings to her Blaze Starr–brand garter belt.

At that very moment, Oscar Wendella arrived at the house in his Coupe De Ville—driving over the curb and honking with two short beeps and one long (Morse code for the letter *U*)—rolling down the right-side windows with the automatic window buttons on the armrest. Max (trying to hide the wallet and the money as best he could) could hear him singing the tail end of a limerick:

> . . . *She had lots of friends,* oh,
> *Because of her ends,* oh,
> *But it wasn't her brains that you diddled*—de de!

Each time Oscar sang the *oh* he threw his head back as far as the headrest would allow and really belted it out, and when he came to the "diddled—*de de*" he slapped the steering wheel with his fat little hands and rolled his eyes back in his head —Belle-Noche *loved* those big brown eyes. Oscar's *favorite* limerick was about some goddamned hairy midget from Nepal who (so the story went)—quote—couldn't get no poontang at all—unquote. Max looked at Oscar's short, fat, little arms and marshmallow fingers and tried to imagine where Belle *got* these guys? What the hell is this, some kind of Grand goddamn Central Station? Belle-Noche thought Oscar certainly was a *prize* pistol. Max, sitting on the top step of the front porch stairs (looking like a cross between Anse Bundren and Major Major), had been putting up with his sister's dreadful boyfriends for thirty years and more—everything from beefcake blowhards to brown-nosing booze hounds to busthead bullshit artists (aggressive and pathetic sexual mooches), though "dreadful" was hardly the word that Max would use; "fuck-ups," "shitheel bird dogs," and "shit-simple fools" was rhetoric more in Max's style. As far as Max was concerned, Oscar was of the "shit-simple fool" variety, but at least he kept Belle-Noche occupied and always had money.

For a couple of years Belle-Noche had been into leather and bondage, then "hung out" with a lesbian meter maid, and then for a couple of years dated a gay football player (6'8", 280, with muscles coming out of his eyeballs) from Notre Dame or Grambling or one of those places. Max thought Oscar should win some goddamn prize for having his head the farthest up his ass. (Maybe that was why his eyes were brown, Max would think to himself.) Sometimes, Max thought— sitting on the top step of the porch, holding the money in one hand and the deck of credit cards in the other—life is such a peculiar and serendipitous mystery a body had to wonder whose fucking idea it was; or as the beer-mug philosophers down at Deadwood Dave's would say, "What the hell's going on here; who made that *brilliant* nitwit call?"

(Deadwood Dave's day-game baseball crowd—some of the city's serious loafers—would have taken one look at Oscar and his Caddy and thought to themselves, That's just the right kind of dwarf, hairy punk that's thirty years old and's still working for his mama; what the hell kind of macho gump-

tion is that—no class, no talent, a nappy-headed city lifer!
Then they'd take a look out the front window at his silly-ass
piss-green Coupe De Ville: "What the fuck is that? Looks like
the goddamn Oscar Mayer wiener wagon to me," some smart-
aleck would say.)

Oscar Wendella, sitting in his car in front of the Nutmegs'
on Ravenswood, took a deep breath. "Hey, Max! How's it
hanging? Hi, Mrs. Nutmeg! Hey, Max, Belle dressed yet?"
Oscar said this all in one breath and leaned over so Max could
see him through the passenger window; Max thinking to
himself, Yeah, she's *dressed* all right—Max thinking, If
bullshit was music, he'd be the whole band!

"Hey, Max, got a joke for ya," said Oscar. "Name three
Chicago streets that rhyme with vagina. Give up?"

Max *always* gave up when Oscar came calling.

"Paulina, Melvina, and Lunt! Haw, haw, haw. Ain't that
a hoot?" (Melvina was named for the town of Melvina, Wisconsin; Lunt was named for Stephen P. Lunt, one of the
estimable partners of the Rogers Park Building and Land
Company.) Oscar sat up behind the wheel, chuckling loudly
to himself. The only other joke he knew, and would trot out
at parties or try out on a new man in the shop, went: "What's
the difference between fish and meat?"—long pause—"If you
beat your fish, it'll die!"; which Belle-Noche thought was an
absolute scream.

Just then Belle-Noche burst out of the house, threw open
the wobbly screen door with the heel of her hand, and
marched down the steps, showing off her frothy tank top,
baggy shorts, and a pair of Red Rooster high-heeled sandals
(and the reddish-purple veins around her ankles). "Don't be
a jackass, Brother," she said without stopping, slapping him
across the top of the head as she passed (instantly reminding

Max of all the knots she used to pound on his head with a dust-mop handle when they were kids): "Keep the money, but throw away the wallet. Set the credit cards aside and let Oscar take a look at them later, maybe we can figure something out. See you in the *morning.*"

Max thought to himself, What's this "we" shit? You dumb broad, you and your cross-eyed, half-bright dwarf of a boyfriend.

"*Oscar!*" Belle shrieked in a high-pitched squeal, and threw up her hands the instant she hit the concrete (as if she just couldn't wait to hop into the sack with lovable, huggable, little Oscar, who, despite his compact bulk, had the loose wrinkly skin of a big fat puppy). She went straight to the car, sliding over next to Oscar with her arm along the back of the seat behind his neck, and gave him a big sloppy kiss (soft, hot tongue, lips and all) on the face. Sometimes, in the middle of the night when both Belle and Oscar were sleepy but still horny, Belle would shove the covers off the bed with her feet and sing, lullaby-fashion:

Fuzzy Wuzzy was a bear.
Fuzzy Wuzzy had no hair.
So Fuzzy Wuzzy wasn't fuzzy,
Was he?

And then jump straight into the air and pounce on Oscar—ready or not.

Oscar, who sat on a folded-up blanket so he could see over the dashboard, glanced at Belle-Noche's extraordinary profile (when the horses came pounding into the stretch and passed the eighth-pole she got so excited her nipples stood up like a dollar stack of dimes), fetched a healthy sigh (he considered himself a *very* lucky man), and told Belle he had a couple of hot tips on some *sure* winners—"Har, har, har" —and they might be celebrating till all hours (which was just fine with Belle, who could still party pretty hardy), drinking what the diehard regulars at Deadwood Dave's called Moscow Lights (half vodka—so ice cold it poured like liqueur—and half rum), because, after a couple of shots of that you could "see the lights of Moscow, and without standing on a chair, you may be sure," as Dave would say, leaning on the Old Style spigot). Then Oscar dropped the gearshift into drive (stroking Belle's leg as he did; she had her feet on the transmission hump) and took off, the car bouncing off the curb as if he were Evel Knievel blasting off from a buffalo jump. Soon Oscar and Belle and the Cadillac (which he called the Great Green Beast) disappeared into the afternoon rush-hour traffic, though the muffler could still be heard for better than a block, and Oscar launched into his story about the evening's surefire daily double—Queequeg's Legs and Death & Taxes, Belle-Noche petting his thighs with playful intention and eagerness.

•   •   •

The moment they were gone, Max relit his cigar, took a swig of Augsburger, and tried to remember where he had left his story, and just as he opened his mouth, Muriel took hold of the wallet and pulled out Loretta's driver's license. Without looking at Loretta's picture she read the address, Snuffy Lane in Northfield. (One of Chicago's very northern suburbs, not too many years ago a quiet town on the North Shore interurban line just west of the North Shore suburbs—a place filled with subdivision after subdivision of overpriced, indifferently produced, upper-middle-class houses that would all blow over and disappear in a decent tornado.)

Muriel said that Max ought to give the woman a call, tell her he found the wallet, and immediately offer to deliver it to her. Muriel thought what horror and mayhem it would be for *her* to lose her wallet—Muriel being especially careful about such things. "It's only money, dear," said Muriel, who had a pure-hearted, Christian attitude about such things; an attitude which included the exasperating belief that honesty was the best policy and rewarded in this world as richly as in the next, and that the Giver of All Good Things squashed dishonesty and wrongdoers like bugs—both in this world and in the next. Which, if anything, made Max take his head, tear his hair out, and regard Muriel as a simpleminded fool best kept indoors, love her though he did.

Agnes-Ruth didn't know what all the commotion was about, but thought the wallet looked exactly like the one that Herman Wallenger, Raenelle's arrogant, loud-mouth husband (who snorted when he laughed), had bought her in 1957, the first and last time Raenelle and Herman had come to Chicago for Christmas.

The money suddenly became a terrible burden to Max, and giving it back was the only solution to the horrible grinding in his gut.

But it's not *only* money, Max thought, squirming and shivering (struggling with the few scruples he had), it's not *just* money, Muriel. It's *money*! Finders goddamn keepers, wasn't that a rule of life? Wasn't that one of the Commandments that Moses brought back from the mountain—those two tablets (one under each arm) and, oh yes, this little bit of a quarry chip. Quote—Just Only Finders-Keepers Money; make it, print it, hoard it, spend it, fold it up and stick it in your mouth and suck on it. Buy-sell-trade money. Even-Steven money. Double-your-money-back money! Money-to-burn money. Send-no-money. Coin-or-paper money. Check-or-money-order-or-Bank-of-England-draft money. IOU money. My-money-your-money, what's-mine-is-mine-and-what's-yours-we'll-talk-about money? Wheel-the-daily-double money. Down-town money. Big-Washington money. Heavy Vegas money. Oil money. Cattle money. Butter-and-egg money. Butter-and-guns money. Nickel-and-dime money. Nickel-and-dime-you-to-death money. Old money. New money. New-money-is-old-money-that-got-away money. Money-in-the-bank money. Money-up-in-smoke money. Money-down-a-savings-and-loan-shithole money. Money-talks-and-bullshit-walks money. Big-time-fuck-you money. Bad-penny money. Sound-as-a-dollar money. One-dollar-and-other-considerations money. Unquote.

Max looked at Muriel (whose whole robust and buxom presence exuded "We have to give the wallet back, dear, money and all") and said that, yes, that's precisely what he was thinking (heaven forbid we should leave sleeping dogs lie), even though he had it in his mind to follow his first impulse and the advice of both Benjamin Franklin and Belle-Noche (it would save a screaming argument with Belle to-morrow). Then he got up, looking like a man dragged out of his house and thrashed with a bullwhip within an inch of his life, slipped the $800 back in the billfold, and, sucking down the last of the Augsburger and throwing his cigar out into the street, went into the house and straight upstairs. He tiptoed through Amaryllis's cats, put the wallet under his side of the mattress, and went out to the hall, where the only telephone in the house hung on the wall between the stairway and the bathroom door.

All the bedroom doors were open, letting in what little light penetrated the windows. Through every doorway a body could see unmade beds, clothes on the floor, hung on dresser drawers, hung on nails pounded into the oak woodwork (painted to death every couple of years in a variety of primary colors), and cats wandering around in gangs and always underfoot. The phone itself was red, a little joke of Belle's, with a long spiraling handset cord that you could stretch all the way downstairs and almost to the kitchen. The wall surrounding the phone looked like the pay phone at Ivory Baxter's Damen Avenue Car Shop—Foreign and Domestic (his business card read: "Besides drinking beer, fixing your hunk of junk is my whole life").

It was to Ivory Baxter's on Damen that Easy Ed and Amaryllis would take their haul of batteries. Ivory, a slightly shady, semi-greasy ex-con, was always in the market for car parts acquired "by art"; they were cheaper and, wouldn't you know it, worked just as well. He claimed he had done time with Jack Henry Abbott. "What an asshole *he* was, bullshittin' those New York writer guys with those bullshit letters of his. What a great line he had. What a scam! They convinced some judge to let him out—it was beautiful! Then he's in New York on parole, taking a whiz back of some café, and the waiter comes out and tells him to zip it up, and move on. So, of course, what else to do when someone tells you to quit acting a fool? Jack shivs him. Way to go, Jack! What an asshole—the one guy on the planet who's *s'posed* to be in jail. A lifer!" Easy Ed and Amaryllis hadn't the foggiest notion who this Abbott guy was, but stood in Ivory's sleazy little office listening to the monologue while he counted out their money. Ivory would clean up the batteries with baking soda and sell them at triple the price.

The upstairs wall of the Nutmegs' house was a mishmash of telephone numbers—everyone in the house had got in the

habit a long time ago of writing phone numbers on the wall
around the phone; visitors said it looked almost like a work
of art, but what*ever* it was, the west wall of the upstairs hall
of the Nutmeg house was a virtual family history reaching
back many years to when Belle's kids were very young—three
of the four children's fathers were still listed. Just last year
Daisy-Lily's father, Durango Ruby, called for a date with Belle-
Noche of all things ("Scoring's easy with that broad," Durango
used to tell Max, though Max didn't need to be told)—and
the instant Belle got on the phone she said, "Listen, Pud"—
she always called him Pud—"you owe me a whole bunch of
child support, and nothing else's changed as far as you're
concerned. I'm still fucking niggers and I'm still a shit-bored
whore, and I wouldn't sleep with you if yours was the last
piece of pork in the whole world!" And then she hung up—
ka-wham!

Max called information and asked for a Spokeshave on
Snuffy Lane in Northfield. There was a moment of electronic
clicks and buzzes, and then a flat computer voice came on
and said that the number was unlisted—*sorry*. But Max had
made up his mind and that was that, and as Muriel said many
times, You just can't keep Max from a thing once he makes
up his mind, even if a person had to help him get busy,
sometimes. She was right behind him with one of Robert's
phone books open across her forearm, thumbing through
the Ps and Qs and Rs as she came up the stairs. She passed
the "Saint-Salad," "Savovich-Sauganash," "Sears-Seaway,"
"Smith-Smith," "Spain-Spaulding" until she came to the
pages "Spencer-Spinner" and "Spinner-Sports." In one of the
middle columns between the Spiveys of Hyde Park on one
side and Sportmart on the other, and just a couple of names
down from The Spoken Word, were the listings for three

Spokeshaves—Arthur E. in Uptown; Emmaline R. of West Roscoe Street near Chicago-Read Mental Health Center (the local nuthouse that used to be called Dunning State Mental Hospital; Roscoe named for the Town of Roscoe, Pennsylvania, on the banks of the Monongahela River); and J.K. out west of Midway Airport (which some of the clowns at Deadwood Dave's thought was halfway to St. Louis).

First things first, that was Max's motto, so he called Arthur E. in Uptown. The phone rang and rang and rang. Finally, a man answered, "Uh—hello?"

"May I speak with Arthur, please," said Max in his most calm and soothing voice, at once straightforward and utterly innocent, the same as when he worked for the Heartland Telemarketing Corporation selling patent medicines and a kitchen table gadget that made afghan blanket squares—

> *In a jiffy!*
> *What a great gift!*

—to little old ladies and shut-in cripples.

"I'm Arthur. Who are you and what do you want? You one of those roofing guys or upholstery guys? I ain't buying nothin' like that. I rent, see? So the roof ain't mine. And all the chairs in the house're just fine. And I ain't looking for a subscription to the *Tribune*, no matter how many helpless, underprivileged little rug-rat pickaninnies go to some goddamn summer camp. I never went to goddamn summer camp and *I* ain't dead. If you're one of those survey nuts, I ain't gonna answer any of your silly questions. Who are you? What do you want?" said Arthur, who lived in the Corngold Hotel on Kenmore Avenue, very near Argyle Street, deep in the neighborhood nowadays called Little Saigon because of all the Southeast Asian refugees who had settled there since the war. (Kenmore Avenue was named for the colonial home of one Colonel Fielding Lewis near Fredericksburg, Virginia; his main claim to fame was the fact that he married George Washington's sister. Argyle Street was named for Archibald Campbell, the first Duke of Argyle, 1701.)

(Down at Deadwood Dave's, when every other form of entertainment thinned out, they'd play street trivia, but how the city came by the names and who was responsible, no one could say. Knucklehead John thought they used a big dartboard; Poky from Skokie, who drove a big, sleek Kawasaki, said, "Some kinda dictionary"; Downtown Raymond suggested it was a trivia drinking game—"Whush da stupides' Irishman you ever heard a? Da boss sez we need a famous Polack. Witcha you guys ever heard of a girl's name? Whoz a dead ward guy from da fordy-turd? Wuzza name a dat guy who put up dem houses Back a da Yards?" Can't you just see it? Some seedy little room in the basement of City Hall at the end of the hallway next to the boiler room, where you've got to duck under the hot-water pipes and squeeze between crumbling boxes of Alderman Vito Marzullo City Council stationery; a bunch of crummy old chairs—the kind you see on White Trash porches in Uptown; big trash cans filled with Budweiser long-neck bottles; a permanent city "commission" of lifers who couldn't get a straight job to save their souls, lounging around, waiting to use the pay phone, and bragging about "real-estate deals" and "insurance deals" and snagging the Board of Education contract for several hundreds of thousands of calculators—at eight smackers a copy—to hand out to every kid in the fourth grade and above in the public schools. What a great gag *that* was!)

Max leaned against the wall, surrounded by Amaryllis's

cats rubbing against his legs, with Muriel standing in the light coming through the bathroom door still with the phone book opened across her forearm; Muriel crowding him as if she's pushing him through a revolving door.

"No, no. I'm not trying to sell you anything. I'm looking for someone," Max said to Arthur, beginning to hold the receiver very tightly.

"What? You the cops?" asked Arthur, standing in the kitchen looking at a sink piled with two days' dishes: canned chili and hot dogs, eggs and bacon, Popeye's Chicken and bratwurst, Wheaties and waffles. "Well, I've already told you guys that Byron left his wife years ago, and ain't none of us Spokeshaves seen hide nor hair of him since!"

"No, I'm not the cops, either," said Max, reminded yet again of all the ordinary horrors of everyday life. "I would like to know if you're related to one Loretta Spokeshave of Snuffy Lane in Northfield."

Arthur switched the phone to the other ear so he could reach the coffeepot. "What happened? She die and leave me a bunch of dough?" said Arthur, who had never heard of any Loretta among his aunts or cousins or nieces, even though the Spokeshaves were a very large family. He poured his coffee and for an instant thought it might be true he'd missed one all these years, but he'd never heard of a Spokeshave in Northfield, wherever *that* was.

"No, no. Nothing like that. I've never met the woman, but I need to get in touch with her," said Max. "Do you know a *Loretta* Spokeshave?" There was definitely no reason on earth to tell this jerk about the wallet and the money, no telling where the conversation might get to; Max felt mighty strange talking to perfect strangers, which is why he hadn't lasted at Heartland Telemarketing.

"No, I can't say as I know of a Loretta," said Arthur.

"Okay. Well, thanks. Nice talking to you. Goodbye," said Max, and hung up.

Arthur looked at the receiver in one hand and the coffee cup in the other and suddenly had to wonder whether a conversation had just taken place—too much daytime TV, he finally thought to himself. Got to get out more.

Muriel sidled up to Max and pointed to the next Spokeshave on the list—Emmaline R., on West Roscoe Street. Max dialed the number and heard the phone ring many times.

Chicago and North Western trains began passing the house at closer and closer intervals, shaking every window as they went, and Agnes-Ruth was lecturing some dogwalker about picking up his dog's shit—"Ain't city living hard enough without you bozos letting your dogs shit all over creation? Ain't there some city ordinance about dog *poop*?" said Agnes-Ruth, taking a moment to wet her whistle with a gulp of ice-cold gin. "You bet there is, young man. Now you just skedaddle on home and get yourself a coal shovel, or a pooper-scooper, or some such gadget, and pick *that* up before I call the cops." Russell Poolaw had moved to the neighborhood with his dog, John Thomas (a happy-go-lucky Labrador retriever, one of the dumbest breeds of dog there is), from Escanaba on the Upper Michigan Peninsula, where winters were *hard* and there wasn't a lick of work; almost immediately he got a job as a yardman at the Gethsemane Gardens, an outfit that sold flowers and shrubs in the spring and summer, pumpkins in October, Christmas trees in December—everything at rip-off city prices. He'd been warned by all the neighbors about the gray clapboard Nutmeg house, which couldn't be mistaken for another household for blocks around, even if Agnes-Ruth never set foot on the porch.

Finally someone picked up the receiver and listened for a long time; Max could hear breathing. He waited for someone to say hello, but no one did.

"Hello?" said Max. "Is anybody on the line? Anybody there?"

And the sweetest little voice replied, "Yes, someone's here. Who's this?"

Max couldn't figure out from the sound of the voice whether it was a very young child or an old woman, as thin and hushed as it was. "My name is Maximilian Nutmeg, and I'm looking for a woman by the name of *Loretta Spokeshave,*" Max said rather loud and definitively, finally deciding that whoever was on the other end of the line was hard-of-hearing. Agnes-Ruth could hear his introduction all the way down the stairs and out the front door; even Russell, holding John Thomas at heel by the collar—the dog was eager to move on to the next interesting tree—could hear Max's booming voice. The cats of the house jerked and looked for a place to hide.

"Loretta? There's no Loretta here, just Emmaline, my mommy. And she's at work. Why did you call my mommy Loretta? That's not her name. It's Emmaline. And why are you shouting? You hurt my head," said little Sophia Spokeshave. Her mother always told her never to answer the phone, but she couldn't resist, though she had stood next to it watching it ring for the longest time, expecting it to jump around, like it did in the Popeye cartoons.

It took Max a long moment, but it finally dawned on him that he was speaking to a child. "Can you tell me if you have any aunts?" Max asked. Muriel had never seen Max being so patient. The things I do to keep peace in the house, Max thought to himself, and imagined the child (he couldn't yet decipher whether it was a boy or girl—Max was not very good at such things) standing at the mother's bedside twisting the phone cord around her finger and hand and arm, making big circles in the air.

"My name is Sophia," the little girl said, pronouncing the word *So-fee-ah*, "Spokeshave," saying it as if it were two words—Spoke-shave—giving the *k* a kick Max never suspected it had. "I'm four," she continued after a long pause. "And I know that my mommy sleeps naked."

"That's nice," said Max in his most fatherly, uninvolved voice, encouraging and exasperated at the same time. "Is your mommy there? May I speak with her?" Max had years ago got in the habit of speaking with excruciating correctness to children—something the bikers down at Deadwood Dave's thought was total bullshit. "How's a kid gonna learn to abuse legal drugs, fast-talk cops, and argue with a bookie with you talking to them like that? Ah-ga-wan!" It was then that Muriel nudged Max (she'd been listening next to his ear). "Max, let's move on" was all she said.

Max hung up, dialed J. K. Spokeshave, and hoped for the best. After all, the third time's the charm, he thought. The phone at the other end seemed to be ringing with a precision that so impressed Max that when someone picked up the phone, said yes, and asked who was on the other end of the line, Max was speechless for a moment.

"Hello?" Johann Kunkel Spokeshave said again, not accustomed to being made to wait. "I said 'Hello!'"

"Mr. Spokeshave, my name is Max Nutmeg and I am looking for one Loretta Spokeshave. Would you happen to know such a person?" asked Max, suddenly straightening his back and standing tall—Muriel still crowding him at the back, cats still *leaning* against his legs as if to knock him down.

"*Loretta* Spokeshave," said Johann. "Loretta?" he re-

peated, and looked out the side window of his forties brick
two-flat, at the brick wall of the forties two-flat next door; he
could hear the truck traffic and express buses on Archer a
couple of blocks north. (Archer Avenue was named for Colonel
William Archer, civil engineer on the Illinois and Michigan
Canal and staunch abolitionist, who nominated Abraham Lincoln for Vice President in 1856.) Johann pondered the name
as if he were trying to identify the difference between inbound
and outbound air traffic at Midway east of him.

"Yes," Max said. "She lives in Northfield. Know her?"

"Northfink? What kind of a name is that for a town?"
said Johann, who had lived in Chicago since his family came
to the United States from Eseldorf, Austria, after the war,
when he was two (changing their name from Kunkelfreud),
and thought he knew Chicago pretty well.

"No, North*field*," said Max, becoming less polite and
more exasperated. "It's north of here."

"Loretta of Northfield," pondered Johann, twirling the
phone cord with his finger. "Let me see," he said, trying
honestly to think.

There was a long pause.

"Well, Mr. Nutmeg, to tell you the truth, I don't think I
have any relatives there," said he (since the Southwest Side
Marquette Park Spokeshaves didn't have any relatives anywhere), and turned around to make a funny face to his mother,
who had come down the hallway from the kitchen to find out
to whom her Johann was talking—the Spokeshaves received
very few phone calls; phone calls (like telegrams) out of the
blue always meant trouble. Perhaps it was Reg Toliver at
Gunnar's work and there'd been an accident (the world was
such a dangerous place); she hoped not, because trouble was
such a bother and gave her headaches. By signs Johann man-

aged to assure his mother that everything was just fine, that the call had nothing to do with his father's work as a switchman for the Illinois Belt Railway (the best job he'd ever had —America was such a *wonderful* place!)—that he would be home in plenty of time for dinner, and that they would play Hearts and watch TV (*Unsolved Mysteries, Night Court*, and *The 700 Club* on Channel 38), just like always. His mother smiled, waved her flour-dusted hands in the air to signify she'd understood (Never mind silly old me), and made her way back to the kitchen—she was making a batch of Elsa Marvenka's *Verwirklichenkuchen* for Rita Moriarty's seventy-fourth birthday (a recipe brought from the old country, though who this Elsa Marvenka was no one could say).

Max hung up and knew he needed another beer right away. Muriel thought he needed a nice hot bath, but was dispatched to the refrigerator (stopping first to clean the cat hairs out of the tub and run the water). Max went into the bedroom to change—a beer and a bath sounded just about right—stashing his panhandling take in his sock drawer without counting it. When he was naked Max looked the picture of health (seeing his tall, lean body always turned Muriel into a "Creamette," she would tell her sister Raenelle), though he always thought that being tall was silly (the only tall guys who had any fun were basketball players)—a body had to keep ducking one's head to get through doorways and in the bathtub your knees always stuck up out of the water, no matter how full the tub or how much you scrunched down. He threw on his bright yellow terry-cloth robe (bought for a buck at a yard sale in Rogers Park) and went to the bathroom. (Rogers Park is the northeasternmost neighborhood of the city, named for Philip Rogers, an Irish immigrant truck farmer.) Several of Amaryllis's cats were standing on the curved edge of the old claw-foot tub watching the water roar, sniffing and poking at the steam.

Max walked in and said, "Okay, everybody *out!*" and took down the bottle of Aqua Velva after-shave and sprinkled some into the water—Muriel *loved* the smell of Aqua Velva. Max threw his robe across the folding chair in the corner—Why do women want a chair in the bathroom, Max thought to himself—and stepped in.

Chicago and North Western commuter trains roared past the house across the street. Max held on to the lip of the tub and put first one bony foot in and then the other. Muriel brought Max's beer and stood in the doorway, admiring his body—he had such a cute little tush, a smooth hairless chest, and a lovely little pecker, which she called Scout (as in "He's such a good scout!"). Max, however, was forlorn with worry and doubt as he settled himself lower and lower into the steaming hot water, gasping with utter surprise. Money, one way or another, had always been a bother and a worry (and he took the bottle of Augsburger dark from Muriel, who was all but licking her lips as his crotch disappeared under water and Max took a long breath through his teeth). Either the Nutmegs were white-trash poor—beans and franks, Spanish rice and greens, corn flakes and instant coffee—or they were on easy street (more or less). Muriel gave Max another cigar—"It's TLC time," she would say at such moments—and a strike-anywhere kitchen match. Since the toilet was right behind Max's head, he could flick his ashes there.

He sat in the bath for half an hour, lost in thought, puffing his cigar and sipping his beer. Muriel kept bringing him another "tall, cold one," which he held to his open mouth, leaned his head back, and poured down his throat. Is there anything more majestic than drinking cold beer in a hot bath, Max thought, tipping his cigar ashes into the toilet. That night at dinner (Easy Ed and Amaryllis never did make it back) they had tofu croquettes with some spicy Greek sauce, Brussels sprouts, and succotash with pimientos (made with the last of Muriel's stash of canned goods she had put up Thanksgiving weekend), but Max wasn't hungry and ate only so as not to insult his wife—good old Max.

The topic of conversation that night was Agnes-Ruth re-telling Bible stories: How the Lord had created the world in six days, *putting* everything in its place; separating the light from the darkness seemed the toughest—Agnes-Ruth drawing a precise line in the dining-table varnish with her table knife and squinting along it as if it were *the* plumb line—the light on one side with the goose-girl bud vase and the *TV Guide*, and the darkness on the other side with the Art Deco Zephyr napkin holder and the Pyrex coffeepot.

Then, rather than sit in the living room and watch TV while Agnes-Ruth (who was on some kind of tear) talked back to the cop shows and lawyer shows and commercials, and lectured the news people about the coming doom (letting Amaryllis's cats lick the salt on her feet), Max—still a little tipsy—went to the basement and sorted through his collection of priceless antique patent-medicine bottles, of which there were three boxes. At 11:00 he came upstairs (Easy Ed and Amaryllis still not home), very discouraged, and went straight to bed. That night, Muriel could not cheer him up no matter what she tried—Beaver & Bear, persuading him by hand, kneeling stark-naked above him (trying to entice Max with her most personal aphrodisia), wiggling around and saying, "Cheer up, Max. Here, help yourself." But Max, worried and troubled about Loretta Spokeshave's wallet and all that money, could not be persuaded to anything.

He fell asleep on his back, laid out like a corpse, and that night dreamed of money: money piled in a bonfire, burning; a country cottage made of money pressed into slabs like Sheetrock; money playing baseball in a parking lot filled with abandoned cars; Gumby and Pokey disappearing into the hardcover copy of the *Grimm's Household Tales*.

For Max it was a sleep filled with money and greed, trouble and woe.

We Don't Want Nobody
Nobody Sent

Loretta (née Horlback) and Henry Spokeshave lived in a large, quiet house on Snuffy Lane in Northfield, a sleepy suburb west of Winnetka—a town on the North Shore more exclusive than all the dickens, as the real-estate amateurs at Deadwood Dave's would say.

Snuffy Lane was named after Simone van der Pohl's prize Shetland pony, and it happened this way: Simone's father, Raymond van der Pohl, had at one time acquired vast pieces of land between the Chicago, North Shore and Milwaukee Railroad interurban tracks and Waukegan Road, old U.S. Route 42A, by buying up foreclosed farms and the odd crummy shack for back taxes in the twenties and thirties (from the small fry having a hard time of it). He was one of those guys nobody ever heard of who made a snug little fortune doing a snug little business representing other rich men (engaged in other businesses, both small and large) in the state and federal courts. By the time World War II came, Raymond van der Pohl had more work than he knew what to

do with from Commonwealth Edison, People's Gas, Standard
Oil, and the New York Central Railroad. In 1945, Mr. van der
Pohl was a very rich man (the war was *good* for business),
owned a good deal of unimproved land, and bought his daughter Simone (aged nine) an Irish-bred Shetland pony she
named Snuffy, a name got somehow or other from his stiff,
bristling mane and sunny disposition. Simone loved the horse
more than her little tongue could tell and rode him often
around the paddock and through the woods. One morning in
January 1952, Snuffy was found dead in his stall, and was
buried on their property in the woods—Simone crying her
eyes out as the stablemen shoveled in the dirt; Thomas, the
foreman, leaned on his shovel and said it was like hauling a
legless grand piano. Then in 1954, Mr. van der Pohl, taking
his family and his money with him, moved to Los Angeles,
where for the next twenty years he worked hard, cheated no
one, died immensely rich, and built a wing on somebody's
museum. When the Northfield holdings were sold—house
and grounds, stable and all—a small, harmless caveat was
inserted at the bottom of the property deed as a binding cov-
enant (and handed over to the buyers with the bill of sale),
to the effect that should ever a residential right-of-way be laid
through the property it was to be named Snuffy Lane—after
Simone's horse. So, the next spring when the group partnership had the property surveyed and subdivided into five-acre
wood-and-pasture lots, they were reminded by the Northfield
Township Real Estate Board, the chairman of the Planning
Commission, and the president of the Village Trustees that
the thoroughfare—a tractor path through the woods to the
"back pasture"—was to be named Snuffy Lane. The partners
had wanted to name it Beatrice or Altoona (names of two of
the partners' wives; they couldn't decide which), or Tree of

Heaven (*Ailanthus altissima*) or Honey Locust (*Gleditsia triacanthos*) or Box Elder (*Acer negundo*), species of fast-growing shade trees that hadn't arrived in this neck of the woods until well after the first white men, a favorite among the local get-rich-quick developers—but van der Pohl had laid plenty of money on everyone before he left, so the partners never had a chance. When they waltzed into court they walked into a buzz saw of legal horsefeathers (as the court-room buffs at Deadwood Dave's would say)—a white-out bliz-zard of objections, legal precedents, and summary overrulings of the plaintiffs' every motion. It was stupid. The partners could not understand for the life of them how the trustees could stonewall and sandbag such a trivial thing as the name of one goddamn little road (they sat in court thoroughly baffled and befuddled; it boggled the mind). Finally, an old bailiff couldn't stand it any longer (the way some clowns can't stand the tingling suspense of someone's not getting the joke), took the meekest-looking of the well-dressed supplicants aside in the hallway, and explained the whole gag. After everyone had had it explained and it had sunk well in, it was *still* stupid. But clout was clout—as they say in the City Hall press room—so Snuffy Lane it was, and Simone (in her later years senile and crabby) was mighty proud. When the weather broke that winter, the easements were surveyed and staked out, the utility trenches excavated along the roadway, the pipe and pavement laid and ditches dug, and the street signs mounted. The lane (sparkling fresh asphalt smelling of tar and as smooth as a tabletop) ran either side of the horse's grave, marked by a gnarly and hideous European buckthorn (*Rhamnus cathartica*), the berries mildly toxic ("And they don't call it *cathartica* for nothing, boys," Tall Paul, Deadwood Dave's afternoon bartender, told one and all). Neither the partnership of speculators nor any of the later residents knew of any such thing as a horse's corpse under the roadway (out front of Robert Salisbury IV's place), and would have thrown up their hands in sheer exasperation at the nonsense stupidity of it if they *had* known. And no sooner had the houses been built (stone and brick exteriors, cedar shingle roofs, and three-car garages with paving stone drives; instant conspicuous consumption) than the elder Mr. Spokeshave bought one and moved Henry in with his new bride—Judy—the *first* of Henry's wives.

•   •   •

The Spokeshaves, beginning with Calvinist James Henry Anthony III, a stern and venerable patriarch if ever there was one, had come to the United States (from the industrial north of England) early in the nineteenth century with plenty of money, long before the potato famines; long before France's gift of the Statue of Liberty; long before the hordes of flat-broke, pathetic-looking, steerage-passage peasants fled the grinding poverty of Ireland and Poland and Russia and such places (or the arrogant and spiteful, idiot ducal wars of imperial Europe). Henry's great-grandfather had long since moved the Spokeshave fortune through the Cumberland Gap into coal, oil, railroads, and shipping, and—when the time came—war manufacture, real estate, and commercial aircraft.

Henry's family had *never* gone without money, mind you, but when it came to divvying up a fortune among five sons, the conversation got mighty quiet and peculiar at the annual Spokeshave Thanksgiving dinner. Henry's father, Anthony, gave his sons plenty of money, each in turn, and a couple of good lawyers to help look after it. So Henry, the last but not least son of Anthony and Alice (née Ruckleshaus) Spokeshave, became the majority stockholder in several Montana coal strip mines and had stewardship (his father's word) of a machine tool company, Jeter International Machine Tools, Inc. (corporate headquarters in Wheeling, Illinois), manufacturer of all sorts of complicated and (it goes without saying) expensive gadgets for General Dynamics, Chrysler, and in recent years Mitsubishi—shiny, handsome, and complicated little things that Henry only dimly understood but thought looked mighty handsome in their crates on the loading dock. Henry was a quiet, sober, and deliberate Yale man who had bored his first wife to tears (she left him for a guy who owned a couple of McDonald's franchises in Tucson); got rid of his second wife, Annabelle (who was "never well"); then married Loretta, fifteen years his junior (she seemed the kind who would always be there—as if told firmly, "Lie down; stay"— just Henry's ticket). Henry had no idea that she was a lustily passionate libertine and would have been shocked—amazed —if he had known.

Almost the minute Loretta moved in, she threw out everything that the other two wives had accumulated and began filling the house with expensive, trashy art and rickety antiques. Everything from large, loud canvases to little snippets of pencil drawings; from clever copies of High Renaissance Raphael fresco cartoons mounted in thick baroque frames to happy-go-lucky *Día de los Muertas* papier-mâché sculptures and Andy Warhol balloons and such like; as well as videos of performance art (some guy snorting water and lying under a slab of bulletproof glass for forty-eight hours, Richard Nixon's "Checkers" speech, head-on train crashes staged for show, and Leni Riefenstahl outtakes of Nazi torchlight parades and Nuremburg political rallies). Early, bad Pollocks any New Yorker would call "pathetic gibberish"; late, senile Renoirs;

really bizarre Dalís; cynical, pornographic Picassos; Miró dream-doodles done on the can first thing in the morning; an entire hallway of Kimmelbergs.

"Who the hell is Kimmelberg?" Henry wanted to know when the truck from the Seven Deadly Sins Gallery arrived with the first half dozen. One of the guys hauling the paintings into the house said, "Don't worry, *pal*, the guy just died. These're gonna be worth a bundle"—Kimmelberg's death the subject of a lengthy Harry Bouras obituary broadcast on WFMT–FM fine-arts radio. Serious and knowledgeable art collectors all over the world wept; investors like Henry jumped for joy—the goddamned things were actually going to pay off. One call to Wally Findlay or the Campanile Galleries and Kimmelberg would be money in the bank.

Loretta's sorties out to the trendy and pitiful, suburban antique and kitchen–bathroom–dining room shops of Long Grove quickly became extravagant binges, and the house filled with loose-legged tables, armoires (made from kits) with doors that didn't hang right and wouldn't close, solarium wicker furniture with the caning coming unwound, a dining-room table distressed with a bike-lock chain, boxes of Mexican ceramic tile ("For the kitchen," Loretta said—when she got around to it), and expensive and arcane dust-gathering *objets d'art* of all sizes and descriptions. Lemuel Cutshaw owned the Seven Deadly Sins Gallery on West Huron (named for the lake; the lake is named for the Indian tribe and in French means "uncouth wretch"), where Mrs. Spokeshave and her redoubtable checkbook often loitered and reconnoitered. Cutshaw thought Loretta's taste was mighty peculiar, but profitable enough for him to send three daughters to college (Smith and Mills)—that woman would *buy* anything (or as the old gaffers at Deadwood Dave's would say, "What's that broad been smoking?"): Wurlitzer jukeboxes, circus sideshow façades (screaming clowns, really fat bearded ladies, and tweedy-looking ringmasters), Union Station waiting-room benches, thirties junk jewelry; obscure, early Illinois section maps showing the locations of scattered homesteads, old French trading posts, and Indian "encampments"; fake African masks done in the 1840s for the safari trade (age their *only* claim to fame)—the tribesmen taking the trade beads and hawk's bells, and laughing last right out loud about those silly white guys who'd buy any goddamned thing a body could knock together between the time you first saw their dust yonder across the savannah and they arrived in the village (asking about water and looking for women).

Every time Henry encountered these monstrosities, all he could see was money—"Perhaps one day all this shit will be worth something."

And on top of everything else, Henry and Loretta had a boat named *Toady* (the origins of which are too obscure and complicated to explain) docked in Burnham Harbor among the vast collection of charter boats and Mafia yachts that dry-docked winters on Goose Island.

The harbor was named after Daniel Burnham, the man who said, "Make no small plans," which is the same as saying, Ignore small, pinched minds (not that easy in Chicago); co-author of the famous Chicago Plan of 1909 (a thing nobody'd seen hide nor hair of since the Great Big War). The harbor lies between Soldier Field (where the Bears play football) on the west, Meigs Field (a small-plane, downtown airport) on the east, the Shedd Aquarium and Adler Planetarium to the north, and McCormick Place to the south.

(This may have nothing to do with the story, but the first McCormick Place—the city's convention center built in

1960—burned to the ground in January 1967, because the fire hoses couldn't reach from the hydrants to the fire, a serious design flaw the city engineers admitted later with considerable embarrassment and professional chagrin. The building was so vast and expensive that it was not insured, a distinct municipal fiscal peculiarity, seeing as how every nitwit alderman and his dipstick brother, every city lifer with any push *or* pull—including Richard J. Daley's sons—had an insurance agency and a real-estate gig or a sham law firm on the side. Daley, who, with his white bread imagination, gave the city much and took much away, always said, "Don't take cash, boy, give them your business card." So it was mighty strange that McCormick Place was not insured—even a little. And when it went up in smoke the city turned around and built another, which looked like a giant pool table with the legs cut off, but the matter of no insurance stuck in everyone's craw. Years later, when the city's reporters got wind of the fact that some of City Hall's vast and lucrative but miscellaneous insurance business went to an outfit that had just hired one of Richard J. Daley's boys, they asked about it with the rhetorical astonishment and feigned journalistic surprise that passes for objectivity reporters are famous for—"*Nepotism?*" The old man stood behind his press conference podium and sputtered—furious—that it was a father's duty, by God, to help his sons, and if the reporters didn't like it, by God, he'd tie some mistletoe to his coattails and, by God, everybody could line up—"Dats wadda gotta say about dat!" he said, and pounded his fat little fist on the oiled woodwork.)

Loretta, as much as Henry—and Jean-Claude—loved her, was just a little wacky, but it seemed to run in her family. For instance, one day in 1919, her grandfather Michael Thomas McSorley was in the Illinois Trust and Savings Bank on La Salle Street (depositing a windfall inheritance from a great-aunt who had died in Duval County, Texas, during the great influenza epidemic). A Goodyear blimp from the Wing-foot Express Company on its maiden voyage over the Loop suddenly caught fire and crashed through the bank's skylight, killing thirteen express company passengers, bank employees, and patrons, including a *Chicago Herald and Examiner* photographer aboard ship who had asked the blimp pilot to hover over La Salle Street so he could get a picture ("What a scoop!"). (It was a terrible tragedy and became known as the "Wingfoot Air Express Blimp Crash of 1919.") Among the unfortunate dead was Loretta's Grandfather Michael Thomas. The Illinois Trust and Savings Bank wrote Rachel, his wife, reassuring one and all of its depositors that the vaults were intact and the bank would remain open during the remodeling; expressed its profound sympathy at the untimely death of her husband, but regrettably declined to honor Mr. Mc-Sorley's deposit, because the cash ($500, a considerable sum in those days) as well as the deposit slip bearing his signature and the bank teller's stamp were never found in the wagon-loads of debris. After Rachel, Loretta's grandmother, got over the shock of the death itself, she became strangely philosophical and would laugh uncontrollably when the subject of her husband's untimely accident came up. "A fiery blimp—Jesus, Mary, Joseph!—falling on his head while he stood making out the paperwork, *that* was just his luck," she would say, standing in front of the open refrigerator. "All that money—may the saints preserve us!—gone!" She began filling the house with odd pets and strays, and hoarded food the rest of her life. Loretta's mother, Ariadne, grew up with a mortal fear of swimming, was an art student at The School of the Art Institute (though she never graduated), and married William

Foster Horlback of Miami when she was twenty—"to get the hell out of the house; your grandmother was crazy," she told Loretta more than once. Loretta went to Barat College in Lake Forest, where Chicago's lace-curtain Irish sent their daughters, and first met Henry Spokeshave at Leona's Pizzeria on North Sheffield in 1982, when a waitress spilled a platter of hot pasta dinners on him; Loretta "just happened" to have a handkerchief handy and started wiping food out of his hair. They were married the year after at St. John's Evangelical Lutheran Church in Wilmette. It was a large wedding—morning coats and top hats—and a lengthy honeymoon in St. Thomas, Hawaii, and Hollywood.

•   •   •

It was the second week of May, Thursday after the full moon, early morning just as the sun rose over the Spokeshave house. Loretta woke to plenty of light in the room and an empty bed. Henry was one of those guys who like to get an early start, so for time out of mind he would be "up and at 'em," as the saying goes, making money before the damp had burned off the grass. Since the Sunday before, he had been engaged in a lengthy business trip that took him from Bogotá to Zurich to Dallas and then to Ottawa. Loretta was accustomed to waking to a cold bed, even on weekends, and had learned to luxuriate by sprawling all over it. As she lay there thinking of good strong coffee and Jean-Claude (today was to be the second of their twice-weekly trysts—Thai bath, feather fan, and dog-collar day), it suddenly occurred to her that her wallet was not in her purse. She got up and went downstairs, pouring herself a cup of coffee, and, stepping over the box of plumbing fixtures in the kitchen, began searching for it.

Loretta was one of those people who are always mislaying

things. Address books and bills, keys and vacation itineraries, several TV remote controls were gone forever. When she came in the front door she would put her keys and coat on the radiator, the mantel, the cedar chest, over the banister railing, on the coatrack with Henry's silly collection of hats. She'd put her keys in the ceramic ashtray, the daily-mail basket, the fruit bowl, in the kitchen among the countertop kitchen machines. It exasperated Henry no end but worried Loretta not a moment—"There are plenty of things in this world to lose sleep about, Henry, but *that* is not one of them," she used to say. Henry was devout about orderly neatness, to the point of fetish, and Loretta's bemused and slightly addled air seemed to him a conspiracy.

That's what Loretta loved about Jean-Claude—aside from his remarkably casual and even cavalier attitude about money—a little sloppiness never killed anybody. Jean-Claude didn't care a snap about money, "not a fig," as Jean-Claude's father used to say, and didn't even seem to know how much he had (the checks came, he signed them over to the trust-fund lawyers—Max guessed right about that)—just that he had *plenty*. Jean-Claude was so devil-may-care! And *exciting*! And *really* rich!

The day before, Loretta had put her wallet somewhere or other and now couldn't find it for the life of her. Henry had an old-world, old-money philosophy about money: go ahead, spend big, but get your money's worth. She knew that if Henry found out about the missing $800, he would be *very* disappointed, to put it mildly—or as the racetrack philosophers down at Deadwood Dave's would say, "He's going to take the $800 out in trade and beat the living shit out of her."

And what was worse, the plumber was coming today—which explained the boxes of plumbing tools and brand-new fixtures in the middle of the kitchen floor—and wanted to be paid in cash. Elmo Dudycz (pronounced "Do-ditch") had studied the engineering physics of the place for most of an afternoon the week before, rattled off half a dozen things (including soil pipes, something called water hammers—a veritable blight on the landscape—and the furnace hot-water radiator returns), rolled his eyes, and said it was going to cost "pull-enty!"—Dudycz's favorite word. He had left boxes of tools and replacement fixtures of every description, scrawled out a work order (which not even careful, steady Henry could decipher), and specifically and loudly mentioned cash. Then he drove off, saying he'd be in touch. He had called the night before (the same instant Max, back at the Nutmeg house on Ravenswood, was climbing into his bath while Muriel watched with tingling admiration), saying he'd arrive the next day, "bright and early," which any homeowner should interpret as sometime between dawn and noon.

Loretta went upstairs to take her shower and make herself beautiful for Jean-Claude, rightly assuming that the minute Dudycz showed up, the first thing he'd do was turn off all the water in the house, unscrew everything, and take every pipe in the basement apart. There'd be filthy pipe grease and that nasty sewer smell all over everything all day, and the next day, too. These workmen never finished on time and always left a mess was what Henry always said, but plumbing *was* plumbing, and there was nothing a body could do about it. Even though the house had been built in 1954, there'd been new roofing to contend with, electric garage doors, an addition in back of the kitchen, and now the plumbing was making noises (and was just "slow," the fixtures crusted with lime). "Ah me," Henry always said when he sat at his Amish-made, cherrywood rolltop desk in the library, adding up the totals on a piece of scratch paper and writing out the checks. Dudycz's wanting cash vaguely insulted him, but the man had good references. Everyone he'd worked for said he came on time, didn't drink or smoke or swear, always ate a bag lunch in the truck, and cleaned up and left by five o'clock. Henry just put this strange business of the cash down to an independent entrepreneur's idiosyncrasies.

• • •

Jean-Claude's father, Stephen Wesley Bouillon, owned God-knows-what, which involved who-knew-whom from heaven-knew-where—but the mailman couldn't help but notice that Mr. Bouillon got mail from the foreign ministries of China and Japan, Denmark and Spain, Panama and New Zealand, Saudi Arabia and Monaco, and, of course, the U.S. State Department—as well as every shop-at-home catalogue known to the United States Post Office. Jean-Claude was a stocky, strapping kid, not afraid of the rough-and-tumble of soccer and rugby. If his father had received less interesting mail and they had had to live in Winnetka, the boy could have had an appointment to Annapolis for the asking and would have wound up flying carrier-based fighter bombers for the U.S. Marine Corps. Be that as it may, he nevertheless went to school in Switzerland. The Boys' School of St. Bernard was so exclusive that the name was not generally known, the deans and trustees did not recruit students, and graduates were asked not to make mention of it in later years—no use troubling the rank-and-file *nouveau riche*. The soccer team went to their matches in a Lear jet—to Tokyo and Hong Kong, Algiers and Capetown, Brasília and Savannah. When alive, the elder Stephen Wesley Bouillon was a charter member of a restored parlor car on the Chicago and North Western nick-

named *Idlehour*—it left Lake Forest early enough each weekday to roll by Max's house on Ravenswood by eight o'clock.
In passing, Stephen Wesley had watched Max's house slowly
fall apart for thirty-five years, while Maximilian Nutmeg was
raised and reached his manhood, married a good woman, and
gladly accepted one and all of his kin into the house (good
old Uncle Max).

No matter what extravagance Jean-Claude treated himself to at the boys' school commissary, then later with British
Airways, Cadillac and Fiat and Rolls-Royce, Brooks Brothers,
the Hilton chain, then later still with sleek young French-
Eurasian chippies and "older" Hungarian widows—no matter
what the item—he never seemed to come to the end of a
running tab that showed up everywhere and covered everything. One summer, when he was barely twenty years old, it
seemed as though all he *really* needed was change for a daily
paper and kroners for taxis; and the next summer he was the
guest of Mr. Augusto Kutachogi on his Neapolitan yacht *Co-
lumbia* with the three Kutachogi nieces—Persian-Swedish
women fresh from their university studies in Paris—who lived
alfresco from dawn to dusk (*avec les têtes au vent*, as the
lusty Riviera French might say), young ladies who took turns
cooking Greek calamari and "Tel Aviv" omelets, and flirted
shamelessly with Jean-Claude. Meanwhile, Uncle Augusto
was off bribing Egyptian oil ministers to leave his tankers and
airliners alone. All Jean-Claude's father said (and bluntly) was
"The Kutachogi girls are highly cultured and beautiful to be
sure, son, so have a good time, but they are not the marrying
kind, so don't forget your 'devices.' " Then one night not too
many years ago, when Jean-Claude was verging on middle
age and whooping it up at Rio de Janeiro's Carnival, the elder
Mr. Bouillon fell asleep reading Barbara Tuchman's *March of*

Folly and quietly died of a stroke—apparently without moving a muscle. Jean-Claude was called home by Emmett Horn, his father's personal counsel. Arrangements were quickly made to inter the body in Provence, alongside his wife, Oriole. Back in Lake Forest, Mr. Horn sat down with Jean-Claude (exhausted from grief and stupid with jet lag) and explained the full array of Stephen Wesley's financial affairs—a conversation that took three days—stocks and bonds, ships and aircraft and real estate, sundry investments and gold reserves, as well as letters of credit and bank account totals in half a dozen countries. When Jean-Claude walked out of Horn's office with the staggering news, it finally dawned on him why he was always running into his father's business associates. He drove back to the estate and shut himself up in his rooms for the better part of a week, writing letters and thanking everyone for their heartfelt condolences and weeping into a towel he kept by the desk ("My father loved me, after all!"), changing clothes many times a day—letting the maid in only to bring the meal trays, make the bed, and tidy up.

And when he emerged, suddenly calling for his prize possession, a mint-condition 1964 Shelby-Cobra Ford Mustang Indianapolis 500 Pace Car, to be brought round front, he drove off to Mr. Horn's office and told Mr. Horn and the other attorneys to incorporate every last business venture into a foundation trust, but, of course, to continue paying his bills as before. He joined the Lake Forest Precision Lawn Mower Drill Team but otherwise became a virtual recluse, working in his garden and greenhouse alongside Pierce, the gardener; puttering with his cars with Audley, the chauffeur; going out little and seeing few.

He met Loretta one evening at an American Cancer Society benefactors' dinner at the Ambassador-West. Henry was off talking with a couple of guys from Boeing. Loretta was standing near the draperies by the French doors out to the veranda, making small talk with several matrons from the Evanston Women's Club and the Greenacres Country Club Auxiliary. Jean-Claude, a man both husky and tall, caught the eye of Helen Brooks (Evanston Women's Club supernumerary, an *old* friend of his father's) and had himself introduced to Loretta right then and there. Loretta, though never having heard his name before, shook his hand politely, looked him up and down, and was mighty impressed. They began seeing each other for lunch a month later, and a month after that were sharing their twice-weekly afternoons in Half Day (a town so named because in the horse-and-buggy days it was half a day's ride from Chicago) in the Presidential Suite of the Montavalo Hotel—which, it goes without saying, Jean-Claude owned lock, stock, and barrel (a real swank place where the Jaycees and Lions and VFW had their meetings, raffles, twice-monthly bingo, and self-congratulatory banquets); Jean-Claude owned all the Montavalo Hotels worldwide.

The morning Loretta awoke to find her wallet missing from her purse, Jean-Claude and Pierce were cultivating the pea vines and the gladiolas, spreading compost around the peonies and raking the last of the leaves—Jean-Claude randy with happy anticipation of an afternoon's fun.

• • •

Loretta took a long, hot shower, then searched for her wallet high and low while her hair dried. She found her Coach purse where she left it sometimes—in the bedroom on the chair between the couch and the vanity. She looked all around the bedroom and in the closet, the upstairs hallway including the drawers of the table where a fresh bouquet of robust purple Queen of the Night tulips sparkled in the crisp and bracing morning light. Her wallet wasn't on the banister, wasn't between the couch cushions, wasn't hanging on the banana tree in the solarium, wasn't in the car or the kitchen. She even checked the Celtic pewter bowl where the mail collected. The wallet was nowhere to be found, and suddenly she was worried, but not panicked—*yet*.

She walked back through the dining room among the Burmese red lacquer screens and the Danish porcelain china cabinet, trying to retrace her steps, rolling her eyes up into her head as if to get a better look at where she'd been the day before.

She'd gone to the Seven Deadly Sins Gallery to look at a new consignment of acrylic on acetate Disney drawings of the Seven Dwarfs, Amazon Indian war clubs, and Maori puberty-initiation headdresses (parrot-feather appliqués and Jesuit-missionary beadwork). She'd dropped by the American National Bank on La Salle to get Dudycz his money (one-third the amount due to start the job)—What *was* that man *doing*? She'd been walking for the train, lollygagging along (eyeing those hideous sculptures in front of the State of Illinois Building), and bumped into this tall man with curly hair, a well-tailored though baggy three-piece suit, and the biggest black wing-tip shoes she'd ever seen. He had explained very simply and clearly his predicament, something about driving all night and a Zion wedding and his car out of gas ("Oh my!"), showing her the gas can and asking for money. Loretta was immediately convinced of his sincerity—it was the China-red tie and the talk about his exquisite sister-in-law, something-something Krautlammer, Grouthammer, one of those German names—then pulled out her wallet and gave him a couple of bucks, taking out some carfare for herself. That's why she hadn't missed her wallet at the ticket window.

I must have dropped the wallet between there and the station, Loretta thought with exasperation. In other words, dearie, we can kiss *that* money goodbye. But good God, *every-thing* was in there! License, credit cards, date book, phone numbers, tax deductible receipts, *money!*, my whole life!—a *wallet* is a *very* personal object.

Belle-Noche couldn't have said it better, except to add, "I ever get my hands on that shmuck who walked off with it, I'll rip his lips off, gouge his eyes out (stomp on those suckers with my bare feet), then kill him with my bare hands!"; Patty the Pushover down at Deadwood Dave's would have said, "Merciful heavens, here we *go* again!"

Loretta stood in the kitchen among the boxes of Dudycz's tools and gleaming fixtures, drinking a second cup of coffee and eating the last of a greasy, crumbling raspberry croissant. She thought of all the 800 numbers she was going to have to call, canceling every charge account (it would take all morning and half the afternoon). What was going to happen in Dallas when Henry hauled out his American Express card and the hotel pegged him for a thief and called the cops? Loretta knew Henry only too well; he'd never let her forget that she stranded him out in the middle of nowhere with $17.00 in cash, the Dallas cops screaming in his face and slapping him around, showing him their pistol belts and rubber truncheons, working on a confession all through the night shift. (Any cop will tell you that an out-and-out confession— or a well-bargained plea—is much neater and cleaner than all that due-process shit, that's what the law buffs and the ex-con legal eagles down at Deadwood Dave's would say, shaking their heads at the sheer beauty of it). Henry'd be speechlessly irate—no telling what he'd do to the furniture, *or* the Kimmelbergs.

What if Henry had found the wallet and hid it as a prank? He was just like that. She gasped and wiped her mouth with a dish towel—"Oh *my God*! What if he found Jean-Claude's letter?" Henry would haul her into the library and have a conniption, slurring his words and bursting the blood vessels in his forehead while reading her the Riot Act. "What's this nonsense about *feet*, Loretta?" she could hear him say as he walked between his cherrywood rolltop desk and the fireplace in high agitation—a romping, stomping, raving lunatic—waving Jean-Claude's engraved stationery and jumping up and down every time he passed Loretta sitting in his favorite wing-back leather chair. "And what's all this nonsense about a *dog* collar? A blindfold? An air mattress? And what does all this have to do with *feathers* and *baby oil* and *surgical* soap? One can *only* guess, my dear!" he'd say, leaning over the back of the chair and down into her face. And Loretta, sitting there burning up, stiff with guilt (found out; ashamed) and worry (what is Jean-Claude going to say?), would hardly know where to begin: "Well, Henry, the feathers and the dog collar and the blindfold go with the velvet ropes that Jean-Claude brings in *his* attaché case"—as if Henry actually wanted a narrative explanation of her and Jean-Claude's afternoon goings-on.

Loretta poured herself another cup of coffee and fetched another greasy room-temperature croissant. The thought of Henry's finding the letter truly panicked her; misplacing her wallet was one thing, but a showdown over the letter was quite another. "As a matter of fact," she'd tell him, sitting up, while Henry stomped around the room in a fine, screaming, mad-fit fury, "as a matter of strict fact, dear, that stuff in the letter is the least of it and utterly tame. Jean-Claude has a large attaché case which he brings to each and every one of our meetings." And as Henry paced around his library tearing Jean-Claude's letter into little-bitty pieces and rolling them into tiny spit balls, Loretta would go on to list every last geegaw and doodad Jean-Claude hauled with him (what Belle-Noche would call industrial-strength marital aids)—each item another nail in the coffin of their marriage: transparent panties and mesh body stockings, corsets and French cutout bras, garter belts, G-strings and split crotch panties, miniature rawhide leather underwear, and other peculiar, colorful exotica: patent-leather boots with spiked high heels, an Argentine cowhide bullwhip, a Chinese Ping-Pong paddle covered with a tight-fitting, quilted oven glove that read *Kiss the Cook* on one side and *For This I Spent Four Years in College?* on the other; flavored body paints and long-bristled sable brushes, a black party mask decorated with sequins, dildos in three sizes, a vibrator with an assortment of "happy tips," a tiny brush and comb, a cock ring and wet-look man's bikini underwear, *ben-wa* balls and a jar of K-Y jelly, rubber suction cups, velvet ropes, FBI regulation handcuffs wrapped in thick knitted covers, a large feather duster, a leather dog collar, tape recordings of remarkably bizarre sound effects, scented oils, packets of Swiss Miss cocoa mix, a half dozen fresh Marshall Field's Frango mints (they melted into a gooey paste more quickly than anything else), and a 35mm film can of the very best garden-fresh Washington State marijuana that Jean-Claude's money and considerable connections could buy.

• • •

Loretta mused—woolgathering—about her and Henry's marriage-ending argument (Henry staggering, twitching and hysterical, around the library, as if gut-shot again and again, while Loretta launched into her list of items and how each was used, and which clothes went with what accessory). And at the very moment when Loretta imagined Henry just about exploding with rage (circling around the room like a balloon let go), flapping his arms and screaming, Elmo Dudycz arrived in his ex-Ma Bell phone company truck with a pipe rack across the top. He waltzed right into the kitchen, where Loretta was finishing her croissant.

"And a good morning to you, missus," he said, and hinted with a great deal of body English for a morning cup of coffee. While Loretta poured him a cup, he fished through the boxes of tools, taking inventory. Dudycz wore polished-cotton two-pocket work shirts and painter's pants, with a name tag over the left-side breast pocket that said D U D —though his wife called him Elmo—and had the look and walk (with short arms and little hands) of what the weekend bikers down at Deadwood Dave's would call a yard-dog litter runt. Loretta and Dudycz chatted for a moment, as if waiting for the other to mention the money, until Dudycz got itchy and said, "When I spoke to your husband last week, I *did* mention that I take cash only, if you recall. I really can't begin the work"—and he cast his eyes down to that corner of the kitchen above the furnace—" 'until we settle this matter of the fee,' " he said, lifting a phrase from a Carpenters' Union brochure. Dudycz didn't want cash because his North Shore customers bounced their checks (as had happened time and time again to other "tradesmen"), and it wasn't because the vast and vagarious subtleties of checking-account cash flow were beyond the calculating precision of a certified union plumber the likes of Elmo Dudycz (though tax time was a breeze); he was just one of those working guys who can deal only with cash, a matter of tactile aesthetics learned in early adolescence, beginning with lawnmowing and snow shoveling. He carried his money in a stiff-leather breast-pocket wallet crammed into his hip pocket, chained to a belt loop.

"Well, Mr. Dudycz," Loretta said while she rinsed her plate and set it in the dish rack, "Mr. Spokeshave is out of town, and I've been running, running, running all week, and I've not got around to withdrawing that much cash from the bank. Why don't you have a cup of coffee, take all this to the basement, get started, and I'll just make a quick run to the bank—I've some town errands, too—and be back in a jiffy with your initial fee." Loretta, exasperated and breathless but nonetheless coquettish, said, "The hell with it," under her breath and then, fetching her keys and purse (out of habit), got into her brand-new, buttery-sleek, stars-and-stripes-blue Mazda Miata and drove away.

Once Loretta was out of the house, Dudycz took his coffee and the last croissant, and snooped around the house. The combination of gaudy "art," thick beige carpeting, and weird antiques knocked his eyes out. He sipped his coffee and leaned on the banister and stared at Loretta's prized Kimmelbergs for a long time—"Shit," he said after a long moment of pondering the colors and shapes, "am *I* ever in the wrong business." He finished off the last of the croissant, knocked back the last of the coffee, then started down the basement steps with the boxes of wrenches, fittings, hacksaws, acetylene paraphernalia and butane soldering contraptions; lead and copper and plastic pipe and joints (Ps and Ts and Ys), adhesive, hammers, and steel wedges, tape measures, portable pipe threader—in short, everything he would possibly need minus his bag lunch and thermos of ice-cold cranapple juice. He didn't have a helper—kids were a nuisance and older guys wanted real money—and having to make it up and down the stairs, through the house, and out to the truck was aggravating (and Elmo always got distracted). Every morning he stopped at Aunt Dot's Breakfast Barn in Lincolnwood and ate with a roomful of freelance tradesmen. All Dudycz's work stories began, "Well, I took my box of tools and went down to the basement, and you'll never guess what I saw there"— as if he had tripped over a horrible, scaly ghoul (with hideous ivory fangs and smoking, noxious drool from *Fantastic Planet*) instead of Rube Goldberg water pipes, P-trap drains, or a maze of antique and deteriorating hot-water radiator pipes, and always the ubiquitous methane smell.

He hauled everything through the laundry room (where Buffy, the twice-a-week Brazilian maid, did the wash, folded the clothes, and ironed) and into "the back," where the furnace and hot-water heater and Henry's pitiful little "workshop" were. Dudycz looked at Henry's silly collection of K mart tools—"Drop-forged cardboard," as the street-corner toolbox experts down at Deadwood Dave's would say—and said to himself, Thank God, there's guys like me in this world who actually know what they're doing. And after he had arranged everything along the walls and turned on the lights, the very first thing he did was locate the water main and shut it off. Then he turned off all the pilot lights and opened all the petcocks and emptied the entire house of hot and cold water. Turning off the hot-water heater and draining the tank, he noticed rust and such around the base, and reminded himself to mention to the missus that a new water heater wouldn't be a bad idea, that he could get a good one at a good price. It was the last-minute, horse's-ass "ups and extras" that paid Dudycz's mortgage.

Then he sat on the clothes dryer and listened to the water

pipes all around him gurgle and clunk—the sound of money to a plumber; this was a three-day job by the sound of it— and in less time than it took him to smoke a Pall Mall down to the lips, the house was high and dry. Meanwhile, Loretta Spokeshave was hightailing it up to the bank with the top down and her hair flying.

My Mouth Wrote
a Check That My Ass
Almost Couldn't Cash

Meanwhile, back at the Nutmeg house, things were as lively as they ever got in the morning. Easy Ed and Amaryllis were busy with breakfast in the kitchen. Agnes-Ruth was busy in the attic talking to herself, today full of regret that Darl Dwayne couldn't have had a more decent burial. Sweet William was already busy with customers in the alley. Robert was busy delivering phone books in Norwood Park, a high-toned working-class neighborhood in northwest Chicago named for, of all things, Henry W. Beecher's novel *Norwood: A Tale of Village Life in New England*. Muriel was busy in the basement working with the last of yesterday's clothes, singing up a storm:

> *Well, when I woke up this morning, baby,*
> *I had to call you on the telephone.*
> *You know when I got up this morning, Sugar,*
> *I couldn't wait to talk to you on the telephone.*

Cooler by the Lake

You know I just couldn't wait to tell you, baby,
Come on and meet me with your glad draws on.

I said I woke up this morning, honey,
I had to call you on the telephone.
As soon as I got up this morning, baby,
I had to call you on the telephone—yes I did!
You know I just couldn't wait to tell you, baby,
Come on, meet me with your glad draws on.

Baby, meet me with your glad draws on,
I want you to meet me, meet me with your glad draws on.
Why don't you, baby, meet me with your glad draws on.

Oh, you don't have to worry about me leaving,
I always be here.
I said, baby, I ain't going nowhere—no I'm not—
I'll always be here.
Because every time I think about the way you love me,
My stuffings get all creamy and my eyes fill with tears.

Hey, baby, meet me with your glad draws on,
Why don't you, baby, baby, baby, meet me with your glad draws
     on.
Come on, sugar daddy, I want you to make yourself right to
     home.

Why don't you rock me, baby,
I want you to rock me all night long.
Why don't you rock me, rock me, rock me, baby,
Get your little red rooster and rock me all night long.
Rock me, baby, like my back ain't got no bone.

Roll me, darling, roll me like a wagon wheel.
Why don't you roll me, daddy, roll me, daddy,

Honey, roll me like a wagon wheel.
Roll me, baby, you just don't know how good you make me
    feel.

Baby, I want you to meet me with your glad draws on.
Yes, I do. Yes, I do.
Hey, baby, baby, baby, meet me with your glad draws on!
I said, baby—hey!—meet me with your glad draws on!
Yeah!

Max was just waking from a shaky night of disquieting
dreams.

At the very moment that Loretta Spokeshave first woke
up and spread her magnificent body from one end of the bed
to the other, luxuriating in warm and enveloping spacious-
ness, and drifted back to sleep hugging a pillow, Maximilian
Nutmeg rolled out of bed and made his weary, tangled way
to the bathroom, staggering through Amaryllis's cats, which
seemed to be playing a combination of hide-and-seek, blind-
man's bluff, king-of-the-hill, and who-could-hawk-up-the-big-
gest-hairball. For Max, this hour of the morning was the moral
equivalent of the crack of dawn. The next instant he stood in
front of the toilet, and once again the mighty sound of warm
urine was heard throughout the house. Good God, Max
thought, trying to grin at himself in the mirror, what am I
going to do? He rubbed water on his face but didn't feel one
notch better, and went back to the bedroom to dress, walking
through the cats with broad side flourishes like a speed skater
("Fuck me running, don't people *drown* kitten litters anymore?"), and went downstairs in search of his coffee. As irk-
some and aggravating as all the cats were, no one had seen

a rat or a mouse at the Nutmeg place since before Amaryllis was four years old.

Easy Ed was sitting at the kitchen table nursing his morning hangover with Boston coffee—black coffee with lots of milk—nibbling toast, and squeezing his eyes like someone who's been reading fine-print heirloom manuscripts day and night for weeks. Amaryllis stood at the stove, whipping eggs and cutting ham for scrambled, swishing her hips back and forth, and singing (to the tune of "London Bridge"):

> *Heaven helps those who help themselves,*
> *Help themselves, help themselves.*
> *Heaven helps those who help themselves,*
> *My dear Eddie.*

Max rifled through the cupboards—the cookware and plates and glasses, the condiments and spices, the whole-wheat flour and the graham crackers, the turkey stuffing mix and Muriel's homemade granola—looking for the coffee mugs.

Right then and there, standing on his tiptoes searching through the high cupboards, he was a man ready to submit to the whim of chance and fate, fortuitous or catastrophic, if only the Giver of All Good Things would show him where the godalmighty, godforsaken, goddamned coffee mugs were. Finally he opened one of the cupboards over the refrigerator, where yesterday Muriel had stored the seldom-used pots and pans, and *there* was his prized collection of mugs and cups. He chose his Baltimore Orioles cup in honor of their remarkable losing streak of twenty-one games to begin the season (the cup, a regular collector's item, got for 50 cents at a yard sale in Pilsen from a couple from Paraguay who ran a Ma-

and-Pa Spanish video store in their basement). Max stood on the brittle ridges of kitchen floor mastic and slapped his stomach—Can't I pick 'em, though, he thought, thinking of the coffee mug.

And when he ladled himself some coffee, it tasted honorably pleasant—cinnamon, grounds, and all.

He went to the basement, where he knew that Muriel was ironing shirts and pants, the board set up underneath the bare light bulb between the furnace and the old Kenmore gas dryer. (Agnes-Ruth, lying in bed and musing about her life of troubles with her smokes and her gin, could hear Muriel singing clear to the attic; Belle-Noche was not yet back from her triumphant back-stretch sojourn with Oscar.) Max sat on the old Kenmore wringer washer with his head low to keep out of harm's way from the overhead rafters. He felt terrible —like a man waiting for a break in a high fever—and looked worse (his face unwashed and unshaved, his hair uncombed), Muriel saw that right away. It was best to get that woman's wallet and her money out of the house, Muriel reasoned with herself as she laid out the yoke of Max's shirt, before her dear wonderful Max shriveled down to nothing, and dropped dead right before her very eyes.

The dust of strangely fragrant spray starch glittered in the air. Elvis, the oldest, fattest, and most world-weary of Amaryllis's cats, sat at the widest end of the ironing board next to the Kelvinator iron, apparently impervious to the heat, and licked starch from the spray can nozzle.

(Max got the iron at a garage sale in Pullman in 1979 and fixed it with a couple of screwdrivers and some wire. So handy around the house Max was, that's what Muriel said many times. Pullman was a community designed and built by George Pullman, manufacturer of railroad passenger cars, as a company town in the overbearing and "paternal" style of all late-nineteenth-century robber barons. When, in 1894, his workers struck, he is reported to have said, "*What?* There *is* nothing to negotiate," and had the federal government—the Attorney General was a former railroad lawyer—break the strike with federal troops.)

The residue of starch and hydrocarbons and whatever else they put in spray starch made Elvis slaphappy and giddy, the envy of all the cats upstairs. He somehow managed to communicate to them that one lick of starch was worth an entire afternoon of rolling around in one of Amaryllis's Hefty bags of gourmet catnip; the other cats managed to communicate among themselves that Elvis was "rather not well," or, as the deadbeats down at Deadwood Dave's would say, "not hitting on all six"—car cylinders, that is—"and as high as a treed coon." Elvis the cat was like the one guy in every crowd who likes liver, much to everyone else's curiosity, surprise, *and* revulsion. After a morning of "helping" Muriel iron clothes, Elvis would feel fine—"just *fucking* fine"; mellow like nobody's business for the rest of the day, was what Easy Ed had observed more than once—and spend the afternoon stretched out on the porch railing with his legs and paws dangling down, staring at the hedge trim, dreamily counting the leaves.

Muriel worked on Max's shirts with steaming hot slaps of the old iron plugged into an overhead socket. She had a workman's ease and a workman's pride: each sleeve crisp, each crease precise, each collar and cuff stiff as cardboard; hanging them on the old kitchen broomstick rigged up behind her over the furnace boiler. Muriel lingered over the shirts the way wind-tunnel model makers linger over an experimental wingspan with #600 grit sandpaper, a half-inch-scale silhouette drawing, and a pair of decimal calipers; she toiled the way high-rise iron workers clamber over their buildings, setting the horizontal beams in place (hanging on to "terra firma" with the fingertips of one hand and reaching out over the sidewalk hundreds of feet below to muscle the next beam home and line up the bolt holes).

In a pinch, Muriel could do a shirt in less than thirty seconds—*wham, slam, wham!* Done! *Time?*—but mostly she loved nothing better than to fuss over them, as if she were making exact-tolerance machine parts.

While she worked they shared Max's cup of coffee, and Max told her of his bad night's sleep (which she well knew) and the dreams he had had—all about money. Max, or anyone else except for Elvis, seldom bothered her in the basement while she was working, so she was surprised and glad he had come down to talk, and knew it was serious.

"I've got to get rid of that wallet," Max said as he began, slumping down, and Muriel agreed with deep and sure, profound nods of her head while she buttoned one shirt, hung it up, and smoothed the next damp shirt out on the board in front of her, sprinkling it with water from an old Coke bottle.

"I had these *dreams* last night. I was in a small Indiana dunes farm town," he said, telling her the first of them. Muriel was not surprised to hear that Max had had a bad night of it, for all the thrashing around, the whining and grunting in his sleep. "Crumbling storefront buildings and a wide, short main drag—a drugstore, some supermarket chain store nobody ever heard of, a couple of bars, and a hardware store. Everything waterlogged and dry-rotted. I was hanging around the bench out front of a bar called Scanlon's Place. I was dressed, and *felt*, like a drifter or a bum. Hungry and tired. My *feet* hurt like hell. Like that time I delivered a '72 Dodge to that jackass in Chippewa Falls and then got beat up and robbed; it took me a week to work my way back here. A caravan of cars comes into town and parks along the curb, bumper to bumper. The men, dressed in muddy, filthy overalls, all get out and take collapsed bags, like grain sacks, into the state bank around the corner. The only brick building in sight. I hear the sounds of pushing and shoving, a scuffle. Shouting. Not a minute later, somebody throws open the screen door. It slams against the potted geraniums, and not a breath later all those guys come running out the door, bent over, ducking bullets, with dusty sacks of good old dough in one hand and shooting behind them with the other—just like in the movies. Money spilling out of the sacks. Everybody jumps into their rattletrap Cadillacs and leaves town, trunks low to the ground and money blowing out the side windows. Bankers in suits holding shotguns and big ledgers, bank tellers in shirt sleeves with handfuls of cash, and patrons with their pockets turned inside out and mouths agape standing in the middle of the street watching them disappear down Highway 20."

Muriel slapped the iron across the back of the shirt up to the yoke (leaning on the iron as if she were "troweling concrete," the construction experts at Deadwood Dave's would say) and looked at Max as a creeping sadness drew down over his face.

"Then I was in a town square with a huge old Gothic cathedral at one end and a town hall at the other. A big old oak tree with drooping-down branches in the middle. Shops and town houses all around. Cobblestones. Little foreign cars parked along the curb. Maybe German. Maybe north Italian. Who cares? It was night. A big crowd of townspeople and country peasants. Iron lanterns and pitch-pine torches. Cops with tall feathered hats and riding boots. Lots of fluffy side-whiskers and high collars. Near the fountain well is a heaping bonfire of money higher than the windows, burning like crazy. The ash of bank notes and cold cash floating upward in the smoke out of the light." Max swirled his arms into the air as far as the rafters would allow, showing Muriel a large and billowing fire. "Everybody grinning and laughing." And Max grinned a big idiot grin. "I'm standing there by the oak tree thinking, This is *crazy*! More and more people stream into the square, bringing handfuls and lock boxes and banded bundles of money. Wheelbarrows. Haycarts. Children and adults fling money onto the fire. Shovel it with snow shovels. Coal shovels. Manure forks. Women fan the thing with their kitchen aprons and rough twig brooms and collapsed cardboard boxes. A band plays. Everybody singing, hooking arms and dancing." Max points here and there in the air in front of his lap, as if laying out toy soldiers by the regiment and soon-to-be-ruined cash crops and farms. "Skirts a-flying. Little babies and small children flung high in the air. Squealing and giggling. My God, Muriel, you would have thought it was some kind of pagan holiday. I was in agony watching all that glowing-hot money." And Max shivered as if the room were suddenly swept with blizzard cold. "The bonfire was sizzling and crackling like green wood oozing sap. I felt like the only sane person there.

"It woke me up and I lay in bed a long time watching a Dick Powell movie on Channel 9, one of those old "Thin Man" numbers—Powell walking around half smashed and trying to solve a couple of murders.

"Then I drifted off again and I was in a city. Like from the *National Geographic*. Victoria City on Vancouver Island. Charleston. New Orleans. Maybe a mountain city in Mexico. All's I know is, it looked plenty odd, let me tell you. It seemed like a Sunday and people were outside. Strolling. Carrying on. It was windy and paper money was swirling up between the buildings with the trash. Money in the gutters. Greasy wads of money clogging the sewer drains. Ice-cream cones wrapped in money napkins. Vendors giving out money hand-bills, and people, glancing at them, walking three paces, then throwing them away. In the park kids kicking through piles of money like it was raked leaves. Like it was spilled popcorn at a movie. Street bums sleeping in deep doorways covering their heads with blankets of money. Money spilling out of everybody's pockets and shoe heels. Somebody would doff his hat and $500 in twenty-dollar bills would fall out. Women would open their purses and $300 in fivers would spill out, and everyone was just as blasé as if it were lint. Buses would zoom by and money would be blowing out the exhaust pipe. It smelled like Valencia oranges and your cooking sage. And me? I'm going nuts trying to scoop up the money in the street. Shoving money in my pockets and in my shirt. And I'm jump-ing up and down snatching at it while it's still in the air. Trying to catch the money that blew out of the office building windows. And it's brittle and dry. And suddenly the idiot thought comes into my head: Why don't these people water it—like it was one of your African violets, Muriel, you know —before they throw it away? And I'm screaming, 'Money, money, money, you fools, this is *money*!' And dripping sweat. And all those people walking by, standing in the street, gawk-ing and grinning. *They* look at me and *they* think *I'm* crazy!

"Then I'm in a Gumby and Pokey cartoon, of all things! *Jesus*, where did that come from? The three of us disappear into a hardcover copy of the Grimm Brothers' "A Little Story about a Good Deal of Money," and everywhere we wander— disguised as money changers—as the story of the foolish peasant unfolds the townspeople had money hanging out of their pockets. Blew their noses with money. Bragged about their money to their brothers-in-law. Manufactured money by sleight of hand. Told get-rich-quick bedtime stories to their children. Made a big show of brimful strongboxes in their root cellars. I tell you, Muriel, we barely made it out of there with our lives, they were going to run us out of town on rails! But the little peasant convinced everybody in town that there were piles of gold bars at the bottom of the lake. Got everybody in town to jump in. One of the most amazing things I ever saw."

Muriel finished with the shirt, slipping it on a wire hanger, laid out the next one (Easy Ed's good Sunday shirt), and went at it with the iron.

"I tell you, Muriel, I don't know what to do," Max said. And sitting there on the old Kenmore wringer washer (still warm and damp), for once Max's motto—What the fuck, it's only a buck—seemed as shallow and hollow, absurd and obnoxious, silly and foolish a phrase as "Wait till next year." Loretta Spokeshave's gray Coach wallet—the money, the credit cards and calling cards and whatnot—was becoming an overwhelming burden of soul and mind (and body) that would diminish him until he dried up and blew away, and Muriel, practical, house-happy (in love with a bungling fool, the beer-mug philosophers down at Deadwood Dave's had said many times), would wind up sleeping alone, sad and inconsolable, for the rest of her life, dying in late middle age of a broken heart. Muriel held up the left sleeve of Easy Ed's white Sunday shirt, eyeing and plotting precisely the crease she was about to lay in (as if surveying the right-of-way for a new interstate highway), and thought that for the health and well-being of the love of her life, the health and well-being of her happy little home, Maximilian would *have* to return Mrs. Loretta Spokeshave's wallet, come what may; never mind and no matter the time and trouble and cost—and it was going to be time and trouble and cost aplenty (*double* the price was cheap enough, according to Muriel's reckoning—Muriel would rather eat dirt than sleep alone). She stretched Easy Ed's shirt sleeve out on the board and sprayed it well with starch, laid the iron on the cuff (the starch bubbling; Elvis the cat licking his whiskers with relish at the sight of a large gooey blob fizzing all over the tip), and pressed down hard, waffling the hot steaming iron as if perhaps trying to screw it into the tapered end of the ironing board. We must return the wallet, Muriel thought (saying it as though she were going to help with the driving), cost what it may—time, money, effort—it was little enough to keep Maximilian near and dear to her. She put the iron aside, went over and stood between Max's knees, put her arms around him. "You poor dear," she said, and gave him a hearty hug and a great big kiss on the lips. "I tell you what. That wallet and that money are not going to give you a moment's rest. We tried calling yesterday, trying to get in touch with that Spokeshave woman." Suddenly Muriel had an extreme dislike for this Northfield woman who didn't have any more sense than to carry $800 in cash on her person.

> *Finders keepers,*
> *Losers weepers*

—wasn't that a decent workingman's rule of life, Muriel thought, but if it meant that her husband, Max, would die of something extreme like remorse and grief, wasn't it better to make the best effort possible, do or die? Right then and there Muriel cuddled Max, feeling the warm bulge of his crotch— he was still wearing just his white cotton Jockey shorts, you understand. Best not, she thought, running her fingers through Max's hair, Max has work to do. Good God, the money and the wallet and the worry had rendered Max strangely impotent last night, and *that* was something that Muriel would put a stop to right now; today; this instant. There would be plenty of time tonight, she thought—a righteous, raucous celebration of hearty, sweaty, whoop-de-do, good-time fucking.

"Maximilian, why don't you do this?" she said, and leaned back, conniving and flirting at the same time (something she did very poorly), holding Max's head up by both ears. "Borrow Ed's tow truck and drive out to Northfield and *give* this Spokeshave woman her wallet. And once that's done I'll fix you your favorite."

Max drooped even further and wanted to groan; Easy Ed's rattletrap of a tow truck (nicknamed Easy Ed, written backward across the front of the hood) was a disaster parked at the curb waiting to happen. Drive out there? By myself? Out into the great shit-stomping, mock-wholesome, holier-than-thou suburbs? The land of cheesy mortgaged-to-the-hilt condominiums, subdivisions of "single family homes" and thistle prairies, commercial zones and snarling traffic, and brain-dead, Goody Two-shoes solid citizens as far as the eye can see—the slums of the twenty-first century? I'll get stomped—Max shook his head in despair—I *always* get my ass kicked when I go any farther north than Howard Street or any farther west than Harlem Avenue. (Harlem Avenue was named for an old westside community that had once put a great deal of money into the Chicago, Harlem and Batavia Railway—"We're going to clean up!"—but lost its shirt.)

Max sat there, utterly depressed and defeated, and would certainly rather have taken a couple of large-caliber gunshots to the head than leave the city and drive north, money and wallet or no, horrible dreams or no, no matter how much he loved Muriel or Muriel loved him. All his life those people seemed to lie in wait for him. Years ago, when he worked as an alley scrounger, he and his rusted-out flatbed truck had been busted more times than he cared to remember. His truck looked "disreputable," *he* looked "disreputable," and the whole notion that Max was one of *them* brought squad cars squealing and roaring up to the scene from far and wide—like something out of *Wide World of Sports*. And while he hauled out his wallet and showed the crowd of cops his driver's license (and they all had to examine it as if it were some remarkable and rare archaeological specimen; in a weird sort of way it was funny to watch them work—*keeping* the peace the way Sherman took Atlanta), they itched to get at him for something ("Soliciting without a License," "Vagrancy," or that brilliant, mighty-fine catchall "Disorderly Conduct")—like half-starved, whacked-out yard dogs with just enough chain wired around their necks to reach the driveway and keep the miscellaneous riffraff and ritual troublemakers (siding and encyclopedia salesmen) locked in their cars with the windows up.

If the late-night regulars at Deadwood Dave's—the serious, melancholy drunks, the booze-sloppy bikers and second-shift working stiffs—had heard what Muriel had in mind for Max and had contemplated Max's inevitable fate for more than a moment, they would have said, "That Nutmeg guy is going to get his ass kicked but good, *no* doubt about it!" They relished it with the same fascinated, bloodthirsty curiosity as the prizefight nuts who lingered over the sound thrashing "Rockpile" Haugen gave challenger Reggie Hedblum—with each roundhouse swing Hedblum's eyes about sprang out of his head with a *pop*, as if he were a cartoon frog, and the sweat snapped loose from his hair, spraying the first three rows. Deadwood Dave had the AP photograph of it somewhere or other on the wall (Haugen's glove squashing Hedblum's face and lips to one side, the air around them filled with sparkling droplets of sweat). All the regulars at Deadwood Dave's would have said that Max would be coming home from Northfield feet first—and grateful for that!

Then Max leaned way back where he was sitting, looking at Muriel with great puzzlement, thinking, "Fix you your favorite?" What the hell does that mean? My favorite what? He immediately had the impulse to ask her what, exactly, she thought his favorite was (taking a breath), but stopped himself—Let's leave well enough alone, that was Max's motto—Let's do this puzzle one funny little piece at a time. Then he jumped down from the wringer washer, kissed Muriel (hugging and rubbing up against her as if for good luck), and said he was going upstairs to dress and talk to Ed, thinking, I'll just have to find this Spokeshave woman, give her back her money and her wallet, get home as best I can, and find out what my "favorite" is.

Max's resolve was invigorating, the plan simple; the execution, however, was complicated and troublesome, not to say threatening to life and limb. But a thing you've promised to do is better done with a light heart (as grim and horrible as the task is)—that was another of Max's rules of life, an infallible motto that got him through many a long night, down many a country road, and through every description of difficult scrape. So upstairs he went, slumped shoulders, dread fear, and all, and dressed quicker than a jiffy.

•   •   •

In the kitchen Easy Ed and Amaryllis were spooning out the cat food into several large, shallow salad bowls. It was the custom in the house that as soon as all the many cats heard the whining grind of the can opener, they would drop what they were doing and run for the kitchen—except for Elvis in the basement on ironing day. The cats and kittens crowded into the kitchen (stopping to tease the ferrets, Big Daddy and Betty), jumped up on the counters, walked across the table (sniffing the salt shaker and sugar bowl, licking up the last of Easy Ed's eggs and bacon), waiting with watering mouths for Amaryllis to serve it up. Some of the cats preferred canned meat and got canned meat; some preferred dry and got dry.

By the time Amaryllis and Ed put the bowls on the floor and everybody crowded around with their tails twitching, it reminded good old Uncle Max of a debris-choked, hard-rain runoff swirling down a street sewer—a slithering, cater-wauling mass of shivering, hairy tails. When Max walked back into the kitchen everyone was slurping and crunching away, the kittens sucking up warmed milk Amaryllis had heated in a double boiler Max got a couple of years ago at a garage sale on North Clybourn (named for Archibald Clybourn, who in 1829 built one of Chicago's first stockyards and a twenty-room mansion right next to it—much to the blinking amazement of his wife; he then made a fortune as a butcher during the Blackhawk War of 1832). Amaryllis stood in front of the sink watching the feeding frenzy with warm, giggling admiration. Max looked at her and wondered what kind of hideous bag lady she would have become if Muriel hadn't insisted she stay in the house until she was well beyond the age of consent. Amaryllis was dressed in a nifty little purple nightie (Ed's Valentine's Day present) with a long fire-engine-red peignoir with fluffy collar and cuffs (It's a wonder she doesn't catch fire and burn to a crisp just scrambling the eggs and frying the bacon, Max thought); the whole ensemble nylon and polyester with Velcro fasteners—tasteless in every sense of the word—itchy and preposterous, though Ed often said it was plenty tasty, if not downright toothsome, once you got past all that nonsense. The cats loved to climb on it, and Amaryllis, cat lover that she was, never seemed to mind. Needless to say, the goddamned cats drove Easy Ed crazy the same as Max. "But," as Ed always said (rubbing his hands together), "you've got to give a little to get a little," and he kept his grumbling to himself.

Max ladled another cup of coffee, by now tepid; the raw cinnamon made his mouth hurt.

"Say, Ed," said Max, sitting down with his back to the refrigerator and getting right to work, "I got to borrow your truck."

So sudden and straightforward was Max's comment (it really wasn't a question) that Easy Ed snapped his head around and sat up all in one motion.

"What?" he said. He was wearing the same logger's shirt, the same wide red suspenders and belt as the day before, but this morning the way he wore his clothes and slumped in his chair looked like a newspaper folded funny and held with a rubber band. He had heard Max's request perfectly well, but seemed to need a moment to gather what wits he had about him. Max started sweeping cats off the table with a wave of his arm and repeated, "I got some chores. I got to borrow your truck." Ed looked at Max as several cats fell off the table like crumbs. "What for you want the truck? I mean, what chores? Amaryllis and me was going back down to Hegewisch. It's easy pickings down there, Max. You ought to come with. Ivory's paying top dollar these days. Batteries. Starters and alternators. Carburetors," said Ed, looking at Amaryllis, who was flashing her legs open and closed, teasing, to see how long Easy Ed could keep his mind on his business. Amaryllis called it "Funnin' Mr. Ed!"; Ed called it silly and childish: "Cut it out, and stop calling me Mr. Ed."

"Well, Ed," Max said with a serious earnestness he knew would impress Ed, dumb as he was, "I got some business up north and the Packard's down, the Dodge needs a timing chain, as you well know, and Sweet William is using the Plymouth out back." The Chevrolet never went anywhere that Sweet William didn't go; it was no use asking about the Chevy anyway, because Sweet William never loaned it to anyone, for love *or* money. "The only ve-hicle on the place is that tow truck of yours. Now I know that you and Amaryllis have important work in Hegewisch today, but this is an emergency," said Max, who tried to look as desperate and prosperous at the same time as his disposition would allow. Ed sat there, waving his coffee cup for Amaryllis to refill, the wheels in his brain grinding away, cracking and whistling and popping. This was something new. Max barely knew how to drive a five-speed stick shift, and here he was wanting to borrow the truck and drive halfway to Milwaukee. Well, he must be up to something; must be in on something; must have his mind busy with some "Max-makes-a-million" brainstorm, otherwise why go to all the trouble of trying to impress him by getting dressed before sitting down to talk. How many nights was it that he and Max would spend in front of the

TV, watching the movies and the news and sitcoms and made-for-TV movie trash, talking back to those fools and shooting the shit, Max lounging all over the davenport in his Jockey shorts. Naw, Max's got to have something up his sleeve, some surefire money-maker, Easy Ed thought to himself. The only thing left for me is to cut myself in somehow; it would be easy money and they don't call me Easy Ed for nothing.

When Max prospered, Easy Ed positively thrived.

"Sure, Max," he said, closing his eyes with satisfaction and reaching into his jeans pocket at the same time, pulling out the greasy keys. "It's still early. How long you figure it'll take you? Amaryllis and me want to get to work, but this afternoon will be good enough; by the time we get down there it'll be nap time and everybody'll be asleep."

Max picked up the keys and said that it was just a run —no use telling him the wallet story, Easy Ed wouldn't have believed him in any case. Drive up. Drop some things off. Drive back. Two hours at the most. "Piece of cake. Thanks," Max said, and went upstairs to fetch the wallet. He wrapped it in newspaper, as if it were his lunch, got his Chicago Bears seed hat and beat-up tan leather sport jacket, a couple of cigars, and then sat on the bed to smoke some dope to ease the pain and quiet the worry—a little dose of post-modern Dutch courage. The leather jacket was one of those numbers with elbow patches he'd got at the Lincoln Park rummage sale for three bucks ten years before; the guy who sold it to him said it had once belonged to a guy named Saul Bellow —Max had never heard of him and wasn't about to ask, but thought he might be some famous dead guy; they were everywhere.

He walked out to the curb where the truck was parked along the embankment under some tall, spreading mulberry trees. Easy Ed's tow truck was a big old Ford with a chain-and-cable hoist and scraps of tires bolted to the back bumper—the whole thing put together on the cheap by a mechanic in Valparaiso, Indiana. On the doors Easy Ed had painted—

*

Easy Ed's
Easy Does It
*

24 Hour Towing
*

But Remember
No Dough
No Tow
*

—which explained why the phone rang day and night since he'd moved in when the weather broke in late winter and why he would come and go at such odd hours morning, noon, and night. Easy Ed, of course, had a CB radio and his moniker, of course, was Easy Ed. He'd met Amaryllis on the CB when she was dating Tulare Tom and a lot of other guys from Deadwood Dave's. (One night, after waiting up for her till four o'clock, Belle-Noche had one of her supreme blowout tantrums, screaming, "Amaryllis, that *hussy*, is in love with twenty guys." The word around Deadwood Dave's was "Want to get laid? Date Amaryllis!")

The truck was itself parked in a famous spot.

Until April (when they finally, apparently, broke up), a young couple would meet there every weekday morning between 7:00 and 8:00. The man, young with shaggy hair, would arrive in a rusted-out Camaro. The woman, very pretty with long blond hair, would arrive walking two spaniels on 20-foot rope leashes. The young man would catch the leashes in the door. The young woman would get in on the passenger side, and ten minutes later the windows would be dripping with condensation. Muriel would sit slumped in a chair in the front-room bay window, looking out over the porch hedge (trimmed with the same precision she ironed shirts and folded laundry), and watch with distracted fascination. For better than a year and a half those two met every workday morning. In warm weather the dogs could wander as far as the railroad tracks at the top of the embankment and bark at the trains; in winter they huddled as close as they could get to the tailpipe—the young man always kept the engine idling. In the late mornings, when Muriel and Honey Jean (James Earl Jones's wife) and Carol Hamner (mother of three youngsters, wife of Leon Hamner, the produce man at the North Broadway Dominick's supermarket) got together for coffee and neighborhood talk, the young couple and the two spaniels were always a topic of conversation. It was obvious that the two weren't married, *or* dating, or seeing each other socially except for these morning meetings. The ladies finally figured it this way. They lived in the same building and he was single—which explained the Camaro. She was married, her husband was probably a graduate student (those kind take forever, never seem to be finished; and are always working late in the library or such places), and she was lonely. She and the young man in the Camaro met in the laundry room. She and the husband had no children ("Not until I'm finished with school, dear"), but he had come from the country, liked duck hunting and pheasant hunting, had grown up with dogs on the place, and insisted that dogs were a good thing—

which, of course, explained the dogs. The ladies on Ravenswood thought long and hard about this matter of who owned the dogs and finally decided they were the husband's idea, otherwise, in cold weather the young woman would let the dogs hop in the back seat—"unless, of course, they need the back seat for you-know-what," Honey Jean Jones had said. Muriel disagreed right then and there, and said that the front seat of a Camaro was perfectly fine and room enough for you-know-what—if a body knew what she was doing, bucket seats and all (After all, Muriel thought, what did these biddies think the wingback chair in their bedroom was for—beyond sitting in and draping clothes over). Then the first week of April— not six weeks before—the young man with the Camaro and the young woman with the two spaniels had met on a Saturday morning. Unheard-of; something was up! There had been many quick phone calls alerting all the lookouts. The young couple got in the car, the windows fogged up, the dogs pissed on the trees. On and on the women across the street waited, talking on the phone—the hand cords stretching about as far as they would reach into the front rooms. Finally, the two young people got out and walked up and down along the curb, heads together and holding hands. Then, very close to eight o'clock, the young man combed through his long, thick hair with both his hands, kissed the young woman on the face, got in his car, and drove off. The young woman, dressed in a parka with a fur-trimmed hood and holding the long rope leashes in both hands, watched him drive north toward Peterson, waving and crying. (Peterson Avenue was named for Pehr S. Peterson, best known as Chicago's Johnny Appleseed, who made a whopping fortune selling curbside trees to the city after the Chicago Fire of 1871.) The two spaniels sat in the weedy cinders, flank to flank, waiting to be walked back

175]

home to a warm kitchen. All the vicarious lookers-on were heartbroken that their daily, early-morning entertainment was over (the young couple had generated plenty of harmless, mindless conversation) and resented Easy Ed not a little for parking his tow truck in that very same spot. Easy Ed, of course, knew nothing about all that, and wouldn't have cared if he had.

.   .   .

Max climbed in, settled himself behind the wheel, slipped Loretta Spokeshave's wallet into the glove compartment (held closed with a bit of rubber band and old Christmas-present string knotted to the defroster vent), put the key in the clumsily wired ignition (there were long loops of miscellaneous wires hanging down from under the dashboard), and cranked it up. He put the truck in gear and drove north to Peterson, a man filled with weary dread and godawful foreboding.

The plan was to drive west on Peterson Avenue to Caldwell Avenue (northwest; named for William Caldwell, born in 1780, the son of a Potawatomi Indian and an Irish officer in the British Army; William did so well moving 2,500 Indians to Council Bluffs, Iowa, that someone named a saloon after him—The Sauganash, Caldwell's Indian name, which means loosely "White Boy"). Then Max would hang a right on Waukegan Road (north) to Willow Road (east), stop and ask some gas station guy where Snuffy Lane was, cruise over there, find the Spokeshave place, knock on the door (Max looking presentable and harmless in his Bears cap and leather sport coat), have this Loretta Spokeshave broad come to the door, introduce himself (as polite as pie), say he found the wallet and show it to her, and (being a man of high moral character and honest as the day is long) give it back to her; hem and haw, waiting for the return compliment of some trifling gratuity (as Deadwood Dave himself might say), then leave and get home as fast as the speed-limit laws would allow. The quicker way, of course, would have been to get on Interstate 94—Edens Expressway—drive north to Willow Road in Northfield and exit westbound, etc., but Max had always had such bad luck with Edens (accidents, tickets from state troopers, driving home in blizzards and whopping spring downpours, when it rained so hard the wind was blowing *down*) that these days he avoided it altogether; the mind-numbing trouble just wasn't worth the time he'd save. Max ciphered it out that the long way was best, come what may.

The tight, high, tow truck springs made everything bounce—Max, Loretta Spokeshave's wallet, tools loose in the back, loose bumper bolts and tow chains, headlights and rearview mirror. How in the hell does that clown get this thing to move, thought Max, having the devil's own time getting from second to third gear, driving with one hand and slamming the gearshift back and forth. If Max had thought about it he would have known it was a combination of worn clutch plates, hand-eye-foot coordination, and original equipment gears (chipped and nicked aplenty), everything loose and sloppy. Easy Ed was a good mechanic, but there's only so much a body can do with a piece of total mechanical trash. Not even Ivory would have bothered—and (for a price) Ivory would fiddle around with anything. "Easy Ed, take my advice, take this piece of shit out somewhere and have it cleaned and burned" was what he said every time Ed and Amaryllis arrived to do a little business. Max made the light at Ravenswood and Peterson (U.S. Route 14) and headed west along with the rest of the late-rush-hour traffic, struggling through the gears—to the exasperation of everyone within earshot.

As he crossed Western Avenue, Max saw a police car with its Mars lights flashing half a block back in the traffic, but it wasn't until he got to Talman Avenue (named for another one of those happy-go-lucky, get-rich-quick, late-nineteenth-century real-estate developers) that the squad car was able to get anywhere near Max and use the PA system speaker mounted on the Mars light stainless-steel fixture on the roof. "*Hey*, Easy Ed! You in the tow truck!" said the cop, reading the name on the steel crossbar attached to the tow cable and chained to the bumper. Even though the cop was talking to Max, every driver within earshot abruptly jerked and twitched and ducked. "*Pull over*. We got to talk!" *Crackle, crackle* went the loudspeaker squelch. Max pulled to the curb in front of the Green Briar Park field house, not a mile from home.

Officer Bruno Hochmuth cut off a Holsum Bread delivery truck and pulled to the curb right behind Max—lights and siren still going—but before he made another move he called in the license plate number to check on whether the truck was stolen or if Easy Ed had any outstanding warrants. Then he slipped his billy club onto his belt, grabbed his hat, and got out, hiked up his pants (sitting made his boxer shorts bunch up in the crack of his ass), and adjusted the wide leather belt with his service revolver (his unregistered "throw down" kept in his K mart attaché case), his extra rounds, his can of Mace, his pack of tickets, his stainless-steel handcuffs, his billy club, and his battery pack for his radio (which he kept clipped to the epaulet of his black leather jacket—his uniform shirt underneath ironed in a way Muriel would certainly admire); if there was one thing on the day shift that Officer Bruno Hochmuth liked to get out of the way it was that first moving violation in the morning: "Greetings to the solid citizens of this fair city," he called it; the sooner the better, "So we can get on with the day's fucking work." Max was already standing by the rear duals, patting all his pockets for his driver's license—Fuck me running, Max thought, I ain't a mile from the house and I'm screwed, blued, and tattooed already. Then as the good officer came within two paces of Max and his pantomime, what should Max come across in his breast pocket but his driver's license—when he'd patted his pockets the first time around, it felt like a book of matches that had gone through the wash, a thing that steady, thorough Muriel would have never let happen.

Bruno stopped two paces from Max and looked him up and down. Max reminded Officer Hochmuth of his old man, who for years wore himself out on the sign-washing crew for Streets and San. (the only municipal sign washing crew in the whole U.S. of A.—this back in the days when you couldn't kick a chair, Downtown, and not knock over some hack payroller), and always said that Mayor Richard J. Daley was the greatest human individual that ever lived, "and a great American"; his first words of working wisdom to his son, Bruno, were "Get a city job, kid, you can't beat it with a stick! It's cushy and the pay is terrific! It's the only nine-to-one, eight-hour day, Monday-through-Thursday, five-day-week job you're ever gonna come across."

"Lemme see your license, Ed," Officer Hochmuth said. He always loved this part, watching the shaky hands, the blood draining from the eyes, the hair standing up on the back of the neck, the apologetic mumbles—the sheer fright and near-panic. He looked at Max's license as if he were checking the numbers of a lottery ticket, with his arms held out at a strange angle (because of all the equipment on his belt), and walked around the truck, kicking the tires and leaning on his

gun. Max followed at a respectable distance, ready to be full
of praise for the men and women in blue (should Officer
Hochmuth seem to need that), glad to be out of the traffic,
and wondering whether not having enough or too much air
in a tire was worth a ticket. Max thought he should have worn
his Chicago Bulls seed hat instead of the Bears.

"Hey, Maximilian, where's Ed? He know you got his
truck? You on your way to a job, huh?" said Officer Hochmuth, making conversation—not really expecting an answer—sizing up Max and eyeballing the truck at the same
time. There was more than one story around the station house
about some punk named Easy Ed and his goddamned tow
truck. These greaseball towing guys were *vermin* who didn't
do shit! Officer Hochmuth thought, preying on innocent,
ordinary citizens who had the misfortune to break down
somewhere, or too lazy and stupid to buy one of them Amer-
ican-built cars. These tow-truck guys were "con-sum-mate
bloodsuckers," as his old man used to say. Max looked at the
back deck and thanked the Giver of All Good Things that at
least Easy Ed and Amaryllis had the brains to get rid of the
stolen batteries from the night before.

Then Officer Hochmuth found what he was looking for,
not Loretta Spokeshave's wallet—And thank God for that,
Max thought—Easy Ed's city sticker had expired. "What do
you guys think this is, some kind of free ride? I'm going to
let you off with a warning about going through red lights, but
I'm going to have to write you up for an invalid city sticker."

Officer Hochmuth was only too glad to whip out his pad
of citations and his official Police Department Bic pen and
write Max out the ticket. "And tell 'No Dough, No Tow' Easy
Ed that he can get a sticker at any currency exchange or
Downtown. Get me? Here," and he gave Max the citation

(which was its own mailing envelope). "And make sure you have a sticker by close of business tonight, because I'll be looking for you two squirrels in the morning. Have a nice day," he said, and chuckled to himself as he got back in his car and took off his hat.

Max stood on the curb, nodding his head, obsequious and agreeable as the day is long, listening with smiling good cheer to Officer Hochmuth's grim lecture and the stern warning, thanking Officer Hochmuth when he gave him the ticket, and grateful that Officer Hochmuth hadn't just kneed him in the groin, spread-eagled him against the hood, and *frisked* him (like squeezing the meat out of a sausage), then slapped the cuffs on and hauled him off to the Summerdale District Police Station.

Then Max was back in the tow truck, making his way as best he could through first and second gear west to Caldwell Avenue, which doglegged severely to the right.

He cruised through the Edgebrook neighborhood with no trouble (except for the transmission. Great balls of fire, Max thought, how does Easy Ed tow cars with this contraption?), crossed the Milwaukee Road tracks, and headed off toward the villages of Niles, Morton Grove, Glenview, and Northfield. Traffic thinned out and sped up. But when he got to the Salerno Butter Cookie Factory at the corner of Caldwell and Howard Streets, Niles Safety Officer Lloyd Lockette took off after him. With lights flashing and siren screaming, he pulled Max over for Failure to Yield Right of Way, Failure to Signal Change of Lane, and Speeding. Officer Lloyd Lockette leaned on the tow-truck hood as he wrote out the citations, ripping each off the pad and handing it to Max with a blunt and officious ceremony that he had learned watching TV cop shows when he was a kid. He, too, felt it his patriotic duty as an officer of the law, as well as an officer of the court and all-around keeper of the peace, to give Max a lecture about the difference between driving in the city and the law-abiding suburbs—Those city cops let these clowns run roughshod all over everything, Lockette thought to himself—but in the village of Niles—"*we* have respect for the traffic regulations, *Nutmeg!*"—which had once been declared an "All-American City" and whose emblem appeared on each and every village marker, both coming and going—

VILLAGE OF NILES
POP. 28,284
ALL-AMERICAN CITY

—decorated with red, white, and blue stripes and swirls.

After Officer Lloyd Lockette returned to his squad car, turned off the lights and siren, and drove away with a squeal of tires and a shower of gravel, Max got back in the truck, threw the tickets on the dashboard, and drove on.

When he crossed Dempster Street into Morton Grove, he was stopped by Officers Alvin Calvin and Barbara Kibby. Officer Kibby stood by the passenger door of the squad car with one hand on her service revolver (talking to "Central" on the radio) while Officer Calvin gave Max tickets for Uncovered Tools and Unauthorized Use of Emergency Lights. "A very serious matter, Mister, uh, Nutmeg. If indeed that is your name," said Officer Calvin, who was a very skeptical young man, though nevertheless proud of his clean, well-starched uniform, his brand-new car, and his many commendations; he had wanted to be a policeman ever since he was a kid, and he was one of those little boys who actually got his wish. As he spoke, Officer Kibby was checking Max out plenty. Max thought he might fit some weird profile that the Morton Grove cops put together for dope dealers—tall, thin, stooped, Hush Puppy loafers, cigar, tow truck, "junk in the trunk." After he was checked out with Central, and Central had checked him out with the Chicago Police Headquarters downtown at 11th and State, the Illinois Secretary of State's Office, the Illinois State Police, and the FBI, the report came back that he was clean. And that's what Officer Barbara Kibby said when she joined Max and Officer Alvin Calvin: "You're clean, Mr. Nutmeg." Max, amazingly, was overcome with surprise. I'm *clean*, he thought, as if after years of mind-frying electroshock and gut-busting hypoallergenic chemotherapy (or whatever they call it) Max was finally declared by an expert team of university physicians to be fully and totally recovered—"He's been a model patient and is now ready to rejoin society, completely cured, and it hardly cost him a dime!" Officer Kibby, who wore a tightly cinched bulletproof vest under her uniform shirt, didn't exactly say congratulations. The tone in her voice was more like "Sorry we can't haul your sorry ass into the station for loose tools in the back and the amber gumballs going like a house afire, but stick around, Nutmeg, *we'll* find *something*! Been a long time since we had a serious threat to orderly society like you to fuck with." The two of them took turns giving Max another scalding lecture about proper driving conduct and courtesy, blah, blah, blah, until they got tired of hearing themselves talk—Max standing tall and staring straight through them, trying to make like he was attempting to get both ears in front at one and the same time, as if to say, "Oh yes, Officers, thank you for pointing out the error of my ways, thank you for pounding sand up my ass over a couple of goddamned wrenches and a cross-wired toggle switch (Wait till I get a hold of that shitstick Easy Ed, Max thought), and thank you, a thousand times thank you, Officers, for costing me another day's work and a couple of days' pay. Much obliged, and I certainly won't let it happen again. You can count on me one hundred percent, sir and ma'am." Max thinking to himself, This is class-A, supreme and complete utter, total bullshit from Bullshit City, a place just down the road between Tap City and Fat City.

After Officers Calvin and Kibby got back in their squad car and cruised off, Max threw the loose tools into the front underfoot, slid back behind the wheel, threw the tickets on the dashboard with the others, ripped the emergency-lights toggle switch right out of the dashboard, vowing by all that's holy to kick Easy Ed's ass the minute he got back to the house, and continued on his way to Northfield.

When he passed Golf Road into Glenview, he hadn't gone a hundred feet when Officer Tangier Middlekauff (originally from Golden, Colorado) pulled him over (on the side of his squad car it read *Justice in a Free Society*) in front of the Jennings Chevrolet dealership, a place surrounded by huge, bright American flags which on a brisk day snapped and crackled like nobody's business. Max didn't even bother turning off the engine or getting out. Just give me my tickets and my ass-kicking and the limp-dicked lecture and let me get on with this, he thought. When Officer Middlekauff came up to the window and asked to see Max's license, Max showed him his collection of tickets. Middlekauff just laughed: Ho, ho, ho, this just ain't your day, huh? Well, let me give you a couple more. No Pollution Inspection Sticker, no Commercial Inspection Sticker, Unauthorized Use of a Commercial Vehicle, and Inoperative Warning and Emergency Lights.

Max was getting boldly, furiously exasperated. "Well, listen, *pal*, just write me up and let me be on my way." Oh,

Max, the guys down at Deadwood Dave's would say, don't never smart-mouth cops. The instant that Officer Middlekauff heard Max's lip he wrote him up for Improper Use of Seat Belts and Insufficient Proof of Commercial Insurance to boot. Officer Middlekauff wrote out the tickets and ripped them off the pad all at once, and Max just flipped them onto the pile. By the time the cop had finished, given Max another lecture—Max sitting stock-still and making a conscious effort not to move a muscle—and got back into his squad car, Max was just about at his wits' end. By the time he got to downtown Glenview, he mused that whatever punishment and humiliation he was going to endure, it wasn't worth all this if he *didn't* find this Spokeshave broad and give her back her goddamned wallet, whether she wanted the goddamned thing or not, and he didn't give a hoot in hell what Muriel thought his "favorite" was, it wasn't worth having to eat all this shit. He'd give Loretta Spokeshave back her wallet, or die. When I get my license back it's going to have so many staple holes, it'll look like the dartboard at Deadwood Dave's, he thought.

By the time Max came to the Marilac Catholic High School and the Holy Spirit Missionary Sisters Convent, he had to wonder what on earth could be illegal in Northfield. The way these people drive I'm liable to get sideswiped, rearended, killed in a head-on, but—well, shit! I'm driving a tow truck with a huge, thick rear bumper and a snowplow in front. I have dual axles in back; I have tow chains and huge tires! How can I get killed driving *this* thing? Max drove on, secure in that knowledge.

When Max got to Willow Road at the top of the hill, he hung a right and cruised down to the Marathon station at the corner of Sunset Ridge Road. He wheeled up to the repair bay, stuck his head out the window, letting the truck idle.

Roy Wimmer, the owner and proprietor since 1957, came out from under the hood of an Audi and asked Max what he could do for him. Max slapped the door panel with the flat of his hand and asked where he could find Snuffy Lane. Wimmer put both hands on top of his head, as if to aid with his thinking, turned on his heel, shot his arm north toward Sunset Ridge Road, and said, "It's that way. Drive past Sunset Ridge Country Club and a couple of other side streets. You'll see a big sign for Voltz Road. It's a *big* sign, you can't miss it. It's *big*! Turn left. Voltz Road—big sign—jogs right, then left. Snuffy Lane is right there. Turn right. Can't miss it. Who you looking for?"

"Looking for the Spokeshave place, thanks. And much obliged," Max said, and drove off. Roy Wimmer, who'd been in business at that corner for more than thirty years, had never heard of the Spokeshaves.

Max had by this time pretty much figured out three of the gears and took off like a shot. Not half a mile on the left was Sunset Ridge Country Club. Fuck me running, Max thought, I completely forgot about this dump being here.

When Max was eleven years old he got work as a caddy—the first job he had in his life. This was where he learned to smoke Camels and play poker, showing up every day in summer at 6:30 a.m. dressed in jeans, high-top Keds gym shoes, and cheap pullover shirts. This was where he learned one of life's most basic but cruel lessons—aside from how to "behave" in front of rich people, never draw to an inside straight, no circle-jerking in the bushes by the driving range, and it's the brown-nosing suck-ups who always get the pro shop jobs: women are lousy tippers, though it was also true that the men weren't much better. This was where he had his first sexual fantasies—about golfing women old enough to be his mother (if they had started having kids when they were sixteen). Bermuda shorts stretched over their rear ends as they leaned over to putt, big feet, and loose-fitting tops with large armholes. Smooth cotton bras and leathery, buxom cleavage. All those women—always referred to as "members' wives"—drove big-ass cars, and the golf bags were always enormous. The leather polished and monogrammed, five woods, twelve irons, and a putter, an umbrella, a collapsible stool, sweaters, socks, wallet and keys, lipstick and compact and other makeup, a dozen and more golf balls, boxes of Tampax and Kotex, wooden tees, date book, old score cards of remarkable rounds, stubby ballpark pencils, loose change, prescription sunglasses and reading glasses. The caddies called these golf bags "trunks"—they weighed a ton and cost a fortune. Max, thin and gaunt (when he was a kid he had a kind of skinny, run-down, and nervous caved-in look), walked the whole eighteen holes with a shuffling stoop in the high grass of the serious rough as the members' wives shanked their drives, fairway woods, and long and short irons zigzag from one side of the fairway to the other, caroming their inexorable and laborious way to the green and the flag, Max unslinging the trunks every 50 or 75 yards. The only time he got any rest was at the green, when the ladies stopped to four- and five-putt with exasperating leisure, kibitzing and gossiping all the while; they did everything but trade recipes. Max would stand to the side of the green, holding the flag (while the other caddies went to the next tee sneak a smoke to be cool and kill their appetites), watching these women lining up their putts—As if they knew what they were doing, he mused driving north along Sunset Ridge Road, thinking, Golf, what a stupid fucking game. (That's why, years later when he worked one, long horrible summer as a beer concessionaire at Wrigley Field, he laughed out loud at those college kids pissing and moaning about the canvas shoulder straps.) And when the foursome finally got to the snack shack behind the tenth tee (near the eleventh green), Max and the other caddies would go around to the back door and wait for the members' wives to signify by vague gestures or nods that the caddies could help themselves to lunch—usually a plain Vienna hot dog and a cold Coke, as well as all the stick pretzels they could wolf down in ten minutes. If for some reason the members' wives did not tell Max that he could have some lunch (added to the members' wives' tabs), Max would have to settle for the stick pretzels (kept in a large, plastic-lined tin near the back door) and fountain water. Under no circumstances could a caddy buy his own lunch and pay cash; the members' wives bought lunch or he went without.

Max thought of all those years of skulking home with heavy rancor and a sore back, taking the $3 with a quarter tip thrown in.

Benito Carbonari, the caddy master, would stand inside his office cage surrounded by heavily painted chicken wire, take the ticket, and lay it on the counter, pull out his cash drawer, recite out loud the amount, "Single bag for eighteen holes, kid; that's three bucks plus the tip," wet his thumb, and dip into the singles drawer (*always* new money), then stroke a finger into the quarter bin and slide out a quarter— Max's tip—on top of the paper bills. Then Carbonari would make a point of looking first at Max and then the money, as if to say, "You're not pleasing the member's wife, kid. You're not hustling your ass. You're not busting your balls. You're making me look bad. And when I look bad, that's fucking with *my* tips."

And with Carbonari it wasn't first-come first-served as

far as the caddies were concerned; getting work had nothing to do with how early Max arrived but everything to do with how late he showed up, how much ass he could kiss, and how much baksheesh he kicked back to Benito. Carbonari's process of selection was exquisite and subtle—it taught Max the way of the world—matching the golfers to the caddies with a handicapper's skill that would certainly have impressed Oscar Wendella or the shithouse lawyers down at Deadwood Dave's. There were certainly personalities to consider, as well as patronage and rewards to dispense, lessons to teach—the likes of "Never spit into the wind," "Never piss uphill," "When playing Hearts always pass the bitch," and all the other time-honored, fuck-your-buddy homilies Max had long forgotten. Carbonari always kept a running tally of punishments to mete out, revenges to claim, and petty, chickenshit caddy-shack scores to settle, some once and for all. Every day for five years Max would show up at 6:30, wait till noon or one o'clock, work till 5:00 or 6:00, take his pissant little pile of singles and his stupid little quarter, then walk down to Waukegan Road and hitchhike south to Caldwell, then east on Peterson, and finally home. Agnes-Ruth was always waiting at the door and took the money; Max was allowed to keep his tips—Thanks, Ma.

When Max first started working there, every couple of weeks some woman from the State of Illinois Labor Department would call and tell Benito that the next day would be a drive-by inspection. The next morning, Benito would break out the bats and softballs, all smiles and chummy repartee, and tell Max and the other underage caddies to get lost the other side of the sixteenth hole and play some softball. And when the Labor Lady had nosed around and left, he'd send one of the brown-nosing pro-shop jocks to shag everybody back. (The State of Illinois Labor Department woman snooping around always pissed off the serious, "no-gimmie" bingo-bango-bongo golfers, until one summer a deputation of members—wearing their longest faces and carrying their fattest wallets—called on the governor and had the Labor Department skip their stop and the woman canned.)

Max thought about all that as he passed the entrance and along the tennis courts and the long, high, out-of-bounds fence (grown through with forty-year-old lilacs), then shuddered (brrr—grrr), and moved on.

•   •   •

The sign for Voltz Road (← T U R N L E F T) was as big as a box car, and Max "hung a louie," as the over-the-road experts at Deadwood Dave's would say. Voltz Road turned right and then left, and then a couple of blocks west there was Snuffy Lane. He slowed up and downshifted, passing some woman going the other way in a bright blue Mazda Miata, the top down and her hair a-flying.

The woman, of course, was Loretta Spokeshave on her way to the bank to withdraw $800 for Elmo Dudycz.

Max slowed down even more, reading the house numbers, matching them to the address on Loretta's driver's license. Finally there it was: the address, the name S P O K E - S H A V E on the mailbox. Max pulled the truck into the driveway. The cedar roof sparkled, the granite paving-stone driveway sparkled, the brass fixtures on the front door sparkled, the windows sparkled, the sod sparkled from a cool night's heavy dew—the whole place sparkled. Dudycz's ex–Ma Bell truck with the pipe rack across the top was parked in front of the garage. Max took one look at it and thought, Plumbers sure are doing okay for themselves in *this* neck of

the woods! He turned off the ignition, gathering what com-
posure he had left, got out of the truck, went to the door, and
rang the bell. He could hear it chiming deeply through some
chords of music.

No one came to the door.

He rang again and waited, backing up several paces to
glance through the side windows as best he could into the
dark house.

He rang again. Finally he heard footsteps on a staircase.
Ah.

Elmo Dudycz came to the door and swung it wide open,
wiping his hands on a rag, looking cross-eyed and humble,
smelling of pipe grease, solder acid, and methane.

"Yeah?" he said, and looked down, his eyes not accustomed to all that good May-morning sunlight.

Max assumed this was Spokeshave and started right in.
"Mr. Spokeshave, my name is Maximilian Nutmeg. I was
downtown yesterday coming back from the ball game, on my
way to the train out to Deerfield," another one of those northern suburban towns that would dearly love to be on the North
Shore, "and I found a wallet in the street. And it's your wife's.
She home? I'd like to give it to her."

Dudycz stood in the doorway, looking plenty baffled. He'd
been in the basement some time and had to take a moment
for his eyes to adjust. And too, he had a buzzing in his ears
from the pipe-threading gadget. But he did hear "Mr. Spokeshave," "ball game," "downtown," and "wallet," and then
looked up at Max's full silhouette—black high-top gym shoes,
khaki wash pants, crummy-looking leather sport jacket, Bears
baseball hat (with plenty of curly brown hair fluffing out
around the ears)—the guy holding the biggest lady's wallet
Dudycz had ever seen.

And the way Dudycz was looking him up and down from the darkness of the house, it finally occurred to Max that his costume wasn't thorough enough; that he should have put on a waxed mustache and snarly, bushy eyebrows, glued on those wing-flap clown ears of his, and worn a regulation hard hat and shoved his hair up under it; that he should have disguised his voice or limped or feigned a hunchback or something. Max's heart stopped, his face flushed, his feet itched to be gone. What if this Spokeshave woman comes to the door, recognizes me from the day before? She'll stall, call the cops, and—to make a long story short—I'll be up shit creek.

Only the most remarkable fortitude Max didn't know he had kept him from fleeing right then and there.

Dudycz wiped his mouth and chin with his hands (thinking, What's *this* bullshit! Who's *this* guy?), going at it as if to smooth down his beard. "What?" he said.

Max stepped forward (only to have Dudycz step back over the threshold into the cool dark of the house. "Is this the Spokeshave house? Have I got the right house?"—Max thinking, It would just fucking figure that after all this I've got the wrong Northfield or the wrong Snuffy Lane, or the wrong goddamned something.

Dudycz said it was, in fact, the Spokeshave house. "*What* you want?"

Max repeated that he'd been at the ball game the afternoon of the day before, that he'd been on his way to catch the train out to Deerfield—where he lived, you see—that he'd come across Mrs. Loretta Spokeshave's wallet, and that he'd taken the morning off work supervising a sheet-metal heating duct outfit on the new Harold Washington Chicago Public Library downtown (suddenly Max thought he should have worn his American flag hard hat instead of this stupid Bears seed hat) to drive all the way out here on a nice warm sunny working day to return the wallet to her.

Dudycz interrupted Max to tell him, "First off, I ain't Spokeshave. I'm Dudycz, the plumber. You think I make the kinda dough so's I could afford this dump?" And he waved his arms around in big circles to signify the whole place— house and grounds, paving-stone driveway, three-car garage, Kimmelbergs, etc., and all. "I been working in the basement." He didn't tell Max about the water hammers. And since he was mighty suspicious of this guy and his funny-looking truck (What the hell's a construction foreman doing tootling around in some broken-down tow truck?), and there are always nuts running around with weird scams, trying every which way they can to get into a body's house (and Max *did* look sort of "hoody," the way city guys look when you stood them up against those "wholesome" suburban guys). Anyway, Dudycz had watched too much television (cop shows and lawyer shows) and seen too many Mickey Rourke and Arnold Schwarzenegger and Clint Eastwood "Dirty Harry" movies not to be pretty suspicious and doubtful of Max (Just look at how strange he's dressed, would you?) and his unlikely story about a ball game and a train to catch and finding Mrs. Spokeshave's wallet. Ho, ho, ho, that's a fat one!

Dudycz took hold of the door, as if to swing it shut, and said, "Mrs. Spokeshave left me here and's gone for the day," holding on to the doorknob with one hand and fingering a pipe wrench he had hooked in his hammer loop on the leg of his painter pants with the other, thinking, If this asshole makes a break for the house, I'll coldcock him with a wrench. Never let it be said that plumbers can't defend themselves. Tomorrow, Dudycz would make a point of telling everybody at Aunt Dot's Breakfast Barn in Lincolnwood that some guy was cruising the northern suburbs in a shitcan city tow truck, dressed in gym shoes, suede leather jacket, and carrying a wallet, trying to break into people's houses with some bullshit line about finding a wallet, which belongs to the lady of the house, and could he just step in and wait for her.

Then Dudycz closed the door and locked it.

Max had been prepared by a lifetime of travails and troubles (more or less) for just about anything, but he wasn't ready to have the Spokeshaves' door slammed in his face. He wanted to protest! He wanted to cuss that Dudycz guy a blue streak! He wanted to explain about the $500 worth of traffic tickets on Easy Ed's dashboard! He wanted, in all Christian honesty, to find Mrs. Loretta Spokeshave, in person, and give her back her wallet, intact, and see the look on her face—he was paying a pretty penny for it, and right then and there wanted his money's worth more than he wanted anything. The least she could do was stand there in the doorway and be astonished and flabbergasted with gratitude. He wanted to stand on the entryway concrete if that suited her with his shoulders stooped and his hands in his pockets and his eyes downcast, as Mrs. Loretta Spokeshave went through her wallet, counting the money, checking the credit cards, seeing that Jean-Claude's letter was still there, that the spare keys and hairpins and other miscellaneous nonsense were still there. Max wanted to see her expression change from gasping apprehension to grateful and humble thanks and honest praise; he wanted her to nearly faint with relief—at the very least, he wanted to see her giggle with embarrassment and stagger back against the staircase (he would have even appreciated it if she fainted). He wanted to see her pick a hundred-dollar bill out of the stack with her exquisitely manicured fingernails, fold it with one hand, and crease it like the backstretch artists do at the track (he'd seen Oscar Wendella do that very thing many times) and hand it over to him: a generous gratuity from a truly thankful and happy woman. He wanted to reach out for it, tell Mrs. Loretta Spokeshave that he hadn't done anything less than any other God-fearing Christian would have done, but was grateful for her appreciation (being as how he was at this moment practically destitute, sending all this money home to Jessamine County, Kentucky, where his ma was taking heart medicine that was $1,000 a month), then take the money, shove it into his front pants pocket, tip his cap, walk back to Easy Ed's tow truck, and drive home the quickest way he knew, before any more of those shit-for-brains small-town cops got some wild hair up their asses and came after him—flashing lights, sirens, shotguns, and all.

Max *wanted* all that, but Dudycz closed the door so hard the solid brass ship-under-full-sail door knocker *klonked* loud and clear (it shook the whole house), and for a moment Max didn't know what to do, he didn't even move a muscle.

What? But I've come a long way and gone to a lot of goddamned trouble for this! You can't do this to me!

But a man can't stand dumbfounded and stock-still for the rest of his life. And besides, Max had learned a long time ago that for every problem and challenge there is a solution and an answer. Max turned his Bears hat backward on his head. Well, fuck me running, he thought, and went back to the truck. In the glove compartment he found a filthy old envelope with Ivory's letterhead in the top left corner, complete with his calling card motto: "Besides drinking beer, fixing your hunk of junk is my whole life." And underneath all the greasy screwdrivers and tire gauges and packs of Trojan rubbers (with reservoir tips), he found a short piece of flat carpenter's pencil and jotted Mrs. Loretta Spokeshave a bit of a note:

Dear Mrs. Spookeshove,
I found yr willet ysterday on the strite and I'd like to geve it bak to you. call me at 744–8263.

> *yours ceneseery,*
> *Maximilian Nutmug*

Max's spelling wasn't too hot, as you can see, and that, along with the fact that the pencil was none too sharp (being made for marking lumber) and Max being angry and pissed off for fair and nervous to boot, it was the best he could do in a jiffy and a pinch. Max well knew by the look on Dudycz's face that he was at that very moment calling 911, or whatever the hell the emergency number in Northfield was, and at that very moment every duty squad car in Northfield Township was hauling ass out to the Spokeshave place on Snuffy Lane to put a stop to this latest crime wave blown in from the big city (and the cops meant to put a stop to it in that public and humiliating way that cops all over the world are famous for)—"Lean and spread 'em, motherfucker!" handcuffs, TV trucks, and well-groomed nitwit street reporters doing a virtual play-by-play, shoving the felon into the back of the chief's car as if they were rolling up a map and stuffing it into a mailing tube (official, uniformed solid citizens protecting their women and their property with macho gunplay, a little persuasion, and volumes of get-the-fuck-out-of-town-and-stay-out village ordinances).

So Max figured he didn't have a minute to lose. He scribbled out the note, signed it (making sure to write the phone number clearly—if nothing else—crossing the 7 the way the English do), shoved it in the weatherstripping, hopped back in Easy Ed's tow truck, and got the hell out of there—backing out of the driveway and taking off down Snuffy Lane (passing the European buckthorn bush marking Simone van der Pohl's Shetland pony's grave) in record time. And sure enough, on Voltz Road he passed a squad car, and on Sunset Ridge Road he passed another, and when he got to Willow Road on his way to Edens Expressway (U.S. 94), the quickest way home, he passed one more. In another instant he was cruising down the entrance ramp, grateful to be out of there with his whole hide. He drove at speed in the right lane, with his shoulders up around his ears, fully expecting that any minute some state trooper in a Yogi Bear hat would haul him over for being too tall or driving *too* slow or some other lamebrained, fucked-if-I-know reason, but sometimes in this world the Giver of All Good Things comes through with flying colors and grants an especially earnest and humble request, and Max arrived home without a scratch, hardly missing any of the lights, as a matter of fact. He parked the truck under the mulberries, took the tickets and the wallet into the house, kissed Muriel a quick peck on the forehead on his way up the stairs through the cats, and went straight to his bed—and spent the better part of the next couple of hours staring up at the mirror above.

Home, safe, and in bed. He would have pulled the covers over his head if he'd thought that would help.

•   •   •

Meanwhile, back in Northfield, Loretta had driven to the bank, walked into the little lobby with her hair going every which way, asked to see Earl Tharp, the executive vice president, and was shown to his office. He rose from his desk, smoothing his tie down over his belly, asked Loretta to please sit and what could he do to help her.

Tharp was an interesting guy. Born and raised in Boscobel, Wisconsin, on the banks of the Wisconsin River, he'd gone to the University of Wisconsin at Madison (called by the higher education gadflies at Deadwood Dave's the "You of Whiz" and sometimes called the "You of Cheez Whiz"), where he had majored in English but had not distinguished himself in any way whatsoever. Class of 1977. He came to Chicago to live with his aunt and uncle in Bridgeport, in a bungalow near the old Illinois & Michigan Canal docks and Stearns Limestone Quarry, and got a job at the First National Bank, rolling money around in the basement on loading-dock carts. Then in 1982, he married, moved to Glenview, and got a job with the Northfield Bank. It was soon discovered that he was the only employee who had a knack with money and could write a decent, readable report, and so he worked his way up to vice president.

Loretta sat, crossed her ankles, and put her purse and keys in her lap. Loretta explained at great length what had happened, even retelling the part about Max's remarkable story about his brother the missionary and his young and pretty fiancée and all the rest; told Tharp about the missing wallet and Dudycz the plumber—a name that the bank vice president seemed to know—told him about Dudycz's insistence on cash only. She left out the part about Jean-Claude's letter.

Earl Tharp listened with the same distracted attentiveness with which he listened to his young daughters and his car salesman brother-in-law. Then he leaned forward on his desk, put his clean, dry hands together—sliding his intertwining fingers into a tight knot—as if in prayer, and asked the good Mrs. Spokeshave (a name he well recognized, though he couldn't place her face) if she had any identification on her at all? Loretta said that no, she didn't—her whole wallet had been stolen, the *whole* thing. Psst! Gone! Money, credit cards, and the famous $800 in cash, all in one-hundred-dollar bills.

Tharp smoothed his tie again and batted his eyes and asked if Mrs. Spokeshave knew the numbers of her accounts. Loretta, crossing her legs and hiking up her dress so that her kneecaps shone bone-china white under her sleek panty hose, said that no, she couldn't just that moment recollect the numbers. Henry, Mr. Spokeshave, usually took care of the money matters in the household.

Then Mr. Tharp asked her to give him a sample of her handwriting on a memo slip to be compared with Mrs. Spokeshave's signature on the account cards—"But being as you don't know the numbers, it's a process that might just take a while."

Loretta, nervous and giddy, scooched up on the edge of her chair, leaned over the desk, and signed the memo with her most careful signature. Tharp asked his secretary, Sally McMurdo, to make the search and comparison, offered Mrs. Spokeshave a cup of coffee, and invited her to sit back for a moment and relax.

Right then and there, Loretta wanted her medication and one of Jean-Claude's back rubs.

Not a moment later, the secretary came back into Tharp's office with several account cards, but they were so old that it was Annabelle's signature that appeared, not Loretta's. Tharp looked up, said that he could not be of any further assistance, and admonished Mrs. Spokeshave—"If indeed you *are* Mrs.

Henry Spokeshave"—to furnish better proof than her bold assertion that *she* was the third and current Mrs. Spokeshave; that Annabelle was a "twitterbrain" and a spendthrift; and that Henry was well rid of her (the fat, prissy bitch). (What he didn't say was that Henry, in his divorce-induced rage and impatient despair, had also told Tharp with good reason that she was a lousy lay—or as the overage gangbangers and loudmouth, sloppy-drunk cockhounds at Deadwood Dave's would say, "A dead fuck.") Then Executive Vice President Earl Tharp stood up and asked his secretary to show "Mrs. Spokeshave" the door, and wished Loretta a good morning.

Well, Loretta was furious. She walked out the door, dodged traffic to her car, threw her purse on the passenger seat, got in, cranked up the Miata, and drove back to the house as if shot out of a cannon. She skidded into the garage and, leaving the car running, went into the house to find her wedding picture album (a white leather and gold-leaf thing as big as an *Oxford English Dictionary*), picking up the portable phone on her way into the hallway to call her most trusted neighbor and closest friend, Sophia Haupt. Sophia answered just as Loretta was muscling the album off the cabinet shelf; Loretta explained her predicament and asked if Sophia would come with her to the bank to vouch for her. Without going into details (time was short; Dudycz had come from the basement for his dough), Loretta said it was an emergency. Sophia said she'd be glad to, except she and Ramona Brierly were cutting up a couple of bushels of Washington apples for the church-bake-sale pies—was it really important?

Loretta set the album of wedding pictures down on the kitchen counter next to the microwave with a heavy *thunk* and, looking at Dudycz (wiping his hands on that rag of his, wiping his face on his sleeve) helping himself to another cup

of coffee at the range, told Sophia that, yes, it was crucial—
never had anything been so important since before they met.
Sophia said she would be right over (after making her excuses
to Ramona, who, Sophia suspected, was a bit of a thief).

Loretta quietly and calmly explained to Dudycz that there
had developed a little glitch, that there was a snafu at the
bank, but everything would be okay "real soon." Dudycz sat
down at the kitchen table, took out his smokes, and said that
Loretta should take her time and get it right, nothing in the
basement was going anywhere—to be sure—but that he
couldn't begin work without the money.

When Sophia arrived, she and Loretta got in the car,
wedding album and all, and drove back to the bank. They
went straight into Executive Vice President Earl Tharp's office
and opened the wedding album while Sophia (whom Earl
knew well from seven years of church pancake breakfasts)
dramatically asserted in no uncertain terms that Loretta was
indeed the current Mrs. Henry Spokeshave. Both women invited Mr. Tharp to flip through the full-color wedding pictures,
Sophia complimenting Loretta about her off-the-shoulder
Alençon lace and panne velvet dress with gauntlet sleeves
and pannier skirt, layered veil, and bouquet of marigolds,
lilacs, and gladiolas (looking like glossy asparagus tips). In
another minute half the bank employees were crowded
around Tharp's desk, ogling the photographs and lavishly con-
gratulating Loretta—Henry had more hair then and looked
positively "delicious" in his swallowtail coat and wing collar
and black bow tie. There was another round of signature
comparisons and balance-toting—a bank statement with Loretta's name and signature had finally been located—to make
sure that the withdrawal was covered by the outstanding bal-
ance (Just in case; you can't be too careful with these addle-

headed rich people, Tharp thought), and when all the forms and formalities seemed to be in order (Loretta signing several pieces of paper, receipts and vouchers and such), Earl Tharp himself got her the money and, closing the album of wedding pictures, counted it out on his desk. Loretta and Sophia left the bank and drove back to the Spokeshave place, immediately paying Dudycz his money, which he stuffed in his shirt pocket as if it were a phone message on a scrap of paper (he'd stayed in the kitchen helping himself to fruit juice and Toll House cookies, thinking how he was going to tell the story of the tow-truck guy and his mighty funny story about a wallet to the guys at Aunt Dot's Breakfast Barn).

Loretta gave Sophia a hug and a kiss and thanked her a thousand times, and as Sophia went to see if Ramona had left anything in her house, Max's note fluttered into the foyer. Loretta picked it up, said her farewells to Sophia, and closed the door.

Prince,

Meet the Boys

Loretta read Max's note immediately, and in an instant knew that her life was saved! "Wallet! Found! Thank *God!*" she exclaimed with a big grin and high feeling, and started jumping up and down on her toes like a jogger waiting for a traffic light. "Yippie!" she shouted, and shook her head in ticklish glee, swishing her hair across her face. In the basement Dudycz heard the commotion and thought she was going to come downstairs and give him thirty million kinds of hell about the water; it wouldn't be the first time, though it would be the first time a customer got fed up and somehow discovered what total hooey and utter bullshit water hammers were. In any case, Dudycz put down his tools, buttoned his shirt, and prepared for the worst.

Instead, Loretta bounced upstairs to get a couple of Tylenols and a swig of vodka (since there was no water in the house), intending to call this Maximilian Nutmug first thing.

Now, it was certainly true that Max's handwriting was just awful, but the phone number was clear—Jean-Claude

crossed his sevens, too. Loretta gulped down the Tylenol with
a two-shot vodka chaser, then circled the telephone by the
bed with many second thoughts (the sharp and unaccustomed
warmth of the vodka rising to her ears), pondering her marriage and her courage: What if this Nutmug is a complete
jerk, one of those weird, slavering perverts who's going to
tease me about Jean-Claude's letter? What if this man has
already told Henry and he's on his way home right this instant? What if Nutmug's going to blackmail me? What if all
he returns to me is the wallet and my driver's license? Oh
my.

Finally, she dialed—what else could she do?—and let the
phone ring a long time, come what may.

At the Nutmeg house, Max was flat on his back, with
the bedcovers pulled to his chin, dead to the world; he never
heard a thing. Muriel was in the basement with Elvis, finishing up the last of the week's ironing, singing (contralto)—

> Why *don't you rock me, baby.*
> *Rock* me *all night long.*
> *Roll me, darlin', roll me like a wagon wheel.*
> Why *don't you roll me, daddy,*
> *Roll* me *like a wagon wheel.*
> *Rock-and-roll me, sweetheart,*
> *You just don't know how nice and creamy you make me feel.*
> *Whoopie!*

—and when she paused to lay out the sleeve of Max's best
dress shirt, she finally heard the phone, faint and far away.

"Goodness gracious, Elvis, who *could* that be? *Mrs.* Loretta *Spokeshave*, perhaps?" she said in her most mock-perfect
voice; it certainly wasn't Easy Ed and Amaryllis checking in

from Hegewisch. Elvis sat on the ironing board with his tail curled around his legs (as mellow as mellow could be), smiling so hard he didn't seem to care who it was. So she delicately smoothed out the sleeve with her hands and marched all the way to the second-floor hallway, leaving Elvis and the can of spray starch to themselves.

The phone was still ringing when she topped the stairs. Muriel stood in a crowd of cats and answered, "Hello?"

Loretta, standing in her bedroom on Snuffy Lane, introduced herself, almost blurting it out. "My name is Mrs. Loretta Spokeshave. I live in Northfield, and this morning I got a note from Mr. Maximilian Nutmug to call him," said Loretta with flat, business-like assertion, giving Max's name a definite and particular pronunciation. "Is Mr. Nutmug there, please?" This was a moment Loretta would recall until the last day of her life, churning regret mixed with a firm desire to have it all over and done with, once and for all. At that moment, she would have promised anything, agreed to the most absurd, picky little thing—Let's just get this over, whatever's left of the $800 dollars safe and sound, Jean-Claude's letter back in my hands and good old Henry none the wiser.

(All of Loretta's speculations about her wallet being intact were, to say the least in this day and age, remarkably optimistic, or as the streetwise, overage gangbangers down at Deadwood Dave's would say, "That Spokeshave dame is sure some kind of strange ginch. She must be one of those broads who sleep late and go to bed early. Northfield must be one peculiar town.")

Muriel, standing in the bedroom doorway with one arm across her ample bosom, looked at Max (sleeping up a storm; surrounded by a dozen cats cuddling the lumps of Max's feet and stretched across his stomach and crotch like exhausted swimmers), and said in her sweetest Sunday voice, "Yes, Mrs. Spokeshave, Max is here. And the name is Nut*meg*, like the spice, the one that's ground from the seed of an Asian evergreen tree. Just a moment, please." In righteous and pleasant excitement, Muriel held the receiver against the side of her breast, leaned into the bedroom, and whispered loudly, "Sweetheart! Max! Wake up! It's the Spokeshave woman! Up! Up!" and went over and shook him by the foot. It was never wise to wake Max too abruptly, but this was important. "Max! *Up! Hurry! Spokeshave!*" she whispered louder.

Loretta, now standing at her bedroom window, looked wistfully out toward Snuffy's buckthorn bush in the middle of the lane down the way and wondered what the delay was. She listened intently, but could hear only muffled mumbles, like heavy breath through a blanket.

Max stirred and rolled over on his side, the dream image clear as day in his head of an uncontrollable coughing fit, hawking up syrupy gobs of pebbly mud and large, limp rubber bands (which he hooked out of his mouth with a finger); God only knew what the cats had been dreaming. Muriel hung the phone on a bathroom hook and went to wake him up good and proper—tousling his hair and tickling him under the arms—"*Max*, get up right this minute and no fooling around. It's Spokeshave!"—which Loretta heard clear as a bell. He rose quickly and staggered out to the hall, ashen and feverish, exhausted with dread worry. He needed to piss right that moment in the worst way, but knew that it might just upset Spokeshave to listen to him talk and whiz at the same time, so he shoveled cats out of the way with his long, skinny feet, sat on the bentwood kitchen chair next to the bathtub, and picked up the phone. Muriel went downstairs to fetch Max a cup of coffee in his favorite mug.

"Yes? This is Max Nutmeg," he said, and glanced at himself (from the eyes up) in the shaving mirror. "Is this Loretta Spokeshave?" Great God Almighty, Max suddenly thought, looking hard at the reflection of his eyeballs, forehead, and hair (remembering the near miss this morning at the front door of the Spokeshave place). This woman is going to jack me around for street hustling, bullshitting her out of a couple of bucks, and snatching her wallet when nobody was looking. She's going to call the State Police and the FBI, get a lawyer, and haul me into court. I'm going to jail forever and ever.

Max wanted to throw the phone at one of the cats, stick his head in the toilet, flush it hard, and drown himself.

"Mr. Nutmeg, I got your note about my wallet, and first of all I want to thank you very much," Loretta said, still standing at the window, looking at the buckthorn bush. "I think it is seldom that one finds an honest and unselfish person such as yourself. Is there some time and place that is convenient for you to meet me and return the wallet? I assume you don't want to trust this sort of thing to the mails"—hope-a-hope-a-hope!

She definitely did not want Max coming out to the house without Henry or some other large, responsible man around; it never occurred to her that Dudycz was plenty big and right handy in the basement, but she wouldn't have wanted him involved anyway.

Max's mind and imagination were foggy and imprecise, to say the least; the first minutes of wakefulness were never a good time to talk business, or anything else, with Max. A convenient time and place? Right that moment the only thing he could think of was Deadwood Dave's Wild West Saloon. He definitely wanted to get the phone conversation over and done with as soon as humanly possible; he had to pee or burst. He did not want to drive back out to her place again—and collect God knew how many more tickets (this time he'd probably wind up in jail straightaway—and they'd throw away the key); and he absolutely, resolutely, irrevocably did not want this Spokeshave woman coming to his house; the Lord only knew what complications that might entail, what with Easy Ed hanging around (and Sweet William able to smell money at a hundred yards).

"There's a place not too far from here called Deadwood Dave's Wild West Saloon. Why don't we meet there? Is there a time that's convenient for you, Mrs. Spokeshave?"

Loretta had to think about that. This afternoon was definitely out of the question; after all, she wouldn't cancel her tryst with Jean-Claude for anything, even to the point of kissing off the $800 (not to mention her marriage to steady, dogged, nicely well-off Henry), and then it would be the dinner hour. She coiled the handset cord around her finger. "Yes, Mr. Nutmug, this Deadhead place sounds just fine. Well, how about nine this evening?"

Max said that would be fine; it would give Muriel plenty of time to finish the shirts, do the dinner dishes, and clean up the kitchen—he certainly wasn't going without Muriel. He'd have time to finish his nap, and nine that evening would be just right.

He gave Loretta extremely precise directions (in another life and with better luck Max could have been an aerospace engineer), which she managed to write down verbatim.

There was just one more thing, and Max was righteous and up front about it. "Mrs. Spokeshave, there is just one more thing. This is to confirm for myself that it is, in fact, *your* wallet I have." Getting up, Max went into the bedroom and opened the wallet. "What is your address?"

"Why, it's Snuffy Lane in Northfield. Where do you think I'm calling from," she said, somewhat testily but beginning to get defensive and, frankly, panicky—what else was he going to ask?

"Describe the wallet, would you please?" said Max.

Loretta straightened her back and shook her head—this was easy. "It's a gray leather lady's wallet, with a coin pocket on the outside, with gold trim. Made by Coach. It goes with my purse," she said, looking over her shoulder at the palomino-colored, cowhide purse on the vanity stool with firm certainty.

"And," Max continued, "what are the contents of the wallet?" Max could hear by the faintly rising, squeaky tone of her voice that he was in charge of the conversation. And just then one of the new kittens began climbing his bare leg. (The kitten held on for dear life, as if it were climbing El Capitán. A solid grimace came over Max's face, a reverberating shudder went through his whole body and somehow communicated itself over the phone, so that Loretta thought he was teasing her with grinning ridicule.)

Suddenly Loretta's worst fear of her and Jean-Claude being found out rose to her throat (as if it were a large, gooey piece of food—curried meat loaf or chicken Divan or an entire microwaved baked potato), and standing in her bedroom she looked from side to side, as if for someone to help get her through this. Where is Jean-Claude when I really need him? she thought. But if there was one thing she had learned from her mother, who learned it from living with *her* mother (cross-eyed, cranky old Gramma Rachel McSorley), it was that there are those times in your life when you simply have to forge ahead, the hell with the money, and never mind the crazy people downstairs (which in this case, of course, was only a figure of speech)—or as the slipshod, itinerant carpenters and plug-ugly, overage hookers would say down at Deadwood Dave's, "Fuck it, bub, just take a breath, hold your nose, and jump."

So Loretta took a deep breath and started in: "There *were* eight brand-new one-hundred-dollar bills," said she, looking up into her head, and then named every last one of her sixteen credit cards—in order.

"That's right, and they are still here, Mrs. Spokeshave," Max said, and when Loretta heard that, her back straightened and a bright and gracious smile came to her face.

"Anything else?" said Max.

"Well, there *was* also a personal letter," Loretta said, wanting to bite her lip, then curl up and die, or climb into one of the Kimmelbergs downstairs and disappear (certain that no one would ever find her).

"What's the name on the envelope?" Max asked, leaning forward over the bathtub as if talking right into Loretta's face.

"The letter is addressed to me," said Loretta, getting irked aplenty—What the hell business is it of yours, Nutmug? she thought.

"And from?" Max said, beginning to enjoy the quiz and wishing it could go on forever.

"It was a personal letter to me from an associate of my husband's, Jean-Claude Bouillon. Engraved stationery," said Loretta, lying badly and beginning to steam, but shriveling with embarrassment nevertheless. Then it occurred to her that if the $800 was still there, maybe this Nutmug character hadn't helped himself to the letter, after all.

Ho-ho-ho, thought Max, that's a good one. Then Max said, "Well, that certainly jibes with what I found on the street," and he couldn't resist mentioning the money again, "including the $800. Well. So. We'll meet tonight at nine at Deadwood Dave's Wild West Saloon, then?"

"Yes," said Loretta, exclaiming in her sweetest, little-Irish-girl voice, "and thank you so very much, Mr. Nut*meg*."

They wished each other well and said goodbye.

Max went back to bed, skipping lunch and dinner, and got up only when it was time to take his bath and get dressed in his most hangdog and pitiful house-repair clothes.

•   •   •

Soon after noon, Loretta, dressed casually as if for an afternoon of golf (with the feathers and baby oil and choke-chain dog collar in her gym bag), left Dudycz eating his lunch in the truck—telling him she'd be gone for the afternoon—and drove to Half Day and the rear parking lot of the tall and sprawling Montavalo Hotel.

The hotel was one of a vast worldwide chain owned outright—lock, stock, and barrel—by Jean-Claude; bought from an impoverished Brazilian entrepreneur who had fallen on hard times in 1985. (Emmett Horn, of Trueheart, Horn & Klinck, had babied the deal for more than a year. There were four copies of the contract: two in English and two in Portuguese. And Horn had exchanged plenty of winks and nods with the Miami and Brazilian bankers and Foreign Ministry gofers, and on his many business trips to Rio de Janeiro had left behind a king's ransom in Swiss francs. Still and all, the hotel deal was easy pickings, "like finding money in your desk," Gabe Trueheart said. Hughie Klinck said, "This Bouillon account sure is paying the rent!")

If, as the saying goes, form followed function, the Half Day Montavalo Hotel should have looked like a cross between a big bag of money and an expense-account voucher. From the highway (U.S. 21—known to the locals as Milwaukee Avenue), it gave the overall impression of being one of those newly minted, minimum-security federal prisons where IRS deadbeats, retired Mafia dons, dope dealers' lawyers, and idiot, hack politicians (too dumb not to get caught) did their time sedately and humanely in air-conditioned comfort—we should all have to endure such punishment. Jean-Claude had nothing to do with the lobby "ambiance" (as the freelance brochure copywriters at Deadwood Dave's would say) and was strangely embarrassed by the concrete carp pond, the potted ginkgoes (*Ginkgo biloba*), and the white-leaved vinca vines and maidenhead ferns hanging from the thick mezzanine rail, not to mention the weird, complicated drinks that were the specialty of the cocktail lounge. (It was never to be called a bar, Montavalo had decreed—only the most common sort "drank in *bars*," old man Montavalo had said many times. "Our patrons pay a pretty penny for *cocktails*.") Many's the time Jean-Claude discussed this matter of the funny-smelling, overstuffed pastel sofas and the virtually invisible elevators, hidden behind a bank of Japanese maples (*Acer palmatum*), which seemingly grew out of the polished concrete floor, but since Jean-Claude wasn't very good at arguing, the manager, Mr. Harold Brueske, was unswerving and firm: the trees and fish and ferns, etc., stayed. All Jean-Claude knew about running a hotel was that a mighty nice check came every month, so he let Brueske do as he pleased. (As far as that went, Jean-Claude knew a little something about how to get money and he knew a little something about how to spend money, but keeping track of it in between had always been a puzzle. "That's what lawyers are for," his father, John Wesley Bouillon, always said, but then the old man had been very good at keeping an eye on lawyers.)

Loretta shouldered her gym bag and made her way through the lobby filled with five hundred bubbling, gibbering Illinois high-school cheerleaders in town for a leadership conference and the semi-annual conference of north suburban newspaper editors (the Kiwanis were chowing down on green salad and prime rib in the Prairie King Room; the Half Day Boy Scouts would arrive at 3:30 for their monthly indoor jamboree—good PR, that); she made it around the maple trees and went upstairs to Presidential Suite #1407. It was 12:45, plenty of time for naughty old Jean-Claude to have arrived and ensconced himself.

And lounging he was, wearing his wet-look, fake-rubber loincloth and a camouflage kerchief around his neck, sprawled across the bed with his suitcase on the sturdy side table, watching soccer on the cable TV (Budapest running circles around Manchester).

After a quick peck on the cheek and a hot shower— Loretta explaining that the plumber had turned off all the water in the house—everyone was ready for an uninterrupted afternoon of erotic high jinks, or so they thought. Loretta dressed in her traditional middle-Thursday-of-the-month, kid-leather rawhide underwear (a very skimpy cut: the undies had a split crotch; the bra had peekaboo tips), and she and Jean-Claude fooled around some, but Loretta was so distracted that her heart just wasn't in it. Soon after they began dancing and mincing around the room, Loretta's eyes filled with tears and she collapsed on the love seat next to the conference table and poured her heart out to Jean-Claude about all her latest travails and tribulations. Loretta thrashed her arms around, cried and wailed, and told Jean-Claude about her latest sojourn to the Seven Deadly Sins Gallery; the man with the suit and bow tie and gas can, his story about his brother and sister-in-law, and how she must have got distracted; the wallet with Dudycz's money lost (explaining at length that Dudycz wanted cash, up front) as well as Jean-Claude's letter; the bother with Tharp, the banker; Maximilian Nutmug's funny little note and her conversation, agreeing to meet Max at a place called Deadhead Dave's Wild West Saloon that evening; and what sort of a horrible dump it was likely to be—all those big-city lowlifes, thugs, muggers, crooked cops, not to mention "the colored"—"city people," tradesmen, baseball fans and hockey nuts at the very least, and God only knew what else. Why oh why, had she agreed to meet at such a place (shudder; sob; whine), even though Nutmug certainly was as honest as the day is long, because the wallet was completely and fully intact. Thank God!

Jean-Claude poured Loretta a big glass of Scotch-and-water and made many trips to the bathroom for tissues while Loretta bawled her eyes out. "There, there, Loretta," he said after each trip. Jean-Claude could tell right enough that Loretta was upset about the letter ("It would absolutely kill Mother, not to mention Henry"), but so what? Big deal if Henry divorced Loretta; she'd be rid of him. And if he made trouble, why Jean-Claude's money could lean on Henry's money anytime, anyplace; he'd never know what hit him.

(Still, it was true that a nasty divorce would get his name in all the papers—Henry's kind were always spoiled and strange enough to make trouble.

BOUILLON HEIR NAMED

IN SPOKESHAVE ADULTERY

Jean-Claude Bouillon of Lake Forest, the only son of industrialist Stephen Wesley Bouillon and sole heir to the vast Bouillon fortune, was today named as the mystery lover of Loretta Spokeshave during divorce proceedings here today.

According to surprise testimony, Mrs. Loretta Spokeshave met twice a week for more than a year and enjoyed a carnal relationship with Mr. Bouillon, the estranged husband, Henry Spokeshave, claimed under oath.

Outside the courtroom, Mrs. Spokeshave said that her husband had mistaken some part-time consulting work for something much more serious and involved. Mrs. Spokeshave, a freelance interior decorator, had consulted with the Half Day Montavalo Hotel management.

Mrs. Spokeshave's lawyer, Naomi Keefer, asserted, "Mr. Spokeshave has a vivid imagination. The relationship was strictly business," and further claimed Mrs. Spokeshave would produce pay vouchers as proof.

Jean-Claude Bouillon, whose worldwide financial interests include the Montavalo Hotel chain, could not be reached for comment.

His representative in court, Emmett Horn of the law firm Trueheart, Horn & Klinck, responded that Mr. Bouillon is away on business. Mr. Bouillon's worth is estimated at more than $15 billion.

Mr. Horn said a deposition would be offered if so ordered by the court.

The Spokeshave hearing, one of the most sensational divorces in recent history, continues tomorrow.

Producing the dummied-up pay vouchers would take some finagling, but then Hotel Manager Brueske was of the straight-backed, boot-licking sort and could presumably be counted on to accomplish everything on the q.t.—or else. Jean-Claude may have lost the argument about the lobby ambiance, but there were some tasks the hired help just shut up and did—what else was hired help good for?)

And as far as Jean-Claude was concerned, it was also true that Loretta's endless supply of anxious and overly theatrical histrionics was getting on his nerves. It was not all that long ago when Loretta got on a tear about her Mazda Miata—what color should it be and whether it had the right sort of audio equipment: speakers front and back? just in the back? just in the front? Then there had been the misunderstanding with Mr. Mikki Moto, Loretta's twice-a-week gardener; where oh where to put the azaleas and cone flowers? Lately, Loretta had got it into her head that their twice-weekly gymnastics were not noisy enough—after all, didn't she and Jean-Claude have the entire fourteenth floor to themselves—and wanted Jean-Claude to take off the gag he insisted she wear. And *now* she was on a found-wallet, big-money, and incriminating-love-letter jag.

Jean-Claude stood at the wet bar running a linen towel under the cold water and thought, Loretta certainly *is* a beautiful woman when she's almost undressed and it *is* true that she's a terrific lay (the kid-leather/rawhide underwear ensemble he had brought back from Berlin certainly made her more than desirable), *and* her divorcing Henry would be no loss to literature (to use that figure of speech), but, my good man (and Jean-Claude looked at himself in the mirror back of the bar), life is not supposed to be *this* difficult and complicated.

Loretta is a wonderful girl, but perhaps it's time to move on. Some say Hong Kong is lovely this time of year.

Even Albuquerque or Managua would do.

However, Jean-Claude was nothing if not the complete gentleman. "Loretta dear, allow me to accompany you to this Dave's Deadhead whatever-you-said," he said, wringing out the towel at the bar. "Besides, it might be fun to meet a man in this day and age that returns a wallet found in the street, intact. Such a man just might be interesting to talk to." How queer, an honest man; why I'd even buy the fellow a drink and shake his hand, Jean-Claude thought.

Maximilian Nutmeg had been called many things in his life, but he had never ever been called "fun" or "interesting," much less "honest." Jean-Claude had a few things to learn in this life, still.

"That would ease my mind, Jean-Claude. You're such a considerate man," said Loretta, still crying but easing up. Lord God Almighty but she loved Jean-Claude.

By the time Jean-Claude came back with the cold-soaked linen towel, Loretta was laid out flat on the bed, still sobbing and gulping, her tears rolling into her pigtails. Jean-Claude placed the towel over her eyes and forehead, gazing lustfully down at her well-endowed, upthrust pulchritude, and decided that he'd better do something and fast if they were to enjoy any of these "carnal delights" the newspaper would speak of so salaciously. So he quickly rummaged through his suitcase of gadgets and geegaws until he found the German-made vibrator.

He'd picked it up in Copenhagen several years ago, a trifling thing about the size of a cricket bat handle. It came in its own ebony presentation box (like a bottle of expensive, exclusive Irish whiskey—Red Breast 20 or Black Bush, say). The vibrator was called *Herr Wunderbar Wilhelm* (or "Wonderful Willie") and came with a deluxe collection of eight "happy tips"—"made of the finest natural Indian rubber that money can buy, in a variety of rainbow colours," according to the worthless English-language product guarantee and owner's manual (written also in Dutch, German, French, Spanish, Italian, Korean, and Japanese).

On a whim he chose Mr. Wizard and the Jitterbug, and slipped one over the tips of the first two fingers of each hand. Mr. Wizard was green and gold with long and stringy, floppy squiggles that closely resembled what used to be called an Afro hairdo; the Jitterbug was purple and brown, with a Tom Mix cowboy-hat-looking top with a broad and stiff, wrinkly brim—as big and thick as a lawn hose rubber washer.

Then, fortified with another healthy drink of Scotch, he walked over to the bed on his knees and stood next to Loretta as she lay flat on her back, pressing the ice-cold, mono-grammed-linen, bar-towel compress to her eyes with the heels of her hands.

Jean-Claude leaned over Loretta's stomach and commenced a little play—what the amateur marriage counselors down at Deadwood Dave's would call "a Punch-and-Judy, fuck-finger psychodrama" (snorting and guffawing)—the "happy tips" on his fingers looking for all the world like Munchkins in funny hats.

Mr. Wizard, star newsman ("The Golden Throat of the Airwaves") for KWOP radio, stands on the corner of Sanguine and Kepler Streets, doing his daily half-hour "Man on the Street" interviews. The question today is "What is money?" Enter the Jitterbug, diddly-bopping and dipping down the street. He's just come out of Grin and Bare It Bar and Grill, and he is definitely half stiff.

MR. WIZARD [*in a voice deeply sonorous and mellow*]: Well, now. Here comes an interesting-looking gentleman. Pardon me, sir, may I speak to you for a moment?

JITTERBUG: Yes, you may.

MR. WIZARD: And what is your name, sir?

JITTERBUG [*smelling of liquor; bowing low; in a high falsetto, Little Richard voice*]: Why, sir! A good afternoon to you; my name is Jasper Jitterbug! My card! And yours, may I ask?

MR. WIZARD [*somewhat taken aback at such sloppy familiarity, not to mention the fumes*]: Why, my name is Mr. Wizard, "The Golden Throat of the Airwaves." I am here gathering information from the great American public on various issues of the day. May I inquire, Mr. Jitterbug, what you do for a living?

JITTERBUG [*grandly chummy; taking hold of Mr. Wizard's arm that holds the microphone; then he steps back as if to get a good look at Mr. Wizard and eyeballs him melodramatically*]: I, sir, am a citizen of the world. A cash-money impresario. An entrepreneur, if you prefer. An international agent of trade. I obtain certain commodities from certain parties who regard such-and-such a commodity as totally useless *for* certain parties who know exactly what to do with certain commodities, for which I obtain a certain, ample fee. I am one of those sterling gentlemen who make the world go around.

MR. WIZARD [*genuinely curious*]: Aha! Let me ask you, was there anything in your background that prepared you for your current line of work?

JITTERBUG (*dancing and dipping and bopping his head*): Well, it just so happens to be true that my family have been horse thieves since before the Civil War. My grandfather heard it from his grandfather that Jitterbugs have been hung for horse thieves since time out of mind. The grand tradition of the Jitterbug line, so to speak. According to the family legend, there's Jitterbugs been hung by the neck until dead in thirty-seven of these United States. Some say it's a record, though I certainly couldn't say. And I do admit, I dearly love the ponies, but only in an aesthetic sense. What's the sense of keeping up a family tradition if it's going to kill you? Answer me that.

M R .   W I Z A R D [*somewhat skeptical; trying to move the conversation along; in the radio biz, time is indeed money*]: And now, Mr. Jitterbug, for the question of the day: What does money mean to you?

"Jean-Claude!" said Loretta, who felt him leaning his wrists across her stomach, had been listening to the dialogue from under the cold compress and could not understand for the life of her what was going on. She raised her head, looked out from under the cold compress (which did soothe her headache) and down between her large, well-trussed breasts toward her stomach. "Jean-Claude! What on earth are you doing?" But then she saw the two "happy tips"—the one with long, droopy squiggles and the other that looked like a cowboy hat—and started to laugh! "What is *this*?" she said, giggling and giggling. Jean-Claude had asked her to do some pretty silly things, dressing up in some pretty silly getups, engaging in some pretty complicated gymnastics, but what was this?

"Why, Loretta dear! Mr Wizard is interviewing the Jitterbug for KWOP's 'Man on the Street' news feature! What else could it be?" said Jean-Claude.

Both Mr. Wizard and Jitterbug turned to face Loretta as if she were part of the gathering crowd and bowed deeply— Mr. Wizard's fluffy Afro bouncing and jiggling, Jitterbug bowing somewhat lower than was necessary. "We're trying to cheer you *up!*" they said together. And with that Jean-Claude went on with his little play, even though the pavement beneath them was rolling like an earthquake.

M R . W I Z A R D [*straightening up after the interruption with the microphone between them*]: Now, Jitterbug, would you please answer today's question: What is money?

J I T T E R B U G [*leaning back again, virtually incredulous*]: Sir, it is a question both gratuitous and absurd, but for the sake of your audience I will comply [*eyeing Loretta with sly regard— her face framed between her hefty and high, leather-encased breasts; the nipples standing up like harbor beacons*]. Firstly, let me say that you have certainly asked the right person, being as I am the progeny of generations of salesmen of opportunity, so to speak, and secondly because only the entrepreneurial individual, that is, someone who handles a great deal of money in all forms, including IOUs and trade vodka as well as plain old cold cash, could answer with any alacrity and statesmanlike poise.

"What *is* money?" Why, every hayseed, every Huckleberry Hound, every tinhorn amateur dictator knows the answer to that! Money is *soul,* boy!

Money is lubricant! It greases the celestial wheels which turn the earth!

Money is last-quarter moonlight. Fuzzy shadows. Give me the deepest darkness. Money is not made in the light.

Money is R-28 insulation! Big-enough, thick-enough piles keep out the cold in winter, keep out the heat in summer, shoo away the vermin, and not only hold body and soul together but keep the riffraff "out the way," as the old song goes.

Money is tits! Beauty, youth, naughty-good fun, and endless healthy grins! Consider: when you haven't got it—when you come to the end of it; when you dole out your last dime—philosophers call that "tits-up."

Money *is* time! If those atomic scientist guys really had their eggs in one basket, had a clock keeping track of the money instead of nuclear *doom*, why it'd be just a touch after four o'clock in the afternoon. Beer call. Cocktail hour. Miller Time.

When you've got big bags of money, you're as happy as a clam, you sleep the sleep of children and eat your fill every time you sit down to a meal. When there's no money to be had, no matter how deep you dig, why, you're always sicker than a dog, can't sleep for nothing, and for some reason or other you get fat. And the less money you have, the fatter you get. Don't ask me how *that* happens. Some strange physics, perhaps.

Money is power, pal. As in kilowatt hours. As in telling other people what to do, i.e., "Tote that barge, lift that bale," etc. And make no mistake, Mr. Wizard, what money can't get [*Jitterbug coming forward to whisper with a conspirator's air*], I don't want!

If money were the World Wrestling Federation, it'd be Haystack Calhoun and Earthquake McGoon against Mr. Peepers and Clarabelle the clown. It'd be "moider" [*Jitterbug rolling his google eyes*].

Finally, money *is* a solid cubic mile of gold [*drawing it in the air, making it solid with his fingers*], all the gold in the world. Imagine standing in the middle of all that. Unyielding and incorruptible, utterly beautiful to hold and behold. The smell of money is the perfume of the gods. Wallowing in money is better than a hot bath and a 90-minute rubdown.

And just at that moment, Loretta sat up (laughing until she thought she'd die), untied and unhooked what clothes she had on, throwing them this way and that, and hoisted Jean-Claude onto the bed, and the two of them commenced a session of lovemaking that staggered Jean-Claude to his toes. But then, money had always inspired Loretta and tickled her in every way.

By 5:30 they were both thoroughly exhausted, their imaginations wrung dry. They showered, dressed, and went their separate ways to change before meeting for dinner at Raul's Italian Steakhouse in Park Ridge, and then drove into the city to find this Deadhead Dave and that saloon of his, and meet this Max Nutmug.

•   •   •

Now, Deadwood Dave's Wild West Saloon was a bar famous both far and wide in the city and a considerable distance into the countryside—though to some solid citizens, vaguely curious tourists out on a toot and amateur crummy-bar buffs, it looked like a cross between a Disney World ride and a south Texas dairy farm. In the Dorchester neighborhood of Boston at a place called Rooney and Mulrooney's Bar and Grill it was known as Dirtbag Dave's, and at the Wheelbarrow Roadhouse outside Oil City near Shreveport it was known (with some tongue-in-cheek) as Dead Dick Dave's. Dave St. Clair grew up in Hancock, Vermont, where his dad worked at the Ballou Plywood Company mill; the closest bar was a twenty-mile drive to Ripton, so everyone drank at home. Dave liked to say (with snappy maliciousness—the only revenge he was ever going to get) that in Vermont if you didn't ski or chop wood there was nothing much to do. He up and left when the State Tourist Board began distributing red, white, and blue bumper stickers that read

VERMONT IS
WHAT AMERICA WAS

"If that's true," Dave would say—when you could get him to calm down enough to talk sense about it—"if that's true, then I shudder with pity for the New England subsistence farmers of the nineteenth century." Dave had knocked around the country during the war, staying one lick ahead of the feds for failing to appear for his induction physical; "Going underground," he called it (anyone else would call it "on the bum"); wound up scrounging work in Jackson Hole, Wyoming—bartending, punching cattle (Dave glancing at his fist, as if his job was to crack them one upside the head as they walked by), and "a little carpentry." He'd done some serious hard time at Folsom Prison, was in the audience for the Johnny Cash concert—

> *My name is Sue!*
> *How do you do!*

—Dave telling everyone there had been a little misunderstanding about some bounced checks, but the fucking prosecutor wouldn't listen to reason and his Public Defender ("*That* asshole") was so dumb he couldn't skip rope and chew gum at the same time. When Dave got out he came into a bit of money when his parents were killed in 1975 (picnic; lightning), so he took the money, came to Chicago (chasing a woman, of course), and set up Deadwood Dave's Wild West Saloon, which turned out to be a real money-maker. He kept bragging that he was going to change the name to Baby Doe's Matchless. There was a great big old varnished-to-death mahogany bar (a prize piece of wood), a Brunswick pool table, good-luck horseshoes over each and every door in the place, enameled spittoons (not all for show), fake Wanted posters, photographs "borrowed" from the Carson City Historical Society, an enormous mounted buffalo head, Denver and Rio Grande Western Railroad memorabilia (rail spikes and Wobbly union cards, coolie hats and dining car menus), Wild Bill Hickok's last poker hand (aces and eights, ten high—the so-called Deadman's Hand), a bleached longhorn skull, and an eight-foot rattlesnake skin (with twelve rattles), and an antique gun collection (a Sharp's Buffalo Rifle, a long-range Henry rifle used by the all-black 10th Cavalry Regiment, the famous Buffalo Soldiers of Fort Davis, and a variety of Colt six-shot revolvers used in the Texas Range Wars of the 1880s). Over the back of the bar was a long, tall, double-life-size painting of a completely naked, remarkably voluptuous woman, with flattened breasts and rose-colored areolae, invitingly sprawled across a velvet couch (about to faint dead away from sheer desire and exhausted anticipation). The week-night bartender, Stale Yale, parked his motorcycle—a big, greasy, virtually antique Harley-Davidson—back by the bandstand. It could certainly make the solid citizens queasy when they'd drop by for a cold one on their way home from work; there'd be this huge nasty bike leaning deeply on its kickstand, smelling of old saddle leather and hot oil.

There *used* to be a country & western jukebox, but it had "gone west," as the saying goes, and was *long* gone. After it disappeared, Tony Maloney, one of the amateur neighborhood handicappers who—like Sky Masterson—would bet on anything, used to say, "What we need in here is some C&W music or there's likely to be some sort of terrible accident, hear?"

To which Dave would reply, "If there's an accident around here, bubba, it'll be your ass in traction for six months, get me?"

Sentiment was not a very long suit at Deadwood Dave's—"If you don't drink beer or booze, get outta here"— and the customer was not always right. When some uninitiated pilgrim came in asking for a Miller Lite, Dave would say, "Shee-it! You know how they make lite beer, fella? Same's they do *Kool-Aid*—they just add water. And we don't serve Coors or Budweiser or Corona. You want that shit, go across the street to that wormhole fag bar Lucy's."

One day the summer before, when the Cubs were bumping along but looked for all the world (with the wind blowing out and a little luck bestowed by the Giver of All Good Things) as if they just *might* finally, *finally*, take the pennant—for the first time since 1945, the year we dropped the bomb on Japan—a couple of west-suburban Schaumburg Cub fans had waltzed in, lost or sick or drunk or something, and bought the house a round out of sheer unbridled glee. Greg Maddux had just stomped the Mets (who seemed brain-dead that afternoon), so everybody from the guys in the Iced Broiler Pit at the Board of Trade to the secretary pool at national headquarters of Sara Lee in Deerfield was feeling mighty fine. Well, truth to tell, Deadwood Dave's serious afternoon drinking crowd would drink *any*thing *anyone* bought; so when those out-of-town white boys offered to buy everyone an Old Style, not a minute later everybody was sucking down a cold one—even though they came in all palsy-walsy, as if to say, "Hi! I'm strange. Please beat me up!" The shorter Schaumburg fat guy started shoving quarters in the jukebox and kept hitting the Cubs TV theme song:

Hey, hey, Holy Mackerel!
No doubt about it!
The Cubs are on their way!

which repeated about a thousand times—blah, blah, blah!—
and even a tone-deaf street bum can only take so much—
ten, twelve minutes, maybe—so a couple of unreconstructed
White Sox fans went over, ripped the plug out of the wall,
and wheeled the jukebox toward the door. Another guy held
the door wide open for them; they rolled it out onto the
sidewalk—cord, plug, records, and all—and over the curb.
You would have thought the thing had gone over Victoria
Falls. Not a moment later one of those crazy Irani cabdrivers,
arguing with some fluffy dish from Sheridan Road in the
rearview mirror about a flat-rate fare out to O'Hare, came
bopping down Granville and ran right into it—*wham!*—
thought it was a refrigerator; thought he was in some very
deep shit, backed up, drove around it, and kept going. The
two guys walked back in (bikers from the Death Skull outlaw
club of Carpentersville), brushing the imaginary dirt off their
imaginary sleeves and snakepit tattoos—"That's the name of
that tune. Thanks for the brewskis, but you two"—meaning
the Schaumburg, fat-boy Cub fans—"out," cocking their
thumbs over their shoulders. And the gold-dust twins looked
at one another as if to say, "Who can argue with that?" So
away they went.

On the other hand, sentiment could take some mighty
strange turns. Above the cash register was a standard 3x5
American flag rigged on a windowshade spindle, and when
somebody played Kate Smith's rendition of "God Bless
America," Dave'd yank that sucker down, hand out Fourth of

July sparklers, and everybody in the place—bikers, welfare hounds, commuters, Loyola University grad students, boozy Sheridan Road widows, crummy bar buffs—would lay into a sing-a-long, swinging sparklers like there was no tomorrow.

Deadwood Dave's catered to a broad variety of clientele, as the *Chicago* magazine restaurant critic might say— homebound El train commuters, overage neighborhood street- corner gangbangers, serious ugly bikers, ridge runners, and urban cowboys who just couldn't get enough of Patsy Kline and Merle Haggard, Willie Nelson and Hank Williams (Sr.), and those guys. The outlaw biker clubs got so bad with all their punch-arm and grabass and generally busting each oth- er's chops that Dave put a hand-lettered sign on the door:

NO CLUB COLORS—GET ME?

It was a hint no one could ignore.

And everybody had a nickname. It wasn't *de rigueur* (as they might say in New York City), the way it was in most biker bars, but everybody came up with a nickname sooner or later. There were Oilrig Sven and Kansas City Lily and Deaf Smith; Fathead John and Jailbird John, Bullshit John and Big Sloppy Dumbass John; Patty the Pushover and Frying Pan Jack, Maldonado the Sailor and Kid Gibbs. There were Biker Bob and Gainesville Bob and Big Black Bob and Bowling Green Bob and Big Banker Bob and Stale Yale, who answered to the name of Bob. (Bowling Green Bob would be standing at the bar, sucking down a Löwenbräu long-neck, and Big Black Bob would swagger in, and Bowling Green Bob would say, "Well, hell's *bells*, it's Big Black Bob!" and the two of them would commence to falling all over the furniture, laugh- ing; a private joke no one understood.) There were Dallas Don and Arkansas Stretch, Mr. Law and Mousy Freta; Little Murphy and Alphabet Asa, Senorita Suzy and Tulare Tom; Slip 'n' Sly and Montana Joey, Indian Richard and Railroad Henderson, and a whole bunch of others. Of course Petunia-Rose and Daisy-Lily, Amaryllis and Easy Ed, Belle-Noche and Oscar, Sweet William, Max, and Muriel used their real names, which Dave and everybody else thought was a real hoot. A lot of Deadwood Dave's regulars never did give their real names, just in case their wives, or anybody else, called. Dave would answer the phone: "Hello? This *is* Deadwood Dave's Wild West Saloon." And the party at the other end would ask for So-and-so—Dwight Mooney, American National investment banker, homeowner and taxpayer, husband, father, and solid citizen, for example—and Dave would put his hand over the receiver and announce to the crowd, "Anybody seen Dwight Mooney? Is there a Dwight Mooney in the house?" And Mooney (trying to put off going home as long as possible; to hear him tell it, his wife was an idiot nag and his kids wouldn't shut up), whose nickname was Boulevard Bill and was at that moment playing eight ball with Big Sloppy Dumbass John, would look around just like everyone else, repeating the name, but no one signified. "Nope," Dave would turn back to the phone and say to Mrs. Mooney—Mary Ellen—"Dwight Mooney don't seem to be here, ma'am, but if he comes in I'll tell him he's wanted home for dinner right away," Dave would say and hang up.

Yes sir, Deadwood Dave's Wild West Saloon was quite a place.

•   •   •

Well, God only knows who said that good news travels fast, but travel it did. Word got around that there was going to be some kind of show—one of Maximilian Nutmeg's deals was going down—and nobody wanted to miss that. By nine o'clock the place was packed, and more were on the way. Arkansas Stretch (on his way south to Memphis) and Slip 'n' Sly (just in from Charlottesville) were standing around the pool table, shooting eight ball and drinking shots and beers. Everybody else was standing along the bar and crowded around the blackjack video game, waiting for things to start. Dave wiped glasses and Stale Yale counted change from his tip jar.

Jean-Claude and Loretta arrived in his Shelby-Cobra Mustang Ford—confident and apprehensive at the same time. He was dressed in a white linen tropical suit, white shirt and silk bow tie, and white saddle shoes with fancy stitching across the toe (the whole nifty ensemble topped with a manila-colored Borsalino hat). Loretta was dressed in a low-cut, stretch-bodice summer dress, bare legs, and Bass sandals; Jean-Claude had to own that she looked magnificent. They asked about Maximilian Nutmug and ordered vodka martinis with a lime twist. Deadwood Dave was so astonished by Jean-Claude's bright red carnation boutonniere that he said Nutmeg would be along any minute, then went ahead and fixed the drinks—which made Big Sloppy Dumbass John gulp his beer, laugh right out loud, and squirt beer up his nose; everyone else furiously busy so as not to look as though they were eavesdropping.

The two of them sat at a small side table underneath Wild Bill Hickok's Deadman's Hand near the bandstand, where Stale Yale parked his Harley, but unlike Hickok, Jean-Claude sat facing the door.

Nothing like the two of them had ever walked into Deadwood Dave's, and everyone gawked for all they were worth, eyeballing Loretta as she sipped her drink through the stir straw; they stared at Jean-Claude and whispered among themselves.

Look at the hooters on that broad! Who's the cat in the bwana suit?

Some out-of-state narc? Big Black Bob came in and passed the word that the guy was driving a Shelby-Cobra Mustang, *the* 1964 Indy 500 pace car. Nobody knew what to make of it. What's Nutmeg got up his sleeve this time?

Jean-Claude drank his martini with distracted politeness, looked around the bar, and thought he hadn't been in such an interesting place in a long while. As far as he was concerned, Deadwood Dave's went right to the top of the list of funky places, along with that bar in Vientiane and that hotel in Moscow.

A couple of years before, he'd been in Laos, trying to sell the Laotian Marxists a bridge over the Mekong River into Thailand—Vientiane, the place where Volkswagen Beetles went to die. The bar, the Sithan Nua (Lao for "big bend in the river"), was built on pilings out over the water—the only place in town open to the public after dark. Heineken's beer (in cans) went for 500 kip (about a dollar), and cheap, heavy Lao beer in plain brown liter bottles sold for 200 kip. In the middle of the room there was a large concrete aquarium, and if you wanted dinner, you picked the crab or fish yourself; the waiter came in from the back, snatched it out, cold cocked the animal right then and there, and carried it back to the kitchen, water dripping from his arm. Twenty minutes later he came back out (the women did the cooking) with the thing on a plate, a side order of unidentifiable stir-fried vegetables, and all the steamed rice you could eat. If you didn't want dinner (and many did not), you snacked on Lao doughnuts, a sort of round fry bread, and drank, sitting in the sodden river air and watching the rats and river snakes between the planks underfoot. Since there was nothing else to do in town, most foreigners managed to drop by of an evening and played something that resembled pinochle, straight poker, and noisy, almost hysterical, mah-jongg with the few live-wire locals. After the poppy harvest, there were not a few dope dealers at the bar, cutting deals and talking shop. On the nights when television reception was especially good, the bartender would turn on the black-and-white and everyone would watch Thai broadcasts of NFL games, *The Dukes of Hazzard*, and a parade of televangelists. The Laotians thought that Jimmy Swaggart was especially uproarious, threw their heads back, laughed till tears rolled down their cheeks, and spit betel juice into the river through the gaps in the woven bamboo shutters athwart the pier.

Then there'd been the year he went to Moscow to negotiate a joint venture with some middle-level government people to import snow shovels—of which, for all the snow in Moscow, there were few; Muscovites got by with a piece of wood nailed to a mop handle. Jean-Claude would clean up, just like Armand Hammer did with pencils back in the twenties (it made Hammer's fortune). He'd stayed at the Brotherhood of River Barge Muleteers' Hotel, or something like that. It looked like a run-down Holiday Inn; served gray, road-kill sausage, day-old bread, and warm Pepsi-Cola at every meal; and street hustlers roamed the halls insisting you sell them the clothes off your back. One morning the kitchen served every table in the dining room a heaping platter of gleaming, piping-hot hot dogs, and the leftovers were cut up and added to the greasy luncheon soup. Just like any other hotel in the world, the bellboys could get you anything, but none of the doors was hung right, the elevators were wired funny, and the hookers were the most pitiable, unimaginative, and exhausted young women Jean-Claude had talked to in a long time.

Yes sir, Jean-Claude thought that Deadwood Dave's was unique, to say the least. He was especially taken with the white kitchen enamel Rock Island Railroad spittoons and Stale Yale's ugly old Harley, the fawning nude languishing above the top-shelf liquor, the shaggy buffalo head and rattlesnake skin, and the tattoos and heavy, flabby biceps of the Death Skull bikers. Whatever happened, he was going to enjoy *this* spree.

Max and Muriel arrived. Max, looking haggard and scruffy—almost grinning with pain—was dressed in his housework bib overalls, flannel painting shirt, and a headband, in the fervent hope that Loretta Spokeshave wouldn't recognize him. He had greased his hair down, parted it in the middle, and tied a black kerchief around it—the springy end curls like a halo around his ears. Muriel was dressed in a plain purple cotton housedress and running shoes. She had the traffic tickets in her purse. The instant they walked in the door, Max saw Jean-Claude and Loretta sitting at the table toward the back; that *must* be them! When Max went to the bar for beers, Bullshit John and Maldonado the Sailor—and everyone else—made plenty of room for him. The whole audience looked Max up and down and wondered where he'd got that outfit.

At the table there were brief and polite introductions, and the Nutmegs sat down—Muriel with her feet flat on the floor, her legs tight together, holding her purse to her lap with both hands, little-old-lady fashion.

But before Max even opened his mouth and got a sip of

beer, Belle-Noche and Oscar Wendella arrived in the Oscar Mayer wiener wagon, which he'd parked around the corner in front of the vacant Devon Theater. They walked in, pulled up chairs, and sat right down, Oscar's feet barely touching the floor.

And before Oscar turned in his chair and called to Stale Yale for a round of drinks, some popcorn and Beer Nuts, Easy Ed and Amaryllis showed up, double-parking the truck in front of the Death Skull outlaw club bikes (with the emergency lights going).

So the scene looked something like this: Max, Muriel; sister, boyfriend; Jean-Claude, Loretta; niece and her boyfriend. And in the background: pool players, bar-hopping drunks; Death Skull bikers, gangbangers and hookers; hang-around-the-fort Indians and barflies; latecomers and passersby crowding in to see what the commotion was. And back of that, Deadwood Dave and Stale Yale, pouring drinks, making change, and ringing the tip bell.

Then the action began.

Max pulled the wallet from under the bib of his overalls, explaining that he'd found it on his way to Union Station, where he sold flowers at the curb; Loretta's eyes filled with sparkle, grateful beyond expression; Max pushed the wallet across the table among the glasses and bottles and basket of well-salted popcorn; Loretta thanked Max long and loud, checked the contents of her wallet (everything was there), and reached into her purse and gave Max a nice new twenty-dollar bill. He took hold of it with both hands and looked down at it for a long time in fully realized disbelief (All that trouble and woe for a lousy twenty). I must be crazy, he thought to himself, but what the fuck, hey, it's only a buck. Max looked at the twenty and wanted to take poison—whatever would get him off the planet the quickest.

Muriel immediately noticed that Max's eyes had glazed over, a sure sign that he was fading. She sat forward, whipped out the tickets, and laid them on the table—bang, bang, bang, bang, bang, bang, bang, bangity-bang-bang! (Muriel dealt the tickets as if she were setting out tarot cards—a hobby of hers and the neighborhood women. They'd get together in the afternoon, have a glass or two of Gallo red jug wine, and tell each other's fortune, looking everything up in a book Honey Jean Jones kept in her kitchen.) She told the story of Max's trials and tribulations, how honest was her husband in this regard, and how he hadn't worked a regular job since he got canned at the Grateful Dead Auto Auctioneers. "What an ungrateful bunch those crooks were, cheating Max of wages, making him work long hours with no consideration—not even a bonus," she said. "One day, zip, fired, gone!"

Hearing this, Jean-Claude took out his elephant-hide wallet, launched into a story about finally meeting an honest man (everybody at the bar trying to keep a straight face), saying something about some guy named Diogenes and another guy named Alexander (the punch line was "Stand aside, you're between me and the sun"), and counted out $20s and $50s to the amount of $500; the pile of money fluffy, springy, well-thumbed; the stack not neat. Everyone was impressed, especially Belle-Noche. "Thank you, Mr. Bouillon," said Muriel, and picked up the money, folded it double (with one hand), and put it in her purse. She sat back, again holding the purse solidly in her lap, as if afraid that if she let go her grip the thing would rise in the air and float out the door with her hanging on for dear life—her toes dragging the floor. Jean-Claude went into rhapsodies comparing Maximilian Nutmeg with the fawning, grasping, well-dressed but conniving lawyers he'd met in his life; comparing Maximilian Nutmeg with dim-witted building inspectors, general contractors, Hong Kong bankers, mayors and aldermen of a dozen municipalities, South American cattle ranchers, and the oil and natural gas ministers of half a dozen Middle Eastern princedoms. Max was embarrassed; Muriel thought that for the kind of money he seemed to have in his wallet he could talk until he was blue in the face, her Max was finally getting his due.

Jean-Claude offered to buy everyone a round of drinks; Belle-Noche offered to help him carry the drinks. It's hard to make eyes at someone and conduct business at the same time, but Jean-Claude and Belle-Noche managed; it was love at first sight. They conspired at the bar while Deadwood Dave poured the beers and booze. Belle-Noche assured Jean-Claude that ditching Loretta would be no problem, that Oscar would get the message quick enough ("He may be short, but that only means his brains are closer to his dick," said she) and would offer to take her home. "They definitely are a pair," Belle-Noche said.

Drinks served, Belle-Noche excused herself to go to the ladies' room and ducked out the back. Jean-Claude suddenly remembered that he'd left something in the car and disappeared, but not before slipping Deadwood Dave a note to give to the lady five minutes after he'd gone. The two of them snuck off in Jean-Claude's Shelby-Cobra Mustang Ford. Loretta, and everyone else, thought it was drag-racing Puerto Ricans outside.

After five minutes of totally worthless small talk and nervous conversation had ensued, Dave delivered the note, bang-ing the brass fire-engine bell the righteous lick he always gonged when someone left an especially excellent tip.

Loretta read the note—

My dear beautiful Loretta,
I've discovered the love of my life. Can't wait around to explain. Ask that Oscar fellow to drive you home. You won't be sorry.

All the best,
Jean-Claude

—and immediately launched into a crying fit, certain that the bar was full of heathen cannibals; that she was going to be taken out back, murdered, her body chopped into a thousand pieces and barbecued on the oil-drum spit in the alley. Oscar comforted her with smooth and ingratiating sympathy— "There, there, Loretta, everything will work out for the best, you'll see"—offering to escort her home. He showed her his union card as proof of his honorable and gentlemanly intentions. She, of course, accepted (beggars cannot be choosers), having already flirted with him for half an hour; Goodness gracious, he's cute, she thought to herself. They soon left and a hundred pairs of eyes followed them out the door.

Easy Ed was perplexed. He couldn't get it into his brain how Max had come out ahead, giving that broad back the wallet, the $800, credit cards and all, and got back $500. The math didn't come out; what's the catch, Max?—"Yeah, Unc, what's the gig?" said Amaryllis. Max tried to explain about the pain in his head, but Easy Ed and Amaryllis still didn't get it. Finally, Max looked at Easy Ed from under his eyebrows and thought, This man is one big fresh-quarried and uncarved blockhead.

Finally, in desperation, Max took Easy Ed to the bar—standing between Frying Pan Jack and Jailbird John—and sincerely and earnestly told him the utter flat-out truth. "Fuck the money. If I didn't give the $800 back, I'd never get rid of the headache I've had ever since I picked up the wallet in the alley yesterday. The pain was killing me. This whole episode is worth a year's pay and a new suit. Thank God, the thing is gone," by which he meant both the wallet and the headache. Easy Ed listened carefully to the argument that Max laid out on the bar with the heel of his hand (drawing hash marks in the beer spills); Easy Ed had watched Max's lips intently and heard perfectly; but it made no sense. Where was the money?

Max looked up at a photograph of Mayor Richard J. Daley shaking hands with Queen Elizabeth at the dock on Navy Pier in 1959; the Queen wore $10,000 worth of fifties flowery Hausfrau clothes, smiling big in the August heat. Mayor Richard J. Daley wore a $30 brown suit, brown shoes, and a haircut that looked as if he got it in prison, sweating bullets.

Max repeated himself, even more carefully than before.

Ed wasn't buying it, and repeated the sequence: the wallet; the twenty; the tickets—"Are those the real article; where'd you get them; a very nice touch, Max"; Muriel's wonderful sob story; the guy giving him a nice piece of dough. Ed worked it out on his fingers and held them up to show Max and everyone else at the bar (Stale Yale and Big Black Bob from the Death Skull bikers went out back and laughed right out loud—haw-haw-haw); according to Easy Ed, Max was out $300. "Is there a big score farther up the road? *What* you got in mind? This is me—Easy Ed. We're pards, right?"

Nobody understood it, not even Boulevard Bill (and *he* worked with big money all day long).

Max repeated for the third time about the headache (he left out the part about Muriel's promise of his "favorite") and flat-out asserted there was nothing more to talk about, got his beer, and sat down again.

Easy Ed and Amaryllis left with an air of puzzlement and hard feeling, and met with Sweet William to smoke some dope and plot their own Spokeshave swindle. They sat in the Plymouth out back. It took them all night.

Max and Muriel went home and she fucked him silly. They slept in and awoke refreshed and chipper, invigorated. Even loopy old Agnes-Ruth got up the next morning clear-headed, wonderfully sensible, and generally feeling mighty fine, as if something remarkable and sublime had been at work in the Nutmeg tribal air.

•   •   •

This is how it all ended.

No one saw hide nor hair of Belle-Noche for a week, until she came back to the house to collect her things and moved to Lake Forest with Jean-Claude. Not long afterward Belle married Panama John (as he was thereafter known at Deadwood Dave's)—Belle "cashing in big," as Boulevard Bill would say. Belle-Noche was in love at last and couldn't have been happier. Panama John turned out to be a loud and serious Bulls fan, a big spender, and a hard drinker—just the kind of guy who was more than welcome at Deadwood Dave's.

Loretta left with Oscar and all but disappeared. Months later, Maldonado the Sailor and Mousy Freta came back from the annual Harley-Davidson blowout in Sturgis, South Dakota, with *this* story. Apparently when Loretta arrived home she decided the hell with Snuffy Lane, the hell with Dudycz, the hell with Henry and Sophia and Tharp, then cleaned out

her closets and jewelry box and took off with Oscar. Maldonado said the word on the CB traffic and around the truck
stops was they launched into an amateur crime spree, knocking over Ma and Pa gas stations and grocery stores in Iowa,
Nebraska, New Mexico, and Arizona. Maldonado and Freta
had taken the long way home from Sturgis and saw Oscar
and Loretta in Las Vegas—dressed fit to kill—betting heavy
and winning big at the crap tables in Caesar's Palace.

The next afternoon, Easy Ed and Amaryllis discovered
they had enough money to buy a new Chevy tow truck with
a hydraulic Willis hoist, which they did (with money left over
for a house), and soon moved to Niles—taking the cats and
ferrets with them ("Thank God and good riddance," Max said
as he stood on the porch and watched them drive away). Ed
got an 800 number and went into business, legit this time,
and started making the "big money" working the interstates.

Sweet William sold the rest of his "garden fresh" inventory, then packed up and left the house for good, driving down
to Tavernier to go into business (a 50–50 split) with his very
best friend, E. J. Cavanaugh, made enough money in the next
six months to buy a cross-country bike shop in Alaska, and
virtually retired.

Robert Nutmeg married one of the Walgreen's checkout
girls, and between the two of them they had enough money
to buy a convenience store franchise in Winona, Minnesota.

Agnes-Ruth moved into Belle-Noche's old room, but still
spent her late afternoons in her car seat on the front porch
with her glass of gin and her smokes, lost in her endless and
dreary, imaginary memoir, lecturing passersby on living right
and dying old.

Daisy-Lily and Petunia-Rose, who always seemed to be
somewhere else when anything happened, suddenly got it

into their heads that they should move to Dallas to seek their fortunes as Dallas Cowboys' cheerleaders, shaking their goodies for all the Texas football nuts. So Jean-Claude loaned them some money and his 1949 black Mercury two-door and off they went.

Not long after, Max got a call from Suedmeyer Brothers Beer Distributors on West Armitage (named for Edward R. Armitage, a Chicago alderman in the early twenties)—would Max like a job driving a truck? Muriel said, "Would he ever!" Alex Suedmeyer said the job was his in perpetuity, on the strong and hearty recommendation of their mutual friend Jean-Claude Bouillon. The early-afternoon barflies down at Deadwood Dave's said, "Nutmeg should live so long," puckering up with envy and derision.

That fateful Thursday evening at Deadwood Dave's Wild West Saloon became a legend—the same as the afternoon in 1932 (third game of the World Series) when Babe Ruth (with an 0–2 count) pointed to the dead-centerfield bleachers, the corner of Sheffield and Waveland Avenues at Wrigley Field, and then proceeded to hit a home run there. Some observers said Ruth was only pointing at the pitcher, taunting; others said, "Naw, he was definitely calling his shot!" Max's wallet gag became an event talked about and analyzed, brooded over and bragged about for months afterward, though, still, no one had the faintest notion of how Max came out ahead.

A body could almost guarantee a round of beers just by mentioning, "I was there the night Max returned that wallet with the 800 smackers to that Spokeshave woman and Belle-Noche met Panama John."

So, that was that.

•   •   •

One more thing:

Across Waveland Avenue from Wrigley Field, almost in line with the third-base foul line, stands Chicago Fire Department Engine Company #78. If United Airlines is the official airline of the Chicago Cubs (for a large consideration), and Canon the official camera, then Engine Company #78 is the official fire station. In front of the station is a fire hydrant with a permanently bubbling water fountain. On days when the sky is too smoky for a between-pitches "lake shot," the WGN–TV engineers zoom in on Engine Company #78's fire hydrant drinking fountain. The firemen sit out front in their kitchen chairs, watch the traffic, and listen to the crowd while watching the game on their portable TV.

And all that summer the firemen would sit there watching the happy commotion of the grinning, homebound throngs at the end of a game, kibitzing about the Cubs finally taking a pennant—"Who knows? We might get lucky?"—and winning the World Series ("Hardy-har-har," the guys down at Deadwood Dave's would say). The firemen hailed everyone—young and old, win or lose, drunk or sober—with the firemen's ubiquitous farewell (exchanged when they struck a fire, hauled the hoses aboard the trucks, and drove away): "See you at the *big* one!"